Ash Rose

Ash Rose Publishing

Contents

Sweet As Sin

First published in Great Britain in 2025 by Ash Rose

E-book ISBN: 978-1-0682707-0-3

Paperback ISBN: 978-1-0682707-1-0

Cover design by Lora Cooray – www.taleswithlora.com
Printed in the United Kingdom

This book is for the other half of me. This book would not exist if it were not for his never ending cheerleading and support of my pursuits – of which there have been a few. Promise this is the last one. Love you always.

AR

Sweet As Sin Playlist

While writing this story and these characters, so many songs and lyrics came to mind. These are songs I had playing or found meaning for the characters in the lyrics. You can find it on Spotify here

1. **Kasey Musgraves**: Butterflies - '*..and out of the blue, I fell for you, now you're liftin' me up instead of holding me down, you give me butterflies.*'

2. **Kasey Musgraves**: Slow Burn - *'good when you're puttin' your hands all over me, I'm alright with a slow burn, taking my time let the world turn.'*

3. **Riley Green**: Worst Way - *'I don't wanna be out of line, but girl, I can't wait anymore. I want you in the worst way, my hands needin' your hips.'*

4. **Chris Stapleton**: Think I'm in Love with you - *'Whatever happened way back when, or if I'll see you again.... I think I'm in love with you. I didn't know it at the time, it's makin' me lose my mind.'*

5. **Lainey Wilson**: 4x4xU - *the vibes of this song*
6. **Lainey Wilson**: Heart like a truck - *the vibes of this song*
7. **Zach Bryan**: Sun to me - *the vibes of this song*
8. **Adele**: When we were young - *'you feel like home, you're a dream come true.'*
9. **Cranberries**: Linger - *'...and I'm in so deep, you know I'm such a fool for you, you've got me wrapped around your finger.'*
10. **Coldplay**: Shiver - *'so I look in your direction, but you pay me no attention do you? ..... I'll always be waiting for you.' - Sean could have written this song for Lucy!! Early Coldplay are my vibe*

Chapter 1

Lucy

"Kate, I'm on my way. I swear, I'm nearly there!"

I slam my hand on the wheel, blasting my horn and gritting my teeth at the oblivious woman with a blond bun in the car in front who slammed her brakes. All those bobby pins must be affecting her brain function. My nose is almost in her tail.

My mama had raised me right or I might have flipped her the bird or served her up some choice words.

"That bakery will be the end of you one day." My best friend sighed, exasperation oozing through the Bluetooth.

"I can't start the party without my maid of honor here."

"I know."

Glaring at blond bun lady, I pull my baby pink Mini Cooper out, passing her and put my foot to the floor.

"I'm only five minutes away. You know I don't have anyone else to cover until finishing time."

I love my best friend but, blow me, this wedding was sending her just a little crazy. The usually cool, calm, and collected Kate Larson was nowhere to be seen, and it's more than a little unsettling. I'm usually the erratic and unreliable one and I was having to pull out all the stops to keep this wedding on track.

The big day is just two weeks away.

"I'm just worried about you Lucy, you work every hour God sends and then some, and I know I've put a lot of pressure on you with the wedding prep on top of taking over the bakery for your mom,"

"Yes," I cut her off, "that's what best friends are for! We've planned this since we were ten years old, pulling white pillowcases on our heads, and parading up and down your bedroom shouting 'I do!'"

Her wicked laugh over the loudspeaker is infectious, and I'm grinning from ear to ear at the memory.

"Be there in five, love you!"

"Love you back."

By the time I get there, the Larson's annual 4th of July barbecue is in full swing. I had to park halfway down the street; the whole town had turned up this year for the joint holiday/pre-wedding celebration.

The Larsons are such a well thought of family in Breakridge. Kate's dad, Mr Larson, owns and runs the biggest hardware store, his dad before him and his dad before him.

The barbecue is a big event on the towns' calendar. The stars and stripes fly high in the front yard, grass cut fresh in front of the bright white wrap-around porch. This was the house I dreamed of living in one day.

I practically lived here growing up. Kate and I have been inseparable since my family moved to the little town when I was only five years old to be closer to my grandma and pops. I remember very little about moving, but I do remember meeting Kate. Her full-on boisterous energy consumed me from the moment we met in the playground,

"Hi, I'm Kate. What's your name?" I was in awe of her full head of unruly brown spirals and the darkest brown eyes.

"I'm Lucy."

"Let's play Lucy, my mom has the best coookies. Do you want one?"

It continued like this for the next twenty-six years. Through the highs and lows of junior, middle, and high school. Through first kisses, prom, breakups, and college. My absolute ride-or-die.

And now she's getting married.

I couldn't be happier for her. She's my sister. I love her.

Am I going to be a little lost without her?

Absolutely.

Music streams through from the backyard, my hands full with the biggest cake box and a pile of cupcakes I'd just finished icing. I had a balancing act with my clutch bag, the cake boxes, and a bottle of champagne. Fighting the door handle delicately, it swings open so fast I almost fall right through the door.

"Whoa, watch yourself there."

Oh-my-god.

The gravel in that voice shot a spike of heat through my core. Who was this unexpected guest? I thought I knew all of Kate's family. I'd been to enough Larson family events, I'd met all the cousins, second cousins, aunts and uncles.

Two broad hands catch my arms firmly, keeping me from face-planting and ruining the cakes I'd spent the afternoon baking and icing.

"Thanks." I look up into deep-set emerald eyes, framed with loose curly blonde hair.

Hellloo tall, blond, and buff.

Trust me to almost fall flat on my face in front of him. The deep emerald eyes narrow, darkening.

"Lucy?" the gravelly voice drawls my name into a question. I couldn't help a smile forming, my insides turning a little squishy.

Jeez, I need a date. How long has it been, four months? Maybe six?

And even longer since I'd dusted off downstairs with anything more substantial than my worn out rabbit.

"I'm sorry; have we met?" If I'd met tall, blond, and buff, I would have remembered. I struggle to form a sentence in reply.

"Lucy!" Kate screeches my name. "You're here!" She rushes me, planting air kisses around the box of cupcakes.

"Dad's just lit the coals. Let's get you a glass of bubbly."

She looks at tall, blond, and buff, "Sean, can you take the cake and muffins to the kitchen for Lucy, please?"

"Sean?!" I sputter the name in shock. My face flushes ten shades of pink and red. I feel a rash burning up my neck.

Have I just mentally undressed Kate's little brother?

Oh dear lord, I'm going to hell. I'd known Sean since he was born, a baby in his mama's arms.

Kate grabs my arm, dragging me to the garden as soon as Sean has relieved me of the cupcake boxes. I sneak a peek back over my shoulder. How has Kate's geeky little brother grown into tall, blond, and buff?

God, I had to stop thinking that! He still stood in the open doorway, cakes in hand; those sparkly emerald eyes pinned on me. He's slightly more menacing than I last remembered. All muscles, tan and tattoos.

How long has it been since I'd seen Sean? The last time he waved goodbye before heading to Uni in Michigan? Yep, like nine years ago?

A lot has changed in nine years.

I manage to get my hands on a glass of bubbles before Kate hauls me over to Josh, her husband-to-be, and his best men. If I had to sit through another night of Kate setting me up, I might vomit in the ice bucket before the night was through.

I know Kate only has the best intentions, and she wants me to be as happy as she is with Josh, but I could just do with a night off from the match making shtick tonight.

It's my own damn fault, I should never have had so much champagne at the engagement party and started wallowing in my self-pity, telling her I was going to be a lonely old maid and stay on the dusty shelf forever, with my dried-up muffins and of course, I'd have to get some cats.

She has since made it her mission to set me up on as many dates as possible until I find Mr. Right. I'm now convinced that Mr. Right doesn't exist, and if he does, I certainly won't find him here, in Breakridge River.

Chapter 2

Sean

She's here. Of course, she's here. She is Kate's maid of honor.

Lucy bloody Davenport.

Nine years. It has been nine years since I left this godforsaken town. The town of Breakridge River where everyone knows your business and nothing is a secret.

The town where I was a gangly teenager that nobody could see.

As soon as I turned eighteen, I was on the first bus out of here.

Gone.

I earned my scholarship to Michigan State, and I never looked back. I'd traveled far and wide. A regular digital nomad. My dad still doesn't think I have an actual job; I'm an eternal disappointment in his eyes. Daddy's princess, Kate, is the angel, the diamond of his eye. Kate owns and runs the local vet. A very successful career, so I'm told at every opportunity. I'm sure he thinks I'm some kind of drug lord with the money I've earned.

"Why do people spend so much money on digital things? They don't actually exist." Dad had huffed exasperated. "I just don't get it."

Explaining the concept again wouldn't make a difference. I'd already explained it several times over the years. I've given up trying.

We'd had this conversation thousands of times over the last five years since I'd finished college and went traveling. It was the most amazing time of my life.

Building the virtual assistant business 'VA4U', sitting with Jude, my travel mate and best friend, in a Tiki bar in Cancun. We didn't know how lucrative the online business world could be. We'd had case studies at college about online billionaires, but I never thought I would come close. I'm no billionaire, but I certainly have a healthy bank balance for a rainy day after I sold my share of VA4U to Jude to pursue more ventures.

With nothing to come home for after college, I decided not to bother. Much to my mother's disgust.

Until today.

Kate's wedding. Mom would've been furious if I hadn't come back. I'd had a daily reminder that I'd missed nine Christmases, nine Thanksgiving, nine 4th July barbecues, and all the holidays in between.

I would need to remind her I flew the whole family out to Bali for one Christmas and to Dubai for another and Paris for Thanksgiving last year.

I just wasn't ready to come back here.

Hell, I still wasn't ready.

But, here I stand, on the outside, looking in.

Nothing much had changed.

I left this place determined I was getting Lucy Davenport out from under my skin, eradicated from my waking thoughts and my dreams.

And it worked for a while. New faces, a new town, heck, a new state. She was just a high school crush, after all. She couldn't dominate my dreams forever.

The years passed quickly. One 365 days rolled into the next. Another continent, another country, another girlfriend, or one-night stand. Now and then she would creep back into my thoughts. I'd wonder what she was doing, and who she was with.

Of course, she'd be married with the perfect little family. An attentive husband, two perfect little children, and a white picket fence.

Did she come home after college? Was she a hotshot surgeon in the city like she'd always dreamed of being?

She was floating around my garden like she owned the place, topping up drinks, and replenishing snacks. She throws her head back, laughing, carefree, and confident, just as she'd always been.

The long pull from my beer does nothing to quench my thirst. I had to pull my eyes away from her. This is ridiculous. From her reaction at the door, she didn't even remember me.

She was so self-involved she didn't even remember her best friend's brother. The boy she'd grown up with, had Sunday dinners with, spent holidays with, joked and laughed, watched movies, and rode bikes up and downtown with.

A firm hand thudded my back, jolting me, my beer sloshes over the sides and onto my boots.

"Still can't take your eyes off her, huh?" My oldest brother, Xander, holds a firm grip on my shoulder.

Irritation hums under my skin. I throw my shoulder up knocking him off.

"Who? What are you talking about?" My attempt to hide is lost on him. His knowing chuckle like nails down a chalkboard.

Xander is the oldest out of the four of us and has always had this innate ability to see right through us all. That's probably why he naturally became the chief of police in Breakridge after leaving the FBI academy for his twins.

Not much gets by him.

Lie to Mom and Dad to get away with something; easy. Try to get that same shit past Xander; it would be easier to tame wild lions.

"Have you really stayed away all these years to avoid her?" He stands an inch taller than me, looking down, his broad arms crossed over his broad chest, beer bottle balanced between his fore and middle finger.

His question slaps hard. Have I stayed away just to avoid Lucy Davenport? Have I stayed away to avoid rejection?

"You think I'd stay away just to avoid a girl Xander, get real." I hope my laugh would seal the lie.

His face stays serious as he stares me straight in the eyes. "Yeah, I do."

"Everything isn't about Lucy fucking Davenport!" I hiss.

"I've been away making a name for myself, building businesses, and packing my bank account."

"Yeah, we all know how much money you've made, Sean." He's so serious.

My big serious brother.

The responsible one, who juggles his job with my niece and nephew as a single dad. The son my dad is proud of.

"But are you happy?" That one cuts my jugular.

Ouch.

Typical Xander, drops a dirty bomb and heads over to the grill to help Dad serve the town hot dogs and burgers, leaving me drowning in my thoughts.

Dad has on one of those quirky aprons with the slogan, '*Kiss the chef but don't touch the buns*'. Throwing his arm around Xander, his smile is full of pride. I don't think I've ever seen my dad look at me like that.

I'm the son who ran away, who didn't take on the family business like Oli, our middle brother, or make chief of police like Xander.

The afternoon gives way to the evening; the darkness making it easier to blend in. How long did I have to hang around before I could cut out without being rude? Oli had only just arrived. Two hours late, but that was because he had been holding the fort and locking up at Larson's Hardware.

My brothers; always working hard.

Still minding my own business, watching a certain redhead floating around, I notice she doesn't come near me. It could be the *stay-out-of-my-face* vibe I was intentionally radiating, but it certainly didn't work for some people.

"Sean!" my little cousin Jack croons, opening his arms to me.

I'm not a hugger.

The awkward man hug is not my thing.

I stick out my hand. He hesitates before grasping it in his weak attempt to pull me in.

I don't budge.

"Long time no see cuz. How's life treating you?" He pauses letting his eyes linger up and down, appraising me from my Cartier watch up. "It's been a while since we've seen you man, how's life treating you?"

He knows fine well every detail of my travels and my business. Mom keeps her sisters up to date with every minutia of my life.

"Yep, just a regular digital nomad." I rarely discuss my business and this usually covered it enough that no one asked too many questions, but not today.

"Aw, man! What a life, traveling and fucking all over the world." He winks, I cringe. The scent of bourbon radiates from him, teasing bile from my stomach.

"Am I right Sean boy?"

Sean boy?

His pointy little elbow finds my rib cage. I glare down my nose frowning, thankful he takes the hint and steps out of my personal space.

If his wife was in earshot, she'd have his balls in a slingshot. Jack was a player. I'm surprised he actually convinced a girl from town to agree to marry him, given his dating history. Cassie was beautiful and smart. Jack was definitely punching.

One thing about this small town, it didn't take too long for Mom to get me up to date with nine years of gossip. I'd already had a full rundown of marriages, births, and deaths since I'd left. Shockingly, Lucy hadn't fallen into the list of marriages. Perhaps Mom had left out a few wedding couples?

Jack's voice buzzes in my ear like an annoying little bug. My attention is firmly elsewhere.

Lucy strides confidently towards my sister, her hips swaying, the light cotton of her skirt sashays back and forth hypnotizing me, a tan skin tone body suit hugged her curves, leaving just enough to the imagination.

And my imagination is running wild.

A gentle breeze lifts her bouncing auburn red beach waves. Her fingers gently tuck the strands behind her ear when she tilts her head down to my mom. Man, I wanted to grab that hair, pull her head back towards me as I....

Jesus Sean, get a fucking grip. You're not a horny 16-year-old kid anymore!

I need to get my head in the game.

I can't go there for the same reasons I couldn't nine years ago. She was a stuck-up she-devil who thought the world revolved around her. No one was good enough for her, and besides, she's my sister's best friend.

And what was this now? Kate, you absolute traitor!

Kate is dragging Josh's cousin Brendan over to Lucy, a clear setup if ever I saw one, and Brendan is lapping it up like a giddy golden retriever.

Actually more like a Saint Bernard with his size and the drool running from his lips.

His eyes popping from his head, he couldn't be more obvious if he was licking his lips like Lucy was a juicy steak. I could stick around to watch the train crash. I didn't want to see, but I couldn't tear my eyes from her.

Brendan grabs her hand in a shake, lifting it. That son of a... his lips touch her skin!

My skin sizzles. A growl rumbles deep in my throat, stuck there.

Across the yard, Lucy lifts her head, looking straight towards me.

Shit, did she hear me?

I don't care. That fucker was touching her, his lips on her.

When did it get so hot out here? Rivulets of sweat trickle down my spine, my chest rising and falling like I've been running through the Sahara in a parka. Her curious eyes burn holes through me.

Something lights in her eyes, a desire I'd seen in many women but never had my body reacted in return, never had it mattered.

I saw her fire light. Was that me she was looking at? My cock twitches taking note of her attention.

She drops her gaze, breaking our connection. Her attention back on Brendan, who is salivating at this point.

If this was a cartoon, Brendan's tongue would be rolling to the floor with hearts pumping out his eyes and Lucy was an oblivious Jessica Rabbit.

I'd have a quiet word with him later about manners and respect.

She watches me watching over his bulky shoulder. A spark of electricity glimmers in my heart, thundering through my rib cage. I've only been back one day, and she has me under her be-witchery.

A cold fucking shower is what's needed and I'm not coming out until Lucy bloody Davenport is gone. Forgetting Jack wittering away beside me, I head for the house.

Chapter 3

Lucy

The barbecue is buzzing; family and friends together drinking, eating and laughing. Mr. Larson is the barbecue king; sporting his '*Kiss the Chef but don't touch the buns*' apron and pouting at everyone as they come for plates of refills. Brandishing a set of tongs dishing out delicious burgers and chicken wings, I grab a burger and a peck on the cheek.

"Thanks, chef. What a success!"

Mr. Larson holds his beer to me for a toast.

"All the extra help from you this year has been wonderful; you've really made the annual grill a wedding party to remember." He winks at me before turning to Uncle Jim and filling his bun with a hot dog.

My stomach objects loudly, gurgling in protest at being neglected since breakfast. I shove a bite of burger in my mouth before the champagne goes right to my head and I'm dancing on the patio like Britney baby. Can't have the maid of honor stumbling around the party. I have to keep everything running smoothly.

Barbs, Kate's mom, teeters towards me in her stilettos, greeting me with air kisses on each cheek. I hand her and her sisters fresh glasses of bubbles.

"Oh Lucy, thank you, darling. What would we do without you?"

She tips her head towards her sisters. "Lucy, Kate's best friend, she's taking all the weight from Kate, so she enjoys her big day!"

"Well, what are best friends for?" I smile politely at the tipsy ladies.

Kate's mom had been a rock for me and Mom when Dad died. Helping with funeral arrangements, making sure we ate and cleaned our house because Mom lost the love of her life. The literal other half of herself. Her soul mate. She never quite recovered to her full-of-life, bubbly self after that day. There's always been a tiny spark missing from her. And two years later she received her diagnosis of multiple sclerosis.

"How is your mom, dear?"

"She's fine Barb, thanks." Always put a smile on; Mom never wants to be a burden, even to her best friend.

"She's gutted she couldn't make it today. She tried, but her body just wouldn't let her."

I try not to flinch the words out loud, "she was sorry and sends all her love to you and Kate."

Barb's head tilts in a knowing and loving smile.

"No apology needed. Your mom has to listen to her body, trying to keep running the bakery and pushing herself. This is the first 4th July she's ever missed."

She says it with the understanding only a best friend could have. I love Kate's mom dearly, with only my mom left; Kate's family has become my family, too.

Speaking of Kate, where had the the bride-to-be gone? I scan the familiar faces of the town in the garden searching for her unmistakable white jumpsuit.

Kate's laughter fills the garden. She's enjoying herself, letting go of all worries with the groomsmen. I catch her eye with a fresh glass of bubbles; she slides me a wink, and I know I should be worried about her wayward intentions. But, she's letting her hair down, and it's beautiful to see. She'd unloaded all her 'to-do's' on me and I have many mental notes stored away.

I still have the bachelorette to plan, the cake design to finish, take the bridesmaids for a last fitting and decide on shoes, pick up Kate's dress and help her finish the favors, and make sure Josh has all the groomsmen's suits sorted and picked up.

I'm sure there will be more and my head is already spinning alongside all the plates I'm balancing. This wedding might well be the end of me, as well as keeping Honeybee Bakery going with Mom's health, taking a tumble down a black diamond ski slope.

Our third generation little family bakery is Mom's pride and joy. It's been her lifeline since Grandma had died. Her legacy. Grandma and Pops had founded the bakery sixty-five years ago this year, starting out in the back of Grandma's kitchen with her delicious loaves, sweet treats, and sticky buns. One year later Pops bought the shop in the middle of Main Street, re-modeled and decorated it with his own love, sweat, and tears, and it's been our family business since.

Mom grew up learning to count and measure from baking with Grandma and then, when it was my turn, I donned the kid-size apron to learn the ropes too.

Honeybee Bakery met every and all bakery needs in town. Local people supporting a local business.

I can't dwell on that now. There's a show to put on, and a wedding to make sure goes off without a hitch.

My best friend's wedding. The day we've dreamed of for each other forever.

It would be damn well perfect.

"Lucy!" Kate's shrill voice gets higher with each glass of bubbles she consumes. She sways towards me. "There you are; I've been looking for you."

I hold out my hand to stabilize her. Note to self: don't let Kate drink too many bubbles before the photos on the big day!

"I've been here the whole time, Kate." My laugh catches in my throat when I notice the broad-shouldered, blued-eyed guy on her side with his eyes firmly trained on my chest.

I tilt my head down; eyes up here big guy! He doesn't even have the decency to look sheepish at being busted ogling my goodies!

"Thish iss Brendan." Her words roll out in a slur; she's propped on Big Guy's biceps. "Josh's cousin from Colorado Springs. He'sh in town for the wedding and..." Kate winks so hard, they get the message as far away as Denver.

"He'shingle!"

Closing my eyes momentarily, I pull all my willpower and strength not to let my eyes roll back into my skull, more matchmaking. My mother taught me manners and by god, I would use them. I offer my hand.

"Nice to meet you, Brendan," his callused hand scratches on my well-moisturized skin like cheap loo roll. Not as soft as Sean's hands gripping my arms.

Where the heck did that come from?

"I would normally say your cousin is a lucky guy, but to-day," I incline my head towards Kate, "he's got his hands full."

Brendan lets out a gentle giant chuckle, low and rumbling, redeeming himself slightly when he lifts my hand to his lips for a gentle kiss.

"He certainly does. Are all the ladies in Breakridge River a handful?" His blue eyes sparkle at me over my knuckles and heat pierces through me.

It wasn't Big Guy's blue eyes giving me the heat.

Over his shoulder, another set of eyes burn through me.

Sean.

What is he staring at?

Why does it feel like a tornado of butterflies has let loose in my stomach?

He's standing on the far side of the yard, tall, brooding, and leaning lazily on the wooden gazebo frame. His eyes, dark and foreboding, never stray from me. I felt his gaze intensify as I had mingled with the party. A consciousness of being observed.

It's no wonder I hadn't recognized Sean when I'd barreled into him, muffins and all. You wouldn't put his 17-year-old shy, skinny, stroppy teenage self and match him with this tall, muscular, tattooed, broad-shouldered, sun-kissed effigy.

Tight jeans and a white shirt unbuttoned to reveal enough chest muscle to excite a woman vowed to celibacy. Golden skin reflected off the bright light of an almost full moon like a tempting golden pastry.

He'd let his hair grow out. What was once tight brown curls, now replaced with thick sun-kissed blond waves.

The butterflies flutter harder. His beer lifts to his lips, eyes never leaving me. God, I wish that bottle were my lips.

Ah, what now, this can't happen!

I can't fantasize about Sean. Sultry, spotty teenager, my best friend's brother, Sean!

But he's not a teenager anymore!

Hmmm...

NO! He's still your best friend's little brother!

Big Guy clears his throat and my eyes tear away from Sean, the spell broken.

Brendan looks like he's just won the Super Bowl, imagining my obvious reaction to his gentle kiss on my hand. How could I dampen the joy in his glittering blue eyes that are doing absolutely nothing for the butterflies? In fact, they were calming the little buggers down.

I can't for the life of me remember his last question; gently I laugh and pulled my hand back, silently cursing Kate. I was going to have to have a word with her.

Many words.

For a start, I don't need to be set up.

I don't need a guy in my life.

And, I'm not lonely.

And I certainly don't have time to deal with a relationship.

"Well, lovely to meet you, Brendan. Guess I'll be seeing you at the wedding."

"You sure will." His wink evokes a cringe deep in my gut.

"I'm back in town a few days before the wedding. I'd love to take you out for dinner?"

Oh hells bells, I'm really gonna kill Kate now.

"I mean, right before the wedding, I'll be super busy with all the prep, the bride, the cake; you know how it is."

Please take the hint, please take the hint.

"Absolutely."

Phew.

"You'll be so busy you won't make time to eat. Can't have you waste away or passing out from hunger at the wedding, now can we?"

He has a really cute, crooked smile. It pulls up on one side. I could have dinner. What harm would that do? A free meal and it would get Kate off my back for a little while.

Hopefully.

"Alright."

I'd be running here and there and everywhere; a scheduled meal might not be so bad, and if I'm too busy, I can always cancel. "Dinner sounds lovely."

Brendan taps his number into my phone.

The butterflies make their move in my stomach again. It wasn't Brendan tapping my buttons.

No, the dark, dangerous, sexy eyes across the yard drag my attention back again.

My stomach flip flops, eyes in a trance. Could he feel the electricity? Heat vibrates from my toes, rising higher.

Excitement, danger, and heat between my thighs have me wriggling for comfort.

As quickly as he had my attention, he rips his eyes away, turning like his ass is on fire, and heads inside the house.

What is his problem?

Chapter 4

Lucy

Dark has blanketed the garden, the moon illuminating the sky. A high-energy full moon in Capricorn. The fairy lights wrapped around the garden light it up beautifully, mirroring the stars. Everyone had left except for a few stragglers finishing beers and the remains of Mr. Larson's amazing sticky chicken wings.

Oh, my days they were to die for. But he wasn't for parting with the recipe.

"Don't be offended Lucy," he teased. "I wouldn't even part with this recipe to my biological daughter. This was granny's, and she trusted me to pass it down the family to someone who won't ruin it," he laughed. "And that ain't Kate!"

Smiles and tipsy giggles leave the garden. Mr. Larson, after a few beers, holds his wife in a drunken, intimate dance under the fairy lights. Barbs crooning with her rendition of Bruce Springsteen's Dancing in the Dark.

I love that song and Barbs is absolutely murdering it with a high-pitched whine.

The Larson's 4th July barbecue come pre-wedding celebration has been an absolute hit. The bride-to-be now wittering sweet nothings into her fiance's ear beside the warmth of the fire pit. Actually, I think Kate might be snoring on his shoulder.

Either way, Josh looks as content as a pig in shit having her there, his arm tucked around her protectively. I sigh, happy to see my best friend happy and only twenty percent jealous it would never be me.

Okay, maybe thirty-five percent. They look so content and comfortable with each other. I've already accepted that scenario just isn't in my future. I'll probably be a lonely old maid with a house full of cats.

Honeybee Bakery consumes every minute of all my days since Mom stepped back last year. Her balance was becoming less steady, and she'd had several tumbles while trying to transport clients' deliveries from the bakery door to the back of the van. I couldn't take the anxiety of potentially finding her lying in the bakery with hot stove pans atop her.

Between Mom's hospital appointments and the bakery, I was still squeezing in, studying pre-med online in the vague hope that I might make it out of here one day. I might make it to the city and become a surgeon.

Yeah, right. That pipe dream crept further and further out of sight with each passing sun set.

Although I knew it would be nothing like Grey's Anatomy, I wanted to make a difference. And who knew, maybe I would find my McDreamy when I was a resident?

Ha, yeah, keep dreaming Lucy.

Mrs. Paterson from next door was checking on Mom before bed, so I didn't have to rush home. I would help Mrs. Larson get cleared up. Kate is in no fit state and everyone else has abandoned the ship. Notably, all the Larson brothers had eaten, had a good drink, and now were nowhere in sight. Typical.

I slip the last sticky chicken wing past my lips before gathering piles of trays for the dishwasher.

The pile of trays crash down on the sideboard. Every area of the extensive marble surface now scattered with open bottles of beer, champagne, and whiskey bottles, and plates piled high, and the smell of leftover burgers and onions lingers in the air.

My stomach makes itself known again with a loud groan.

"Man, we drank a lot tonight." I say out loud to myself out of habit. The bakery was always quiet, so I chatted away my thoughts or sang along to the radio. I'm partial to a bit of Kasey Musgraves or a rock out to Evanescence. It was how I always loved to process my feelings.

Hands-on hips, I stand staring at the carnage. I was going to be here all night getting this place sorted. I couldn't well leave it for Kate and Barbs. What a state that pair will be in the morning.

"Well, I *am* the maid of honor." I sigh, glancing at the time.

One am.

I need to open the bakery at eight am.

"I better get a wriggle on."

Bent over the dishwasher, ass in the air; a throat clears behind me

Shit.

I know exactly who it is because that's how much God hates me.

"Do you always talk to yourself in the kitchen?" The deep drawl sends a shiver through my core, a little warm and satisfying feeling sparking low in my belly.

Aw crap!

Could I stay ass in the air and pretend I didn't see or hear him? I couldn't deal with his intense stares for another second. I might melt, like I actually might end up in a puddle on the floor.

I turn around, Sean leaning casually against the fridge, eyes smoldering. His arms across what I had peeked earlier was a very toned, very hard chest. It was now covered in a very snug cotton white tee, with low-rise jeans hugging those thick thighs.

Oh-my-gawd.

My belly does a bit of a somersault, my thighs clench.

What the hell happened at college? Did they inject heat and smolder out there in Michigan?

This couldn't be the same guy. This could not be the same boy I ran around the lake with, splashing in the water in our pants. The sulky teenager who grunted goodbye at me before he left for college without a second glance.

My brain struggles to put the two together. My brain is struggling to do much right now. Too many glasses of champagne.

Damn Barbs for topping up my glass too many times!

Fresh out of the shower, the welcome smell of pine and lavender fills my nose, messing with my senses. His tumbling sun-kissed curls pushed back slick and wet, accentuated his high pronounced cheekbones. Those emerald eyes pin me to the work surface.

Pull yourself together Lucy.

It's Sean.

My face flushes with heat like I've just stepped into the sauna on an icy day.

"Sorry, I thought everyone was gone."

Quickly, I turn breaking that sizzle and hiding my blush at being caught talking to myself.

"It's great to see you back." I glance over my shoulder with a quick smile. "Your mom has missed you so much, believe me, we've heard about it every day!" I laugh easily.

"Ha, I know." His smile seems sad. "The longer I stayed away, the easier it was to not come home." He shrugs, stepping closer to grab dishes, he stacks along side me.

"Oh, I bet it was easy with all the beaches, cocktails, and women."

Shit, that last bit just slipped right out! It wasn't my business how many women he'd dated while he'd been away.

"That wasn't all I did, Lucy." Disappointment laces his eyes when he catches mine. He throws a dish towel over his shoulder before continuing to stack sticky barbeque plates. Why is that so sexy?

What did I say?

That's what everyone said.

"I traveled for business, I enjoyed different cultures, I made friends and enjoyed myself, and made a little money while I was away."

He carries on crashing the dishes into the dishwasher.

"Sorry Sean, I didn't mean to judge." I say sincerely, "You must've enjoyed it a lot to stay away for so long?"

We work through the chaos until the kitchen is sparkling, chatting easily and laughing. I try to keep a distance.

It's easy listening to him chat about some of the places he had been and experiences he'd had. I would give my left leg to go skydiving or see Machu Picchu. I could listen to him for hours.

While we worked away everyone had headed straight past us and up to bed.

Josh had carried a comatose Kate upstairs over thirty minutes ago, and Mr. and Mrs. Larson followed them up not long after. Barbs gripped her son in a vise grip before she headed upstairs to bed still humming Bruce Springsteen.

I put the last dish away. An awkward silence fell like a dark drape cloaking us.

"Well, I'd better get myself home to bed; I need to open the bakery in five hours." That reality almost brings tears to my eyes. "Thanks for helping me tidy; you didn't have to stay up with me."

Glad you did though!

By the time I drive home, wash all my makeup...

"You're *not* driving home."

Sean's voice bursts through my mental to-do list. "You've had far too much to drink; I saw you earlier sipping on the champagne."

I saw you seeing me earlier, is what I want to say but thankfully keep my brain in check.

"It's only across town; I'll be fine. Besides, there will be no one else on the road."

I start the hunt for my bag with my keys, scanning all the clean surfaces. I remember seeing it in here when we were tidying, where did I put it?

"You aren't driving." His deep, gravelly demanding voice strums through me. Who the hell did he think he was telling me what I was and wasn't doing?

I can't stay here.

Sean's hand is high above my head, dangling my keys.

"Not funny Sean, pass my keys."

I hold out my hand hoping he'll just give in and drop them in.

No chance.

A twinkle sparkles in his eye when he shakes his head back and forth slowly, his blond curls loosely falling free.

"No keys, no driving. You might not hit someone else, but you could hit a tree or a street light and kill yourself."

I'm not having this, Kate's little brother *teasing me!*

Hell no.

"Come here and look me in the eye."

That command stops me in my tracks. I look up as he bends looking down, leaning forward into my space. If I wasn't drunk before I might now be intoxicated by the scent of pine and lavender flooding my brain.

"What?" I stutter.

"Look - into - my - eyes." He over pronounces each word like I need help to understand.

I'm transfixed, staring into the deep pool of green. My lips part on an exhale. A smile pulls at the corner of his lips and I do the only thing I can think of; throw my arm high to grab my keys, "Give - me - my - keys!"

Of course that's exactly what he's waiting for.

With his opposite hand he grabs my wrist firmly holding it above my head.

Holy shit. A spark of electricity burns from my wrist through my entire body. The coolness of the fridge behind me is doing nothing to cool me down. I'm trapped, my arms pinned high, his eyes never leave mine.

My chest presses against his with the strain. With every breath, my hard nipples graze him. The friction sends me wild. I have nowhere to look but up into him. The laughter gone.

Those pesky butterflies rampage with vengeance. My core like a furnace waiting to erupt. A fiery wave of desire pulses through me.

In that moment, if he presses those soft full lips to mine, I would be helpless to refuse.

Chapter 5

Sean

I hold the keys high above my head, out of her reach. My other hand grips her wrist above her head, backing up against the fridge, her face tilts up to me, her neck elongated and so tempting. I know I should step back, I know I should let her go.

But I can't drop my gaze, I can't pull back.

She is even better than I remembered.

I can't take my eyes from her, her solid nipples pulse against me with every inhale.

I am rock hard. There is no way she can't feel my body's reaction to her.

All those years, I thought I had a clear memory, a clear vision of who she was, and how she affected me.

I had no fucking idea. Time and distance had made her more potent to me, if that was even possible.

The anger has drained from her eyes and something else lingers there.

Is my imagination creating what it wants to see or is that desire in those deep brown pools of chocolate?

She is so close, the scent of cinnamon from her skin is glorious. Does she bathe in the stuff? That tan body suit has teased me all fucking night. I'm dying to rip it off. Her round chest presses on me with every rapid breath, the sheer material doing nothing to hide her rigid nipples. The sweet scent of champagne tempts me lower, sucking me in.

I could kiss her right now. I could fulfil my teenage fantasy, the stuff my wet dreams were made of.

I drag my eyes lazily from her red toenails to her pouted lips, my brain flashing images of what she could wrap those lips around.

I want that curvy, thick waist in my hands, her soft skin under my touch. My hands itch to get closer, pull her against my throbbing cock tighter. She is everything I ever wanted and every feeling I shoved down deep, every tiny tingle I'd ignored my whole life, smacked me upside the head in that second. All the teenage angst, all the unexpected boners when she walked into the house, which had been *a lot.*

The way she's looking up at me right now, eyes wide, pupils dilated, lips parted; one hundred tiny fireworks light my heart on fire.

My fingers slip easily around the back of her neck, her soft red strands caressing; I pull her closer.

I pause, waiting for her to put a stop to this. Waiting for my dream to shatter.

She doesn't.

Her eyes flutter closed, beautiful lips part, she tips her chin higher. I dip so close my nose kisses her; her skin like velvet.

The moment shatters.

Lucy yelps like a wounded animal, nearly hitting the roof, diving so fast out of my grip to get to the other side of the kitchen island.

"OH my god!" She's a deer in the headlights. Backing away like I've grown horns and started breathing fire.

Gone are the dreamy chocolate eyes, replaced with large black saucers,

"Holy shit, what are you doing?"

Wait what!?

"What! What am *I* doing?" I don't believe this. "You lunged at me, threw yourself right on me!"

"I did NOT!" her shriek pierces my ears.

"I had to hold you in a death grip to stop you from attacking me." I laugh.

"Ugh, I would never, I have never..." she splutters, not impressed, the words caught in her throat. It was cute. "You're Sean."

"Yes, I'm aware." I can't help my eyes rolling.

"You're Kate's little brother."

"Not so little now though, am I?" I raise an eyebrow. Her tan skin pale and flushed as she pats down her skirt, eyes roving for her handbag.

"I have to go. I have to sleep and work."

She's muttering about too many bubbles and bloody Barbs. Still holding her keys, I swing them in the air, out of her reach.

"Looking for these?"

"Please give me my keys, I really need to go to bed."

"You could crash here you know? There's a spare room."

Why the hell did I say that? How on earth would I sleep with Lucy Davenport in the next room, especially after that little firework display?

"I need to get home." She stands tall and firm, arms crossed under her round breasts, pushing them high and firm. Jeez, she was going to kill me before I could leave after Kate's damn wedding.

"Now - give - me - my - keys - Sean." My name on her lips is so soft, it feels like home.

"No." I'm smug. There is no way she's getting her hands on these keys tonight.

Anger flashes in her eyes again, she's ready to pounce. I hold up my hands in surrender. "But I will drive you home. I only had one beer earlier."

Really?

Is my brain taking stupid pills? With that toxic cinnamon scent filling the car. I might as well drown in a bottle of whiskey!

"Honestly, you don't have to do that. I can drive myself, Sean, really, I'm fine." I might be more convinced if her eyes weren't half shut.

"I insist." She has no reason to argue, but I can see her mind working hard to conjure up an excuse.

Was I that hard to be around?

Reluctantly, I see the fight leave her before she gives in. She stomps past me towards the front door. All I can do is follow.

What the fuck. Her car is tiny. I can see cramp in my near future.

An old banged-up Mini Cooper in pink. Not my usual mode of transport. My six foot four-inch frame wasn't built for such a confined space. As I guessed, my knees almost touch my chin before I pull out of the drive.

It's not a long journey, a few blocks to the bakery, but man, I would likely be cut in half by the time we get there and I still had to run home.

"So you still stay above your mom's bakery?"

She'd lived there her whole life. I remember being in the apartment with Kate when we were little. The wonderful smell of bread and pastries always lingered in the air.

"Well, it's technically my bakery now." Her shoulders slump. "After Dad died and Mom's MS started progressing, she signed it all over to me."

"And you're not happy about that?"

She wriggles, clearly uncomfortable, tucking stray hairs behind her ear.

"I just didn't imagine still being here when I was 31. It's not really how I planned my life." She shrugs.

"But you know, shit happens. People get ill, people die and I'm here to pick up the pieces."

"I thought you stayed because you love Breakridge?"

I lift my foot off the accelerator. We're getting closer. I could still drive around town like I'd never been away. I want to stay in this cramped space with her intoxicating cinnamon smell, asking her about what she's been doing for the last nine years. How long could I draw out one block?

She lets out a weak laugh. "Nope, I had big plans to run out of here as fast as my little legs would carry me."

I'm so curious.

"What changed? Why are you still here?"

"We can't all run away, Sean!" her head snaps in my direction.

"Sorry I asked." Foot back on the gas until I pull up outside the bakery.

The silence hangs thick in the car.

Her words sting.

"I wasn't running away." I defend myself.

Liar.

"Some of us have responsibilities. I wish I could run away." Her sigh is so full of regret it fills me with sadness.

"Sorry, I rarely get on this topic with anyone. It's a bit of a sore one."

The suffocating quiet lingers. Neither of us making a move to get out.

"Sorry I pried."

No, I wasn't, but... manners.

"Well, I got you home without wrapping us around a tree." I rub the back of my neck. "I'll need to extract myself like a contortionist out of this midget car."

"Hey, don't hate on the car. I never forced you to drive me home." Her laugh is like smooth honey. "Ol' Betty has been good to me for years."

Rubbing the dash lovingly, "she could be your Tesla's grandma and she'll be here for many years to come."

"Well, I'll stick to my truck or Tesla from now on if you require a chauffeur, Miss Davenport."

Our eyes lock.

That flush on her face has the blood in my head rushing far south, reducing my leg space. I need to get out of this tin can.

Breathing is getting difficult.

"Right, well, I better get into bed."

That visual isn't helping. I bet she wears little satin short pajamas. She turns, stepping out of the car, leaving me with a picture of her full, round ass.

God, is she trying to end me right here on Main Street with no witnesses in sight?

Every bone in my body creaks and cracks as I extract myself. Staying put behind the safety of the car, fearing she sees what must be a bulge in my damn jeans that could support the leaning Tower of Pisa. I feel like the horny teenager had returned, hiding from her again.

"Thanks for the ride, night Sean."

She waves and spins away, disappearing through the bakery door.

"Night Lucy."

I've never run with a hard-on before. This will be a new, uncomfortable experience.

Chapter 6

Lucy

"You look tired, darling."

Mom studies me across the counter. Despite her condition, she insists on coming to the bakery most days. Standing behind the counter for as long as her legs will hold her up, then giving in and criticizing me from the sit-in tables at the window.

"Yep, I'm pretty tired, mom."

With both hands full of fresh blueberry muffins, I flip the oven door closed with my foot. "I didn't get home until almost four am."

I sink my teeth into a muffin filling my mouth with blueberry juiciness before I say something I'll regret. Closing my eyes as the warm, soft, gooey texture comforts me. The brief rush of dopamine that floods the system with the joy of delicious cake is second to none. I keep my eyes closed savoring the feeling as Mom mutters away behind me. Being hangry is not the time to deal with my mother. The hot sweetness of blueberry bursts into my mouth.

I smile, satisfied with another tasty batch.

The problem with owning a bakery is you have to sample the goods, which is why I have always been a little round in the rear and hips. Who can resist home baking, though? I'd grown up with it my entire life. I was destined to be a little rounder in the rear. My grandma was, my mom is. It was in the genes or the cupcakes!

Life is not worth living without dessert. What a bore life would be to say no to every sweet treat or carb. I just keep a moderate diet of everything else and grab a gym session or a run or two a week to keep a good balance.

"How many times do I have to tell you, you can't burn the candle at both ends?" She looks at me with her scolding face, "you know, you're not getting any younger."

Oh damn, here she goes. I can almost recite this speech by heart and can't help my eyes rolling back in my head.

"Don't roll your eyes at me, lady." She saves a sharp tone just for this occasion. I'm the only one who witnesses sweet Sandie serve up a tongue lashing.

"You'll never entice a man with dark rings under your eyes and falling asleep at seven pm to reruns of Friends!"

"Mom, there are no men left in Breakridge to entice. It's fine." Exasperated, I gather all the ingredients I need for the next recipe placing them to the side. A batch of banana bread for tomorrow. Some with pecan, some with chocolate chip, and some plain old banana. I keep my hands busy as my ears burn.

"There won't be any with that attitude." She sips her tea, tentatively holding the cup to her lips. Her gaze fixed out the window on a young woman walking by, pushing a stroller in one hand and holding a toddler's hand in her other.

"I won't be here forever Lucy, will I ever see my grandbabies?"

I purse my lips concentrating hard on carefully filling the previous batch of vanilla cupcakes with frosting from the piping bag, so I don't lose my shit with her.

It's not her fault I'm useless with men, it's not her fault every man within a hundred-mile radius is a pig, a sleazeball, or lives with his mommy, and the ones I have dated have fizzled out faster than a New Year weight loss resolution.

"I don't know what to say, Mom. I can't magic myself a man." I swish the pipe bag for effect, sending frosting flying.

"If I could have, I would have."

"Well, Kate bagged herself a little hottie."

Cringe!

"Mom! She met Josh through work. Kate goes back and forth to the city, getting further than the town boundary. The last time I left Breakridge was cousin Jack's wedding in the city last year. And Mr. Right isn't likely to waltz through my bakery door, is he?" I'm still brandishing the pipe bag, jabbing it towards the door.

She looks at me with a point to make.

"Yes, I remember. You were a bridesmaid there, too." Somehow, she manages to turn that into an insult. It's a skill.

"Do you want me to marry just any old jock to give you some grandchildren? They might have eleven fingers and three ears!"

My spatula is working overtime in the bowl, creaming butter and sugar furiously.

"Lucy, I don't care if they have two heads. If I could cuddle them and know them before it's too late and I'm too weak."

She really knows how to get me where it hurts.

Ugh!

"When I meet him, I'll know."

Mom's sigh could have shaken the walls.

"What?"

"Love isn't like that honey, it builds and blossoms," her hands flutter around her for effect. "You have to plant the seeds to let the flowers grow and blossom."

"Not for you and Dad."

She smiles bright as she always does when we talk about dad, "and not for Grandma and Pops. You both have told me the feelings of love and passion you had for each other from the beginning. You knew Dad was the one from your first date."

"We were childhood sweethearts dear, we grew up and had our first date and I knew your dad was my forever, but we hadn't just met." Her sympathetic eyes raise my blood pressure.

"Well, Grandma and Pops met at a dance." I say petulant-ly. "Their eyes met across the empty dance floor and Pops marched over and asked her to dance. I want that. I want that spark, the butterflies and the fireworks, never having eyes for anyone else, being happy when he comes into the room fifty years later, just like Grandma."

"It's hella hard to get to fifty years when you haven't met Mr. Love at first sight and you're already thirty-one!" She punctuates her point with a sickly sweet smile and the raise of an eyebrow. "You've dated lots of men."

"Thanks, Mom!"

She dismisses me with her hand. "You know what I mean, you've been in relationships, I thought were serious relationships."

"You hadn't picked out China, had you?" I point the spatula in her direction accusingly.

"Don't be sarcastic, Lucy, it's not becoming. I'm saying the guy shows signs of getting a little serious and you back away like a scuttling raccoon."

Oh boy, I was *not* mentally prepared for this today.

"That is not true, Mom."

It was a little true. "The guy always gets weird or stops calling."

Her eyebrows are in her hair before she starts.

"Ben,"

Oh, here she goes.

"I don't need a lis...."

"He got you a key cut for his apartment. You ended it faster than a lightning bolt through the sky; Jay," there is no stopping her now.

"He invited you to dinner with his parents after dating for three months and you sneaked out the back before dessert was served!"

My face burns hot.

"How on earth did you find out about that?!" I'd only ever told... "Kate! I'll bloody kill that little gossip."

She continues to list the last five boyfriends I've dated for longer than two months and why I'd run away. If there wasn't an element of truth, I might have objected sooner. There were never any sparks, fireworks, butterflies, or swooning with any of them.

I raise my hands in surrender attempting to put a stop to the attack. "Mom, when he comes into my life, I - will -know."

"How will you know?"

Her questioning eyebrows are nearly on her crown now. "How will you know if you've never felt love before? Not love from me or Grandma, but this almighty, gut-wrenching, all-encompassing love that's going to sweep you off your feet and turn your world upside down?"

How do I counter that?

The bell above the door tinkles. Thank the lord, a reprieve from the roasting Mom is serving up today.

"Sean!" Mom shrieks.

My heart jolts.

Wait. What? Why did it do that?

As if this day couldn't get any worse, the awkward memories of last night come flooding back to the forefront, playing like a drive in movie in my head.

Here.

In the bakery.

With Mom in the room.

She was like a coyote. She might smell the hint of lust and be on me like a wounded rabbit to set up a date!

Oh, my days. Her face is ecstatic. Why was she so excited to see him?

Could the world just swallow me up right now? I could come back as a dung beetle. That would be preferable to being here right now.

"Come over here and let me see you!" She croons to him. Mom pulls herself out of the little wicker chair, her arms waiting open.

"Mrs. Davenport, so lovely to see you." His words are so warm I could melt like butter in the sun.

He bends low grasping my mom in the softest embrace. Her arms stretched over his wide shoulders and around his muscular neck. She looks so petit in his large all encompassing grasp.

"At least *you* remember me." He grins over Mom's shoulder. Pulling back, she places her hands on his face squashing his cheeks like he was five again.

"Who would forget this face?" she smiles lovingly. My eyes can't help rolling again.

"Your daughter, that's who."

Mom turns to me dramatically, her mouth gaping. "Lucy! Did you really?"

Why does he have to stand there looking so smug, in his thigh-hugging Levi's and another muscle-hugging white t-shirt? Does the guy not own any other shirts? I thought he made a lot of money with his business. He needs a memo for more colors and a not-so-tempting fit.

What the hell!

My brain is back firing today!

All this talk of dating and failed boyfriends has sent my brain on a crazy loop!

"Well, you're a lot taller since we last saw you." She places her hands on his chest looking up at him, "and broader in the shoulders too!"

Sean chokes on a laugh. "Thanks, Mrs. Davenport... I think."

"I didn't forget you." I attempt to defend myself, "I had fallen in the door with a handful of cupcake boxes." I huff my hands across my chest. "I didn't get a chance before Kate grabbed me and whisked me away."

It sounds lame, "and Mom's right, you are a lot taller and broader." I cough out the last word.

"Hmm," his eyes darken, my tummy does a summersault. What is he staring at?

"What can I get for you, Sean?" I continue to cream the butter and sugar, slowly adding the whisked egg; I keep my eyes down. That's all I need to do: avoid eye contact, avoid seeing, avoid any contact.

"What's on offer?" My attention immediately on his eyes.

Damn it, I failed.

His eyes are full of mischief, a golden glint in those green eyes, his eyebrow-raising in a cute arch.

Mom, as light on her feet as I'd seen her in months, bounces around to the back of the counter, "I have your favorite, rhubarb pie, fresh out of the oven this morning."

"Oh yes, Mrs. Davenport, I can't remember having pie as good as yours. Nowhere in the world serves pie like yours, and I've been a few places around the world."

Mom blushes like a schoolgirl. Actually blushes!

"Well, let me get you a large slice then, son, you can sit and enjoy it here."

Finishing icing the cupcakes, I ring up his bill.

"Is that all?" His eyes rove over me sizzling my skin like magnifying glass in the sun. Eyes trailing from head to waist; he pauses at my chest, eyes hungry, wetness pools between my legs.

Damn traitorous body.

Oh, my goodness, it's getting hot in here.

He reaches over the counter. What is he doing? Is he going to kiss me? I freeze, rooted to the spot. His thumb grazes the edge of my lip. Electricity sparking, my heart thunders in my ears.

His thumb, warm and soft, held on my lip for a second before he presses firmly, wiping then stuck it in his mouth.

He groans quietly.

“Frosting,” he winks, “yum.”

Well, fuck me if that wasn’t the sexiest thing I’d ever encountered. And it was in broad daylight, in the bakery, with Mom standing obliviously behind me.

Chapter 7

Lucy

The last hour drags by, each second feeling like an eon. Every mouthful of rhubarb pie spooned slowly past his lips, my brain doing crazy leaps as he pulls out the spoon slowly, eyes close like he's imagining something else entirely between his lips. Every time he does, he glances over at me with a half grin like we're both in on a dirty little secret.

My butterflies are ready to burst free. I'm in desperate need of a cold shower and a fresh pair of panties.

Sean has to leave the bakery.

Now.

Unsuccessfully I try to act cool, I'm flapping around, I've dropped spoons and spatulas while he and Mom are shooting the breeze and he catches her up on the last nine years, between sexy smiles and mouthfuls of pie.

Mom laughs along asking so many questions. I try not to listen in, but I want to know where he's been and what he's been up to. What was so amazing was that he didn't want to come home for so long.

As much as I feel trapped in Breakridge, I can't imagine leaving while my mom is still here. I'm all she has. I suppose Sean is lucky he has three other siblings. Kate is just getting ready to move out; Xander lives in town, and Oli has his apartment above the hardware shop. Their parents had a full family to take care of them. No worries if Sean decides he's staying away for years at a time.

Oh, to be so carefree.

It's Saturday afternoon, so thankfully I can kick him out and shut the doors at three pm sharp. Mom still enjoys independence while she has it and insists on walking the short distance to her little one-bedroom bungalow. Her MS is progressing, but she's adamant she's still capable herself and I have to believe her.

"Darling, the day I can't walk myself home is the day you can stick me in a nursing home. I need to keep this old body working and I enjoy the fresh air."

She smiles before heading tentatively down the small step and out the door.

I love coming home to my apartment above the bakery. The apartment Grandma and Pops left for Mom and she had signed it over to me with the deeds to the bakery.

A homely little one-bedroom, no room to swing a cat apartment. I'd called it home my whole life.

Since Mom left, I've loved putting my touch on the place, my colors, and my choice of furniture. My beautiful yellow sofa I'd saved over a year to buy was the centerpiece in the lounge and open-plan kitchen. Eye-catching and comfy.

The bath water running, bubbles bubbling, and the scent of bergamot filling the air coming from the bathroom. A deep breath and a bubble bath are exactly what's in order. Something to calm my nerves.

"Damn Sean and his tight Levi's." I thump my fist on the kitchen island. "Damn his face and his swishy blond hair."

He isn't the guy I knew before. The cute, awkward teenager is long gone. He isn't surly or spotty. He is hot, and he is sexy. And obviously a very smart guy. He's made something from nothing with his business and it has been mega successful.

Successful, kind, smart, sexy....

Ugh no!

This is wrong. Sean was like my kid brother.

I need a date, that's the problem. I need some male attention and satisfaction. My worn-out rabbit just isn't doing the job right now. I should give Josh's cousin a call. What was his name again?

Brendan, yep, Brendan seemed really keen.

Maybe a bit too keen, but hey, the pickings were slim in Breakridge.

That should satisfy an itch that's needed scratching for a long time.

Picking up my phone to message Brendan, he'd of course put his number in my cell and made sure I'd given him a couple of rings, so he now has my number.

It vibrates in my hand; Kate's name flashing with an image of the two of us clinking cocktail glasses from last summer in Florida.

Kate? I thought she was out at her final dress fitting in Denver?

"Hey girl, how's it goin'?" I curl my feet under me on the sofa, preparing for a minute-by-minute rundown on the big fitting.

An unnatural whining noise with intermittent sobs fill my ears down the line.

"Kate? Are you okay? What's wrong?" I jump to my feet, knocking the bowl of chips from my lap all over the floor.

"The...dress .... Is .... A.... disaster!" Sobbing and snotters punctuate each word.

I inhale deeply, tuning to my rational brain for her. "Kate, calm down. I'm sure it's not a disaster, so you might need to have it altered to fit better. It's not the end of the world."

I love her but she could be a real drama queen when she wanted to be.

"Not .... The .... Size!" she shrieks, "Wrong .... Fucking.... Dress!!"The sobs progress to whaling.

Oh, dear lord.

"Right, I'm on my way. Where are you?"

I grab my keys and shoot out the door like my ass is on fire.

I am the worst maid of honor in the world. I didn't make the last dress fitting to see Kate, and I didn't make sure the right dress was ordered.

Deep down, I know this isn't my fault. The junior shop assistant getting one digit of the order reference number wrong and making a whole other dress to order with only two weeks until the wedding, is something I couldn't have prevented or changed.

Kate was home now, still sobbing into the dress that was a disaster. If it wasn't a disaster before, it certainly is now with tears and snotters down the ivory train.

"I can't. I just can't wear this dress!" She stands up, arms wide, pleading with us to agree.

I catch Mr. Lawson's eye roll before he heads for the kitchen as far away from the dress dramatics as possible.

Barbs holds Kate in a tight hug.

"You look exquisite, darling!" she tries to comfort her. "It's still a bespoke dress, made just for you." Kate's misery drowns out her words.

"It's not *MY* dress!"

A stream of fresh tears pour from her. "The wedding is in two weeks and I don't have MY dress and I can't get it made on time!" She drops to her knees in the very expensive ivory dress.

"There's nothing else for it." Her eyes look up into mine, large doe brown eyes. "We'll have to postpone the wedding!"

And then more whaling erupts from her. It's a wonder she isn't passing out from dehydration.

Oh, for the love of god, why is my friend such high maintenance? The dress she has on fits her perfectly and, of course, she looks absolutely stunning in it. She will take Josh's breath away when she walks down the aisle with it on. She could walk down the aisle in a garbage bag and Josh would have the biggest grin on his face that he's marrying his best friend.

However, I know Kate as deeply as I know myself, and she would postpone this wedding if she wasn't happy.

I am the maid of honor. It is my job to make sure this damn wedding goes to plan and the bride has her perfect dress.

"Kate." I drop to my knees beside her, clasping her hands in mine. She sniffles, looking at me with mascara smeared eyes.

"Remember when we were eleven years old, and we put white pillowcases on our heads to walk down the aisle?"

"Yes, white," she sobs, "not ivory!"

Oh boy.

"Yes, white pillowcases. Remember, we promised we would be each other's maid of honor and make sure we each had the most perfect day possible?"

She nods, rubbing her nose on the ruined ivory dress.

"Well, it's my turn to step up and make sure you get the wedding of your dreams," her eyes light up, "and that means your white wedding dress, on your big day."

I lift her chin, looking right into her panda eyes. "Your wedding is in two weeks and you will have the dress of your dreams. I will make sure of it!"

Kate's eyes light up. "You mean it Luce, do you think we can do it?"

I would make damn sure my best friend got the wedding of her dreams because she would do the same for me. With her grit and determination, she would move a mountain for me and I am darn well going to do the same for her.

"Absolutely." I grip her in a fierce hug.

"So no more talk of postponing the event of the year. Heck, the event of the century!"

She's sobbing hard again. "You're ... the ... best ... friend ... a.... girl ... could ... have!"

Now what the hell am I going to do about getting the perfect bespoke dress in two weeks?

My phone vibrates between us.

Crap, that must be Brendan returning my call with the worst timing. I don't recognize the caller ID.

"Hello?"

“Eh, Hello, is this Miss Davenport of Honeybee Bakery?”

“Speaking.” Weird.

“This is Deputy Dwayne Collins of Breakridge Police. We need you to get back to your bakery immediately.” His southern twang disarms me slightly, but the words have my heart racing.

“What’s happened? Is it my mom? Is she okay?” I’m on my feet and scrambling to find my car keys. Everyone’s eyes are on me, including Sean’s, who I didn’t even know had appeared.

“Eh, no ma’am, your mom isn’t here. There’s been an incident at the bakery and we need you to get here immediately.”

Chapter 8

Lucy

Water pours from what was once the ceiling of my bakery. Where the cake display unit was this morning, my now soggy yellow sofa sits not so proudly.

Bricks, wood, and debris scatter the floor in a dusty, sludgy mess. My mouth hangs open, Kate holds a firm grip on my hand. I Squeeze her fingers so hard her circulation is at risk.

My words are stuck somewhere in my throat, my lungs burning. My beautiful bakery, my pride, my home, my life all in one place; gone.

My heart feels so heavy, I struggle to breathe.

Deputy Collins' lips are moving, but I can't hear a word he says. White noise fills my ears. My knees wobbling; Kate keeps me supported, her arm tight around my back.

Decades of work, blood, sweat, and tears; a family legacy gone because I forgot to turn off the damn bath tap.

"It's gone," I sob, dragging breath into my lungs in gasps. "What will I tell my mom?"

A tremor shakes my body violently, my eyes hazy, a blackness envelopes me...

"Lucy! Lucy!" I waken to *his* voice.

My name sounds strangled from his lips.

"Oh thank God, she's opening her eyes." Kate yelps.

I'm wet and cold.

Why am I wet?

Why is Sean leaning over me looking so worried?

"My bakery!" The words rasp through my dry lips. "It's gone."

Tears stream down my already moist face.

"Shh Lucy." His fingers stroke my wet hair as I lay on the floor of my bakery with my apartment caved in around me. From this unique position on the floor, I can see the giant hole in the roof.

"We'll sort it, don't worry." He continues soothing strokes, shushing me.

Don't worry! Is he crazy? I have nothing, not one thing left, nowhere to sleep and nowhere to go. I can't go to my mom's. She lives in a tiny one bedroom, just big enough for her. Could I sleep on the sofa?

"Come on, let's get you off this wet floor," Sean scoops me to my feet like I weigh nothing. He grips my shoulders, stooping to look at me. "Are you hurt? You fell down hard there."

I rub the back of my head where it feels fuzzy. "Ouch, I have a bit of a bump."

Yep, an enormous egg is rising. Could this day get any worse? Sean gently caresses the back of my head where my fingers felt the lump.

"Ow!"

"Oh, that's a big bump alright, we need to get you to the ED."

"No!" My head is pounding like tiny ants with tiny hammers were going to town in there. "I don't need the ED, it's just a bump. I'll be fine,"

"You could have a concussion."

"They would just observe me anyway, nothing they can do." I insist stepping out of his reach.

"Sean's right, Lucy. You should get checked out." Kate rubs my arm, sympathy in her eyes.

And have another medical bill to pay, no way.

"Look guys, I'll be.."

"Ms. Davenport?" A large fireman draws my attention grunting my name.

"Yes, that's me."

"I'm sorry, but you won't be able to stay here right now. Do you have somewhere you can go?"

No shit, Sherlock. The tears spring free again, pouring down my face. "I - don't - know.."

"I - uh," where the heck am I going to stay? "I'll get a motel."

"Like hell you will!" Kate interrupts, turning to the large fireman. "She'll be staying with us."

I spin to look at her; a stabbing pain like a knife shoots through my head. “I can’t!”

“Stop, Lucy,” her hand up in the air. “I won’t hear another word, and neither would Barbs,” she ends the argument with a firm nod. “You’re coming with us.”

I don’t really have much choice. Sleep at a cheap motel for god knows how long or Mom’s sofa. Kate's firm arms, a bear hug around me are reassuring.

“Let’s get you out of those soaking clothes, and a wine in your hand!”

“I might need more than a wine to fix this one.”

“It’s a start though,” her arm still firmly around me, Kate leads me out of my soggy bakery.

The fireman is talking to Sean. I hear something about the roof and pipes as he points up into my apartment before Kate drags me out the door.

Sean

Well, this was not what I had planned for my two-week return home. A raging hard-on for the next fourteen days until I could get out of here again. It was challenging enough to stay away from Lucy Davenport when she *wasn’t* living under the same roof.

At the barbecue, she was so damn irresistible. Then, dropping into the bakery because I was ‘in the area’.

Yeah, I had been in the area because I drove there to see Lucy again. I'd walked past the bakery on the other side of Main Street three times before I found my balls and walked in through the door. I'm surprised she never saw me creeping by like a stalker. Main Street is never what you'd call busy. No hiding on the sidewalk of pedestrians.

I watched her bake. I saw her smile at customers, a smile that lit up her entire face. She helped her mom round to the front and served her a cup of tea.

I really was a stalker.

Go in, or go home, Sean.

I had to go in.

Of all the tasty cakes and pastries, she was the most tempting thing in there. Her fiery auburn mane piled high in a messy bun, some soft wisps escaping, surrounded her face, enveloping her like a red halo. Curves wrapped in the cute yellow apron embroidered with her name, and to top it off, a little blob of frosting had sat teasingly on the edge of her lips.

It took every ounce of restraint I'd had not to pounce over the counter and plant my lips on hers. For the frosting, of course.

I've never kissed Lucy, ever.

Well, not in real life anyway.

I've dreamed of her soft, full lips a thousand times. Even that couldn't prepare me for just how soft her lip was under my thumb when I reached over and wiped that frosting.

Did I see a spark in her eyes? If I did, it burned out fast. She wasn't interested. She couldn't get further away from me at the bakery and didn't even want to look my way. As soon as the clock struck three pm, she practically shoved me out the door.

And now, Kate invited her to stay in the house, in the same house. I mean, she didn't have anywhere else to go and Mom would never hear of Lucy staying at some motel. But how the hell am I going to avoid her? She's in the next room right now. And she would be until I left.

Fuck.

Hiding in my room was not an option. As a twenty-six-year-old man who's only home for two weeks, I'm expected to attend all the events with the maid of honor. And now she will be here when I sleep. When I eat. When I shower.

She's my sister's best friend. Kate would be devastated if I did anything to ruin her big day.

Nothing more awkward than a hostile bridal party.

Nothing was going to happen with Lucy Davenport.

No way. I will do everything to keep out of her way. I'll head out early in the morning and opt for an early bedtime every night.

I can do this. I'm leaving in two weeks.

Only fourteen days to survive. Well two days down and twelve days to go. I could avoid her for that long, couldn't I? It wasn't like I hadn't had practice. I'd done it for years.

Whatever worked, I'd do it. Stuff my feelings down, deep down, shut them in a box, and stick them on the shelf next to my old baseball card collection.

Nine years had done nothing.

Nothing except make her more tempting. Those curves, her hips, the scent of sweet cinnamon floating behind her wherever she went.

What I needed was a distraction. There must be someone in town. I'll ask Kate if she has any friends to take to the wedding.

I just needed someone else to focus my energy on. And I appeared to have a lot of energy.

The sound of Lucy's sobbing came from the front room. Barbs and Kate were fussing over her, while Lucy cried on the phone with her mom.

It took all my energy not to rush through and grab her in a bear hug to soothe her, shoving my face in that auburn mane of cinnamon.

Ugh .... This was going to be a long twelve days.

"Dude, what's with the long face?" Oli pulls a beer from the fridge. "Want one?"

"Sure," I don't have anything else to be doing, might as well try to numb myself a little.

"So... what's with the long face?" God, he's annoying.

"Nothing, I have nothing to complain about?"

"Well, you really should tell your face that." He laughs at his own joke. My face remains straight. Oli has it so easy. He'd finished college and started working with Dad. Never had to apply himself and work for anything. Lived in the apartment he let from Mom and Dad above the store, worked in the store, and had time for his furniture-building hobby on the side.

"Are you still pining for her?" His head inclines towards the tears and sobbing. What was with my interfering brothers?

"You'd think you might have gotten her out of your system while you were globetrotting."

"I'm not pining!"

My protest is vehement. Too strong.

Oli's eyebrows lift. He's not buying any of it.

"I need a date for this wedding."

I need to change the subject. "Any girls in town you might not have screwed already?"

"Ha! Jealous brother?" He takes a long pull of beer. "I have a few girls' numbers I could recommend."

He's such a male hussy. Oli Larson left a trail of broken hearts behind him. It was the same through high school and into college. And from what Xander said, not much has changed.

"Never mind, forget I said anything."

The last thing I need is to call up some girl who's still hung up on my brother. That's a drama I can live without.

This damn bed is so uncomfortable. I have tossed from one side to the other and back again. My back, my front, round and round. Sleep is not coming easily tonight.

How could I sleep with Lucy next door? Thinking of her in her pajamas, little shorts probably, no bra restraining those amazingly curvy breasts. Cuddled in bed, her hair spread across the pillow.

Damn, I'm killing myself.

Hard as a fucking oak tree.

My clock reads 12.24 am.

12.56 am.

1.28 am.

1.50 am.

Still awake.

I give in when the clock hit 2.30am.

Hauling on a pair of shorts, I head downstairs for some warm milk. Mom always made that when I couldn't sleep. Funny, sleep was never an issue the entire time I'd been away.

No warm milk required. Slept like a baby.

I tiptoe as quietly as a 190lb guy can. Surprisingly, I remember where the creaky stairs are.

Light seeps out from under the kitchen door.

Weird.

Kate must be up. She'd always been a restless sleeper.

Keeping quiet, I push open the door.

Shit.

Lucy has her back to the door. I'd guessed right- little pink pajama shorts only just cover the glorious globes of her ass. Two round buns sway back and forth in front of the stove. She's humming to herself. The red satin waterfall swishes with her hips.

I can't help myself. I step closer to inhale her.

My inhale is too loud.

"What the fu..." she whips around, the wooden spoon in her hand misses my nose by mere millimeters.

"Jesus Red, it's me!"

Red? Where did that come from? I like it.

"Sean, what the hell are you ....?" her gaze drops to my chest.

I can't hold back the grin that pulls my lips up.

Oh yes.

Chapter 9

Lucy

Oh, sweet Jesus. He's here.

He's practically naked. Just a pair of shorts. Thin shorts.

And so close.

His tanned chest is so broad and defined. I fight to restrain my hands at my side, wanting to run my fingers through the soft scattering of light hair and trail my fingertips over the valleys of his chest. My fingers tighten around the wooden spoon, gripping until I feel the wood bite into my skin.

Do not reach out, do not touch his chest, Lucy.

So close, and I'm in my pajamas. My Minnie Mouse Disney pajamas. Why didn't I own any sexy nighties? And my face, my makeup-free, swollen red face from crying. Why does he have to be here at two am? I thought I was safe and alone in the middle of the night.

I really must look ridiculous with my mouth gaping open.

"Uh, what are you doing here?"

Oh my God!

Prize to Lucy for the stupidest question ever!

His eyes twinkle in the muted under lights. He steps closer, the scent of his skin warm and musky screwing with my brain.

“I live here Lucy.” My name is a purr on his lips.

Of course, I'm the intruder here.

Why have I never noticed how deep and gravelly his voice is? It is a panty dropping voice. He rolls the L in my name into at least three syllables, sending a shiver up my spine.

“Of course you do.” I'm bumbling. I step back trying to clear my head of the intoxicating musky pine scent and bump into the stove.

“Sorry, I didn’t mean to wake anyone up. Why are you up so late?” My traitorous heart thunders in my ears, my fingers finding the edge of the stove I grip on, wooden spoon still in hand. I'm ready to put it between us if the need arises.

“Funny thing..” his smile is cheeky, like he has a secret he wasn’t sharing. “I couldn’t sleep.” One eyebrow raises. “Why are you up so late, Red?”

When did it get so hot in here? Why is he so close, smelling so good? And Red? Where did that come from?

“Red?” The word is a question, my voice raspy.

He reaches out for the bottom of my hair, grasping a few strands and flicking them.

“This hair is a waterfall of red fire.”

I stare at him. I must look like I'm having a seizure. Why are words failing me?

Brain, WAKE UP!

I feel bereft after all the drama of today. Someone has cut something from my soul. I'm up because I couldn't lie crying any longer. But somehow that feeling is being diluted with something entirely different. Heat burning between my legs. His intense gaze has my nipples standing to attention, tight and grazing the inside of my Minnie Mouse t-shirt.

His tongue slides temptingly along his bottom lip. My imagination throws me images of his tongue along my bottom lip, along my jaw, pinching the bottom of my earlobe.

Maybe his tongue along *other* areas.

With that mental image, my core tightens in anticipation.

He looks ravenous, as if he's a starving man. I'm sure he never experienced a shortage of beautiful women on his travels.

But he wasn't on his travels, he was here. In Breakridge River, with me.

Looking at me.

His eyes devouring me.

My throat dry, my voice raspy; "I thought some warm milk might help me fall over to sleep."

"Yes, I came down for a sleep remedy." Again with the sexy eyebrow.

"Do you have any suggestions to help me relax?"

Oh sweet jesus, do I?

"I can make you some milk if you like? Or something else..."

The silence is suffocating, Sean's face is laced with indecision.

The silence broken by the sizzle of milk bubbling over onto the stove behind me.

Sean

Or something else...

Is she joking? Yes, *something else,* please!

How can a woman look so delectable in a pair of Minnie Mouse pajamas? Those full thighs ready to wrap around my waist. My eyes pin her, drinking her in. The auburn mane I'm dying to dive my nose in and feel her scent permeate through me.

That's not the only place I want to dive my face into. I'm so close to her, I can smell her arousal and see her nipples hard as steel, fighting for freedom from the snug top.

I don't miss the way she eye fucked me when she turned. She liked what she saw and that's a huge stroke to my ego.

One more step and my chest touches hers. My head tips low, she doesn't pull away. Her back arches, pushing her breasts closer to me. I itch to lean in and suck that nipple deep in my mouth.

I'm hungry for her.

Starving for Lucy.

Since the day I'd noticed her as a woman and not my sister's best friend, she was my desire. I'd played this moment so many times, in so many ways in my head, and in no way did they come close to the way she's looking at me right now.

She sucks a sharp breath through her full lips when she looks down and notices my cock, full and erect under my shorts.

Out of control.

For her.

Her eyes draw languidly up my body, pupils blown wide. Meeting my eyes, hers darken.

Fuck it.

I swiftly close the distance between our lips, grabbing her hips and pulling her tight against my solid cock. She welcomes me, wrapping her arms around my neck. I crush my mouth against hers. I imagined a soft and sensual kiss for our first encounter, lingering.

Nope.

Not a chance.

This is hot and urgent.

An urgency I've never experienced with any other woman. I can't get enough of her fast enough and my god, she's responsive. Her hands through my hair, tugging and pulling me closer.

It's making me feral.

A deep growl rumbles through my chest. Taking her lower lip between my teeth, I bite down and suck that full lip.

Her answering groan is guttural, spurring me on. My tongue explores her mouth further, deepening the kiss, my hands on her full ass. I pull her closer still, her tongue meeting mine, pushing and pulling, searching.

I pinch one of her solid nipples between my fingers pulling. Her gasp is satisfying.

"Oh Sweetness, I knew this would be fucking amazing." I continue, twisting her nipple, her head dropping back, chest swelling against me.

Trailing kisses along her open neck, I whisper, "You have no idea how long I've wanted to do this." I work my way up to her earlobe, kissing and nibbling her soft skin.

She stills under my lips.

"What?" Pulling back, she glares up at me, those eyes still wide and beautiful.

Shit, I shouldn't have said that.

"What do you mean, how long you've wanted to do this, do what Sean?"

How can I get back from this?

"Well," I hold her firmly, refusing to let go, "have you seen you lately?"

The blush that flushes her face is sexy. She really doesn't know how gorgeous she is.

"That's not what you meant."

There are no more words. I need those pouting pink lips back on mine. I need it more than I need my next breath.

Dipping my head, I kiss her along her jaw line up towards her lips. She welcomes me, humming in satisfaction. The noise is an electricity volt right to my cock.

This time she lifts on her tiptoes, meeting me, pulling me, my mouth devouring her. Soft, warm hands on my chest, grip my short hair. The heat beneath her palms has me weak.

This woman could have me on my knees in a second.

I place my hands on the stove behind her, pushing off to move down her body.

"Shiit!"

I leap back, grabbing my left hand, pain shoots through my palm like a bitch.

"What's wrong?" Lucy gasps.

"I put my hand on the fucking stove!" I flap my hand, trying to get some cool air. Lucy springs into action.

"Give me your hand." She demands.

I'm flapping when she grabs my arm, hauling me over to the sink.

"Now this will feel cold and uncomfortable," is the only warning I get before she sticks my hand under the blasting cold faucet.

"Mother fu..."

"Shhh!" Her free hand clamps over my lips. "Do you want to wake everyone up?"

My head spins; the pain not easing. I look down at Lucy, still holding my hand under the faucet. She's staring right up into my eyes with what looks like confusion.

Is it regret?

"You'll need to keep this here for at least 15 minutes. It'll stop the blistering."

We stand by the sink in silence; the faucet deafening.

"You don't have to stay down here. I can sort myself." I can feel her tension. The moment between us has well and truly passed.

She's desperate to get away from me. Her body is rigid. Except for her hand on my arm holding me firmly, she avoids any other parts of our bodies touching. She has put a chasm between us.

Shit, what have I done? I've scared her.

"I'll get you bandaged up before I go back to bed." Her voice a whisper.

She avoids my gaze.

Does she regret kissing me?

I feel the loss of her touch when she finally drops my arm. Moving around the kitchen like it was her own, she gets the first aid kit, bandages, and antiseptic cream ready.

With minimal skin contact, she finishes taping the bandage.

"Keep that dry for a day or two, redress daily, and put the antiseptic cream on." Her voice is a flat whisper, meeting my eyes now, the fire smothered out.

"Night Sean." She turns and leaves the kitchen, not looking back.

Chapter 10

Lucy

My hair is rumpled, my lips are full, and my chin is a little red from the scratch of Sean's stubble. The woman staring back at me from the floor-to-ceiling mirror is a disheveled mess. Yet surprisingly satisfied.

She grins back at me with pride in her eyes.

What the fuck just happened? I felt like a woman possessed downstairs. If Sean hadn't burned his hand on the hot stove, who knows how that would have ended?

I certainly wasn't in my right mind in the Larson's kitchen in the middle of the night. If he'd have stripped me off and bent me over the island, I struggle to say if I would have objected.

That's not me.

I don't get lost in passionate kisses. When I'm kissing, I'm usually making a list of to-do's for the next day in my head.

I don't let go of my inhibitions in a public place. Okay, not public, but anyone could have wandered downstairs at any moment and caught us. Why does that thought send a thrill through me? Who knew I was such an exhibitionist?

Not me, that's for sure.

And I certainly don't make out with my best friend's brother.

Pressing my fingers to my lips, I feel a longing I'd never felt before. A desire that pulls in my stomach urging me back out of the bedroom and downstairs to where Sean is still in the kitchen.

He hasn't come back up the creaky stairs to his bedroom next door. Only one wall between us.

It doesn't matter, anyway. Nothing is ever going to happen again. It was a complete lapse in judgement. I can't be with Sean and he doesn't really want me.

He was probably just bored. Board of being back in Breakridge after having access to so many beautiful women falling over him wherever he went.

I'm the only woman in the house who isn't his mom or his sister.

Convenience.

I can't have my heart broken.

I don't have the time or the bandwidth for a broken heart. My body is nothing like the usual bikini-clad stick insects Sean would usually make a play for in Hawaii or Maui or wherever he was.

I was little dumpy Lucy from Breakridge River. Owns a bakery,

Correction;

Owns a destroyed bakery and is stuck here forever.

He's only here for two weeks for his sister's wedding and looking for some entertainment. Well, I couldn't let that entertainment be my heart.

Nope, not happening.

There's no way I'm getting any sleep now. I grab my laptop, thankful I could save that from the disaster that was my home and livelihood. A happy accident that I'd left it in Ol' Betty.

My next job, fix Kate's dress disaster.

I'm *the* maid of honor for my best friend and she doesn't have her dream white dress to walk down the aisle in just two short weeks.

Kate would have her dream dress, and I was going to make it happen.

The next morning, Kate and Barbs are chatting away at the kitchen table over Eggs Benedict. The wedding dress saga is still the number two topic after my flood disaster.

Kate's voice raises an octave with her stress levels any time the dress is mentioned. Mr. Larson continues to hide with his coffee behind the morning paper. I smile to myself behind the fridge door, grabbing the carton of milk.

I sat up for hours researching the perfect dress last night. Of course, it was off the rack. I was maid of honor, not a magician with two weeks to work. As well as baking, my grandma was an amazing seamstress and had taught me a thing or two.

Enough that I could alter and adjust Kate's dress to make it perfect for her. Personalize it with a design of her choosing. It would be a blank white canvas and I can't wait to surprise her with it tonight.

Ready for a drive to the city, dressed to impress in Kate's skinny jeans, leopard print suede ankle boots, a fitted tee, the look finished off with a blazer. I feel a million dollars swishing around the kitchen gathering my breakfast. No eggs for me, I'm more of a cornflakes and toast kinda gal with a strong coffee to set me up for the day.

"Thanks for letting me borrow your clothes today, Kate."

"No problem; I can't let you wander up and down in your thongs now, can I?" she giggles and Barbs swats her arm.

"Kate, you can't make light of Lucy's situation," Barbs scolds.

"Sure she can, Mrs. L. I need a laugh." Kate was my sister. She knew when to laugh and when to be serious.

"I'm heading to the bakery later today to see what I can salvage."

"Aw sweetie, that will be tough. Do you want me to come with you?" Kate asks.

"No, it's fine, you'll be working, I'll see you back here tonight, I have a surprise for you." I can't keep the mischievous grin from my face.

Her eyebrows shoot through the roof. "Lucy, you know I'm no good at surprises!" She whines.

"Ha, you'll just have to be, because I'm not telling." I stick out my tongue, grab my coffee, and walk straight into a solid torso.

"Shit!"

My coffee sloshes all over Sean and his classic white t-shirt.

"Oh my god Sean, I'm sorry!"

A low growl hums in his throat. Those emerald eyes sparkle, pinning me in place.

"Don't worry about it." His voice is dismissive. With one hand, he pulls the stained t-shirt over his head, revealing that solid, sun-kissed body.

Again.

Sweet Jesus.

"Did I burn you?" I ask, grabbing a towel and soaking it under the faucet. I place it on his chest, where his skin prick-led red. Through the towel, I can feel the heat. I can't help but look up.

His face stony. Had I imagined last night? He places his bandaged hand over mine, grabbing the towel. "I got it. Don't worry about it."

What the hell was that all about? He couldn't have been colder.

I did just burn him with coffee.

Still, no need to be rude.

"Pretty boy will survive, I'm sure. Lucy don't sweat it."

I have completely forgotten we aren't alone in the kitchen this time.

"As long as you didn't get coffee on my Levi's, that would be a disaster." She grins at Sean and he flips her the bird.

"What was that racket downstairs last night?" Mr. Larson asks from behind the broadsheet paper. "Did anyone else hear it?"

I choke as a cornflake lodges in my throat, gasping; coughing. I look up at Sean. He's as cool as a cucumber, and doesn't look my way.

"I couldn't sleep, got up to make some warm milk." he shrugs so nonchalant there should be an award.

"What was all the crashing?" The broadsheet now lowered; Mr. Larson's eyebrows are curious. Sean holds out his bandaged hand.

"I dropped the pan after I burned my hand on the stove."

"Hmmm," one eyebrow raises. "Nice job bandaging yourself up, son."

Mr. Larson looks right at me. Kate and Barbs are back in conversation about wedding flowers and seating arrangements.

I need to get out of here.

A Starbucks drive-thru it would have to be for my morning coffee hit. I grab my purse,

"Right, see you all later. I'm heading to Denver this morning."

I avoid any eye or body contact with Sean, waving at Barbs and Kate as I leave.

"Drive safe." Mr. Larson shouts as I sprint out the door.

Chapter 11

Sean

Denver? What is Lucy heading to Denver for?

A two-hour drive to the city, on her own. What could she possibly be doing in Denver when her bakery is sitting in tatters back in Breakridge River? Would her beat-up little Mini survive the journey there and back?

Probably not.

I pull my dad's old truck into the gas station before I head to Denver. I could have said to Lucy to hold up and I'd give her a ride. One of my business contacts is flying in to meet me for lunch, a new venture. Something to get my teeth into. Something to distract me.

But that would have meant being confined in the truck with Lucy and her skin-tight jeans and breast-hugging shirt for four hours, and I'm not sure my poor cock would survive. I'm not sure my restraint would survive intact.

I need my head in the game for this meeting.

The truck was bigger than being squashed in the pink Mini, but four hours was long enough to have my balls turning blue with her at my side.

No way. I need some space from Lucy Davenport and her bewitching cinnamon scent, her bouncy, swishy red mane.

The kitchen this morning was the last straw.

Throwing a coffee over me without so much as a 'good morning' and I still wanted to smash my lips to hers. Audience be damned.

"Hi Sean."

The cute blond behind the counter flutters her extra long eyelashes my way. "It's great to see you back in town again."

"Hey, yeah, it's great to be back." The confused look on my face must be a give away.

"It's Melanie," she brightens her smile. "Remember, from senior prom?"

So it is; she was my prom date. The years had been kind to her. Skin smooth as it ever was. The first girl I got to third base with at the back of the bleachers on prom night.

"Of course, sorry! I've bumped into so many faces I can't place."

She scans my few items. "I bet. You were gone a while, a lot has changed."

She looks out the window and laughs. "Well actually, not really, nothing much changes around here."

Her laugh was sweet, and I can't help but chuckle with her.

I hand her a $50 to pay, she grasps it along with my hand, leaning far over the counter. I have a birdseye view right down her v neck tank.

"I know this is forward, but I'm sure you're not in town long. Do you want to catch up over dinner sometime?"

Hell, this was one thing I was afraid of coming home. I didn't want attention, didn't want dates. I just want to get to this wedding and get out of here.

But...

The thought of getting Lucy out of my head for a few hours sounds like a great idea, and I might even get rid of my blue balls with a bit of luck. Sign me up.

"Sure, that sounds like a great idea."

Her smile beams a hundred watt. I honestly don't know whether to be pleased with the reaction or scared.

On the road again, after swapping numbers with Melanie, I feel a little spring in my step.

Melanie has probably heard how well I've done for myself. If I remember back to prom night, she wasn't that into me. The guy she wanted to go with had a date with the head cheerleader, so she didn't have a chance. I'd asked her because she looked sad in Spanish one morning and I needed a date.

Besides, she was hot.

I couldn't exactly ask Lucy to go to high school prom with me. She was at college. The memory leaves me feeling lacking.

Fuck that.

I'm Sean Fucking Larson. Self-made millionaire, app developer, and investor.

I'm not that little kid anymore.

I hit the gas, gaining a bit of speed; The Eagles playing out about taking it easy, I tap the wheel and my foot in rhythm. Nothing brings me back to reality and home like listening to my dad's favorites with the open road ahead.

"What the fuck is that ..."

Dead ahead, flashing lights on a little pink dot on the horizon.

Getting closer, I palm my face.

Of course.

It's Lucy Flippin' Davenport's banged-up pink Mini.

Lucy

"Are you kidding me!!"

I smash my fist on the wheel as Ol' Betty splutters, very un-lady like, and rolls to a standstill in the middle of the road.

What did I do to piss off the powers above this week?! First, the flood ruined my bakery and apartment, then I have Sean Larson thrust at me with nowhere to run, and now *this!*

I mean, there has been a little light on the dash for a week or so, but it usually just goes away.

Had it been there a week, or was it longer?

Ugh!

I need to call the dress shop. They're expecting me in an hour. It took me a lot of begging and sob stories to get an appointment at this boutique. Even for an off-the-rack dress.

It's a high-end bridal boutique. I was lucky they had a cancellation and bumped me up on the wait list.

“No, no, no!” I shake my cell, holding it high. “Not one bar of signal!”

I scramble out of Ol’ Betty, waving my cell around for some kind of signal. I slam her door, the tiny car vibrates at the violation. She started it. I don't have time for this today.

“Well, this is just fan-fucking-tastic.” My boots kick up road dust as I rage hop around the ground, pacing up and down the edge of the road.

“No way I’m getting to Denver on time now. Kate will never get her dress, and it’s all my fault.”

The open road swallows my words, fields stretching for miles on either side. Not a soul around to hear me.

I could get abducted and no one would notice. No one would miss me until dinner tonight, and I’d be dead and buried by then.

I hear an engine roar in the distance.

“Yes!” Fist pumping the air, I flap my arms up and down in an attempt to wave down the driver. I could borrow their cell and get a tow and hopefully save my dress appointment.

Or…

Knowing my luck, it's a creepy murderer with a hacksaw and a penchant for red heads who will drag me into their truck, chop my limbs off, and stick me in a suitcase, never to be found again.

Shit, hide!

I sprint round the back of Ol' Betty, flattening my body on the ground. Kate is going to kill me for lying in the dirt with her new Levi's on.

That's if a psycho stranger doesn't kill me first. Hopefully, they didn't see me jumping around like a crazy person and just drive on by.

Please drive by, please drive by.

The truck slows, pulling up beside the Ol' Betty.

Oh my god, this is how I'm going to die. Why do I watch so many true crime documentaries?

I'm imagining all the ways someone could drag me to my death right now at the side of this lonely road, my mind races at a thousand miles an hour.

Heavy footsteps scuff in the dirt. My heart beat thumping into the ground, my eyes squeeze shut.

"Eh, Lucy?"

Wait...

"Sean?" I squeal.

Sweet relief! I leap from the ground around the car and throw my arms around his neck.

"WOW!" The breath huffs from his chest. My heart races until I realize what I've just done.

Did I just feel his face in my hair?

I jump back, knocking myself off Ol' Betty's hood.

"I'm so sorry! I'm just so relieved I'm not going to be murdered in the middle of a lonely road!"

"What?!"

"Well, I'm out here on my own, with no signal. You could have been a psycho killer."

He stands in all his gorgeous glory, hands out at his sides, and a very cute, angry face.

"Do I look like a psycho killer to you?!"

Hands-on my hips. I stand my ground.

"I don't know. I've never met one in person before."

"So let me get this straight. You were going to let the only car with a signal or some kind of help for miles to drive by you?" he scoffed.

Oh, he looks more than a little mad. "Well, I was worr..."

"You were worried?" His hands are in the air. "No one else could have driven out of or into Breakridge for hours. You would have been stuck!"

Who the hell does he think he is? Telling me off.

"Women are abducted and killed at the side of the road every day. I will not be one of those statistics."

I cross my arms firmly over my chest, feeling petulant but secretly glad he drove by. He is right, and I would *never* say that out loud. I could have been facing hours here before the next car drove by.

"Okay, we could do this all day, but I gotta get to a meeting in Denver. Do you need a ride?"

His cheeky side smile returns, creating a dimple I'd never noticed before. "I'll call a tow for your car."

Why does that feel like a loaded question? Another hour to Denver and two hours back in the car with Sean. Why does my heart skip at the prospect?

Chapter 12

Sean

"Okay, so where are you heading in Denver in such a hurry this morning that you nearly gave me third-degree burns with your coffee?"

We drive through Lincoln County on the I70. The terrain is flat as far as the eye can see. The surrounding grass tainted brown from the heat. Coming into mid-July, a bead of sweat trails its way down the side of my face.

Its sauna-level heat in here. The AC is non-existent, Lucy has fiddled with the buttons for the last five minutes, finally giving in and opening the window. Warm air blasts in, blowing her fiery mane around her face.

I need to focus today. This meeting is the next big move in my career. I've been waiting to pitch this idea for months and they've agreed to meet with me in person because I'm back in the States.

I can't fail today.

And here I am with Lucy and her witchy cinnamon scent, unable to concentrate on anything except how electric that kiss was last night and how much I want to slam the brakes and do it over again.

We're in the middle of nowhere. No one would catch us here. Does she want the same thing?

"Sean.. Earth to Sean!" Her voice punctures through my dirty thoughts of a reclined truck seat, milky white thighs straddling me with a face full of red hair as she leans low.

"Sorry, I was a million miles away." Understatement.

"Clearly. I was apologizing for the burning." Her voice is sincere and too serious.

"The first or the second time?" I snicker, holding my bandaged hand up.

She flushs the sweetest shade of rose pink, staring me right in the eye

"That was all you, bucko!" Crossing her arms in defiance in that stubborn way she always has.

"Eh, I believe there were two of us in that hot tangle last night."

What the hell are you doing? Drop it.

Thankfully, Lucy doesn't say a word. The silence thick, she reaches and turns the stereo up.

I'm such a shithead. Why did I have to bring that up when we're stuck together for the rest of the afternoon?

"Where did you say you were going?" I ask, breaking the tension.

She won't look my way. "Last night, I found the perfect dress for Kate. I called early this morning and thankfully they had a cancellation so I can go along and pick it up." Her mood lightens immediately after talking about Kate and helping her.

"That's amazing Lucy, Kate will be stoked."

She spins towards me, her face so serious, "It's a surprise, swear you won't tell her before the big reveal!"

Her eyes sparkle with excitement. "I can't wait to see her face; she's going to love it!"

The excitement is infectious. When she cares about something, it exudes from her pours. "You're an amazing friend to Kate. You must love her. With so much else going on in your life and you're taking the whole day to sort out her dress mess."

She looks at me like I've grown two heads.

"She's my best friend, more than my best friend; my sister. There's nothing I wouldn't do for her."

She really would do anything for Kate. I believe that. Would she stay away from me because of Kate?

Why do I care?

"Right, well, let's get this dress."

I wipe another bead of sweat from my brow. My hair is slightly damp and wavy. Damn busted AC in Dad's old truck.

"I'm meeting a client on East Twelfth in the city at two pm."

"The boutique is on East Third."

"I'll come with you and then you can hang around during my meeting and we can head back to Breakridge after that.

I'll call the tow company. Your car will be back before we will, probably."

The sooner we get to Denver and get back, the better. I need some space between me, my dirty thoughts and Lucy. I'll call Melanie from the gas station as soon as I'm back.

Lucy

With the ting of the bell on the door, the blast of air conditioning inside the bridal boutique is heaven. A combination of summer heat, no AC and the heat radiating from Sean, you could mop me off the floor. I stand for a second too long under the air conditioning appreciating the cool breeze on my skin. Sean walks into my back with an, "Oomph."

"Sorry," I turn. "I was appreciating the frosty air after such a hot ride."

His eyebrow lifts, the dimple deepening.

"Get your head out of the gutter. We're in an upscale boutique!" I whisper-shout at him.

"It wasn't me talking about *hot rides.*" He waggles an accusing finger at me.

"What are you, sixteen again?" I prod my finger at his hard chest before turning to admire the beauty of the store.

It is stunning. I'm completely under dressed. How can I be under-dressed to buy a dress? I'm not sure, but I certainly feel like I should have dressed up a bit. Or at least not rolled around in the dry dirt at the side of the road.

The crisp white of the gowns on display contrast the royal navy velvet wallpaper on the back wall elegantly. The entire room alight with fairy lights. I'd walked into a wonderland. If it was my wedding, there was no way I could afford a wedding dress from a place like this.

Thankfully, I'd had a quiet word with Mr. Larson this morning and he is in on the secret and more than willing to help with in the surprise in the form of his credit card.

Eyes wide, I wander further in, grazing my hand over the satins and lace. So luxurious, so expensive.

I catch sight of myself in a full-length mirror, sweaty and awestruck. I may never be in a boutique like this again. In the reflection, Sean's eyes follow me across the store, a curious look on his face. He doesn't say a word.

I've dreamed of a wedding day, like every other little girl does. I've imagined what kind of dress I would wear, the veil covering my face as I walk down the aisle towards my husband-to-be. He's had many faces over the years, some were dates from high school, some were boyfriends who might have lasted longer than a few months - there weren't many.

Right now, when I close my eyes and imagine walking down that aisle, my mom giving me away. Her arm linked through mine as we step tentatively towards the altar. There stands a tall gentleman with his back to the room, his thick wavy blond hair tied back neatly. Would he have the deepest emerald eyes when he turned to see his bride?

Oh, hell's bells!

Get a grip, Lucy!

"Hello darling, can I help you?"

A smartly dressed woman in her sixties appears from behind a display, interrupting the train crash that my imagination was heading for.

"Hello, I'm Lucy. I called this morning for your cancellation appointment."

"Oh yes, Lucy, I'm Mable." She grasps my hand in her papery fingers.

"Oh, your hair is beautiful. Will you be wearing it down on the wedding day?"

Ha, she thinks I'm the bride; I wish!

Did I wish?

That was something else to break down later in the confines of my room with a full glass of wine and my journal!

Mable doesn't give me a chance to correct her, she elegantly sweeps over to Sean, grasping his hand. "You must be the groom, so lovely to meet you."

She turns back to me with a conspiratorial look on her face. "He's handsome Lucy, a little unconventional to bring the groom, dress shopping dear. Where are your bridesmaids?"

Sean is grinning from ear to ear with the mistake, his look asking, *do we correct her?*

My entire face is flushing red. I catch a glance in the perfectly placed full-length mirror. Stuttering, I choke out,

"I *am* the bridesmaid."

Mable's eyes float between Sean and me. Looking back at Sean, she has to tilt her head far to reach his face.

"I see." Did she just wink at Sean? What was that?

"I mean, I'm the maid of honor; my best friend, Sean's sister, Kate, is the bride."

Nervous, I'm babbling now. I hate when I do that.

"You see, she had a dress disaster, and the wedding is in two weeks. I'm trying to find her perfect dress, but at such short notice, you know that's a challenge."

Where had the AC gone? The river of sweat returns to the crevice down my spine.

"I found your boutique online last night with a gorgeous dress, of course, off the rack, but I can alter and embellish."

Mable's hand flies up in protest, her finger held up to pause me. "No one alters or embellishes my dresses, dear."

"Oh, I didn't mean to insinuate it wouldn't be perfect, just that Kate isn't here for a fitting and it's a surprise."

She smiles at me like Grandma used to, that all-knowing smile of life experience.

"We will have a perfect dress for your Kate and it will leave my boutique as it is intended to glide down the aisle."

And on that note, Mable starts fussing around picking out dresses, holding them against me, asking my opinion.

I catch a glance at Sean, who is finding this all very amusing. He's sat on a plush velvet couch with a cup of espresso and strict instructions not to leave the chair with the coffee.

I scan all the dresses, the materials, the textures, the smells and have to admit I'm having fun wedding dress shopping. Even if it was for Kate.

Then I find the one. The perfect dress for Kate I had seen online.

"This is it, Mable, this is the one for Kate." I point excitedly, too scared to take it off the rack.

Mable is at me in a flash. She's sprightly for an older woman.

"Wonderful, dear. Let's get it on you and see what it looks like." Arm around my back, she guides me to the changing area.

"But it's not for me. I couldn't possibly do a fitting for Kate. She's a size smaller than I am."

My objections are futile.

"Nonsense dear!" Mable's firm hands shove me behind the curtain and she follows behind me.

"We need to see it on a lovely woman's body. It's no good on the hanger."

Dumbfounded, I stand like a mannequin letting Mable almost strip me of my clothes before she manhandles me into the white satin gown.

"You'll be able to tell me where on the dress you want embellished and I can alter the dress to your size before a last fitting with Kate next week."

She explains all this with pins between her teeth, expertly pulling the material snugly around my body, pinning me inside the heavy yet comfortable material.

Mable is an artist.

She pulls my waves around to one side of my face, sliding an eye-catching diamond clasp on the other side to secure the hair down, elongating my neck. I can't help but straighten my back, correcting my posture.

I don't recognize the elegant woman staring back at me in the mirror.

"Wow, Mable, you are amazing."

She smiles and tilts her head in thanks.

"Are you sure this dress is Kate's?"

"Of course, she will be a beautiful bride in your gown."

There's a pang of something inside, sadness maybe, that the dress would never be for me. But Kate is going to love it and that's all that matters.

"Turn towards me, dear."

I swish the full gown around, facing the curtain. I see a glimmer of something in her eye. Is it mischief? Before I get a word out, she grabs a handful of the curtain and whips it back.

Sean startled, gasping mid-sip of his espresso.

His mouth hangs open.

I blush under his intense stare, but something stirs deep in my belly. I feel a rush of satisfaction at the way his breath catches puffing out his chest. I feel beautiful, and I want Sean to see me.

Mable beams from ear to ear.

“Doesn’t she look wonderful!”

Chapter 13

Sean

Speechless.

I can't form words. Lucy looks mind blowing in a crisp white gown, the bodice hugs her curves in all the right places, down to her hips, cascading around her as she walks on a cloud.

Sexy yet elegant.

Her wild auburn mane tamed down one side of her face, flows over her full breasts, lengthening her neck and bringing my attention straight to her deep chestnut brown eyes.

Time stands still.

With each breath, her chest rises and falls. I'm enchanted.

She's as shocked as I am when that little minx, Mable, whips the curtain back; but there's expectation in her eyes. Expectation of what? It takes my whole willpower to keep my ass on the velvet sofa, not to run over and kiss the bride.

The little woman clears her throat.

"I said, doesn't she look wonderful?"

"Umm, yeah, of course you look great, Lucy." I need to get out of here. My heartbeat thunders in my ears. The blood flowing somewhere too far south.

"I'll just wait for you outside."

Lame and awkward, I sprint for the door.

"I've ah, got some prep to do for my meeting."

That little minx of a woman, Mable. She knew exactly what she was doing. When she saw my reaction, her face lit up like a Christmas tree. A smirk lifting one side of her lips until I hot-tailed it out of there.

No relief from the heat out here on the busy sidewalk. I'll be lucky not to melt onto the sidewalk by the time Lucy has changed and paid for the dress.

What was I doing in a bridal boutique with the girl I've wanted as mine for as long as I can remember? I feel like a cartoon version of myself where my tongue rolls along the floor and hearts pound from my eyeballs.

What an idiot.

This was a mistake. I should have left her at the side of the road.

Yeah, that would have been real gentlemanly, Sean.

I pull out my cell and the number from Melanie at the gas station and send her a voice note.

"Hi Mel, it's Sean Larson here. Great bumping into you again today. Do you fancy drinks this Friday? Let me know, and I'll get us booked somewhere."

Just drinks, casual, no strings. Yep, that's what I need. Mel was just what I need right now.

Keep telling yourself that, jackass!

Project 'Get Lucy Davenport out of my head,' in motion!

Now just the biggest meeting of my career and a two-hour drive home with my balls feeling like they'd been trapped in a vice. I don't know which one I was more nervous about.

Lucy

"Oh-my-god!" Kate gushes.

She squeezes me in the tightest hug I think I've ever had. I swear my eyeballs nearly pop out of their sockets. And my mom gives some pretty firm hugs.

"You are without a doubt *the* bestest friend a girl could have!"

Her excitement is so contagious, like a five-year-old has gotten a pony for her birthday. She skips and jumps on the spot, her eyes glaze over, admiring the blown up image of her dress I've projected on the wall.

"Mable said she can squeeze you in for a fitting this week so she has time to alter before the wedding. You just need to get to Denver."

After Mable told me under no circumstance was I altering her dress, I had to make a new surprise plan.

Thankful for Mable; who was I kidding that I'd have time to alter a dress in time for the wedding with all the insurance and renovation work I still have to sort at the bakery on top of being maid of honor. The wedding was less than two weeks away.

"Are you kidding me? Of course, I'll get there."

Her arms grasp me again. "I don't know what I've done in a past life to deserve a friend like you."

The love in her eyes right there made it all worth it. The drive to Denver, the hot, awkward drive back with Sean. My best friend was so thankful at that moment, I would have moved mountains for her with my bare bleeding hands.

With the help of Barbs when Kate was finishing work, I set up the Larson's lounge with balloons and champagne with strawberries and the projection of the dress filling the back wall. I invited the rest of the bridal party around and my mom. Kate's cousin Becca and another girl we went to school with, Lisa, were the other bridesmaids making us a trio. They were both so relieved I'd dealt with the dress disaster so they didn't have to.

Kate walked in blindfolded for the big revelation. She's such a drama queen at heart, she loves a big surprise. But her face when we took off the blindfold was worth every hot, awkward minute of the day.

Her tears of joy fill my heart. My best friend is happy, I'd found her the perfect dress.

My heart fills with pride.

The memory of standing in the dress projected on the wall is bittersweet. I've never felt so special or beautiful in my life. I wish my mom had been there to see it. She would definitely have had tears in her eyes. The eyes that had seen me, however, didn't have tears in them.

Those glistening, emerald eyes filled with raw heat and desire.

Remembering that moment when Mable whipped the curtain back and his eyes met mine, my body flushes all over again at the memory. I thought he was going to rush me. Instead, he up and hightailed it out of the boutique, like his ass was on fire.

"Are you okay, dear?" Mom pulls me towards her around my waist, wakening me from my trance.

"Sure, just tired is all." I smile down at her, "lots of driving today."

"Oh yes, that long drive to Denver. It's a good job Sean had been heading that way. God knows what would have happened to you stranded on the side of that road."

"Yes, a genuine hero." I can't stop the sarcasm dripping from my voice or the roll of my eyes.

"You better watch it or those eyes will get stuck at the back of your head, lady." Her tone is more concerned than scolding. "What's bothering you?"

Why are moms so intuitive?

"It's nothing. I just have a lot in my head with the bakery, and the wedding is all."

"Uh-huh," she isn't buying it. "Did your car get to the garage?"

"Yes, Sean had it towed to Marshall's."

Marshall's is the local garage in town. He knows everyone's car inside out. Has fixed Ol'Betty more times than I could count in the last year.

"Oh, he did, did he?" Her smile split her face. "He's such a nice boy, Lucy."

She pats my arm before leaving me to gush over the wedding dress with Kate, Barbs, and the other bridesmaids.

After I get Mom home safely in Kate's Mercedes, I enjoy a glass of champagne. The rest of the bridesmaid crew are gone, they headed home after the bubbles ran out. Only Kate and I left, sipping a Jack D on the rocks.

I'm so happy for her and Josh. When he'd proposed on Christmas Eve last year, it was the most romantic thing ever.

We'd all rented a lodge on Mount Evans for the holidays. The snow was thick, and the air was crisp. He'd confided in me a few months before about his plans and asked me to help him pick out the ring.

What a guy. I couldn't think of anyone else more suited to my best friend.

When they announced on Christmas morning that the wedding would be the next summer, I nearly fell over. I thought there was no way we could get the wedding Kate had always dreamed of pulled together in seven months.

But here we are, less than two weeks to go and we're almost ready to get her down the aisle.

“Lucy, you know I couldn’t have done all this without you.” She places her hand on mine raising her glass; I clink mine with hers, laughing.

“You’re more than my best friend; you’re my sister.” There’s the sparkle of a tear in her eye.

“Don’t go getting all soppy on me after a couple of glasses of champers now.” I giggle.

She smiles. There’s something she’s not saying.

“Out with it,” I demand. “I don’t get to sister status without knowing when you’ve got something on your mind.”

“Ha, you can read me like a book.”

“Sure can.”

“Well, I was worried about you after the bakery flood and you’ve been stressing about my wedding so much.”

She’s rambling and I’m certain I’m not going to like where this is going.

“I thought you could use a night of relaxing and being pampered. Maybe even get you laid.”

I almost spray my mouthful of Jack in her face, barely making it back into the glass.

“What have you done, Kate?” I close my eyes, drawing in a deep breath, waiting to hear the damage.

"When was the last time you had sex Lucy, or even went on a carefree date to let your hair down?" She demands gently. "You never stop working or caring for everyone else."

"Well, I've kind of had a lot going on lately, my best friend's short-notice wedding, Mom's MS getting worse."

Is she trying to make me cry?

"And oh yeah, big update. My business and home are in soggy tatters. I haven't really had time to think about anything else right now. Especially dating or getting my leg over!"

"I totally get that," her face is sympathetic. She could try to get it, but her wedding was going to be amazing. Her high-paying vet salary keeps her comfortable every month, and she and Josh had just secured a house in town for after their honeymoon.

She didn't get it.

"So I thought I'd treat and surprise you because you're so good at it for everyone else."

"Okaay, what did you have in mind?" I know she was telling me because I hate surprises and Kate can't keep a secret to save herself.

"I've booked us into the Cedar Spa on Friday afternoon, massage, nails and hair, the entire works." She's animated now, "aand Brendan is in town this weekend and is dying to see you. You made such an impression on him at the barbecue. Josh said he keeps asking about you and if you're available, what flowers you like, your favorite food."

The last part came out in a rush of words. Her eyes are wide looking for praise. She's such an optimist.

“Kate! Tell me you did not agree I’d go on a date without asking me?!”

At least she has the decency to look a little sheepish, but not enough that she was going to regret it.

“He’s a great guy, Lucy; I think you two will hit it off.”

My eyes tell her I’m not impressed.

“Don’t look at me like that. If the tables were turned, you would do exactly the same thing for me.” She huffs, shoving her folded arms over her chest. “You should give it a chance. You need a day of relaxing.”

“The spa sounds great, just what I need, but I’m not sure about a date with Brendan. The first thing he did when he met me was stare at my tits.”

“Well, you have a great rack!” I can’t help giggle at that and she knows she’s lightened the mood.

“Are you coming to the spa with me?” I ask.

“Of course! Would I miss a day at Cedar?” she mocks shock.

“Alright, I suppose Brendan-blue-eyes wasn’t that bad to look at. I’ll go on Friday.”

Kate punches the air for the win before we burst into fits of laughter.

Chapter 14

Lucy

I don't know if I've ever seen this much pain in my mom's face. Her heart breaks before we walk through the door of our soggy bakery. She pauses outside the door, tears streaming down her face.

All I can do is hold her from behind. Reassure her, I'm here.

"Mom, I'm so sorry." My apologies have been long and repetitive, I'm positive she isn't hearing them anymore.

"It's all my fault. You know I'm going to make this right, don't you?"

"Darling, I don't blame you." Her words bleed between sobs. "The contractor said there was damage done, and this was the last straw. I'm just glad it never happened when you were lying in your bed, sound asleep."

I pull her into a hug from behind.

"Let's get this over with."

I step in front pushing the door open. The shock hits me just as hard as when I'd arrived the other night to water dripping everywhere. Thankfully, the dripping has stopped, and the contractor has placed some machines to start the drying process.

A lot of rubble has already been removed. My sofa is gone from the front of the window. I pick up the little bumble bee bell that chimed whenever a customer stepped in the door.

"Right Mom, I'm going to pile up what we can't salvage and save things that can."

I don't know if it's my imagination but Mom looks even more stooped and frail. She was always the strong one. The decision maker. I loved my dad dearly, but my mom was the business, she was the driving force.

To see her so frail, helpless, and now fractured further, is breaking me inside.

"Honey, I'm not sure I'm going to be much help." She shuffles around some soggy magazines, fallen from my living room.

"Mom, you're a help just being here to support me. Being here all alone would be too hard." I pull out the deck chair I'd brought for her with a flask of her herbal tea to keep her calm. I dust down a table that still has four reasonably sturdy legs.

She rests wearily down.

"Look, this can go in the salvageable pile," I joke, showing her the bell, pulling a small smile from her lips.

"Always a bright side, Lucy."

"Is there any other side? That's what Grandma taught us."

Grandma was forever looking on the bright side. It didn't matter how horrific any situation was; she was rarely deterred.

I was going to have to summon up my inner grandma to get me through the next few hours. Mom pulls out her wireless radio from her bag and set it to her favorite country music station.

"Shoulda brought my boots?" I laugh, kicking up my heels.

"Well, no better way to work than with the beat of a great country song."

For the next hour or so we work away, Mom standing and picking bits, then resting herself back down in the chair.

I've worked through the rubble and debris on the floor and had it cleared. A lot of the steel pans and utensils were recoverable.

The big industrial ovens had taken a hit, the electrics flooded beyond repair. The insurance was going to cover all of this. I had to keep repeating this to myself to stop the onset of a panic attack.

Running my dusty hands down my jeans, I'm hitting a wall. Hair clapped to my head, sweat trickling down my back.

"Time for a break, I think, sweetie." Mom's sympathetic eyes point me toward the second folding chair and a wax wrap of sandwiches. Then she offers up my all-time favorite cinnamon swirl bun.

"Well, how can I say no to that?" I laugh, my stomach rumbles in anticipation. I haven't eaten for hours, my head feels fuzzy.

"Have you been baking at home again?" I try to scold her. Although, I can't be too mad because she made my favorites.

"Young lady, the day I stop baking is the day I die."

"That's not funny." I stick a ham and cheese triangle into my mouth.

"Helen next door was in and made sure I was safe."

"Praise the Lord," I sigh with sarcasm. Helen was a well-meaning lady. She would give you her last cent. However, her very advanced arthritis had her hands like claws did not make her the best candidate for a very suitable supervisor.

"Honey," the catch in Mom's voice has me nervous as she fiddles with the wax wrap, folding it and re-folding it. "What are you planning on doing?"

"What do you mean?"

"When the insurance money comes through."

Am I so transparent? Have I even said out loud that I don't know if I'm going to open the bakery again?

I can't hide anything from Mom. She's a human lie detector. Even with little white ones. And besides, she deserves to know everything about the bakery. It might be mine in name now but it is our love, our passion.

"I'm not sure I have a choice," I whisper the words. "The bakery is our life. It's our family's legacy."

Mom leans in, squeezing my knee in her weak hands.

"The bakery was Grandma and Pop's dream, and then it was mine and your dad's. We put our blood, sweat, and tears and our whole life into it, but I've never expected you to do the same, my honeybee."

Tears brim the edge of my eyes, ready to break free. How could she be so understanding?

"I can't be the one to let it go, to let it close after all these years. How could I live with myself?"

The warm blobs drip slowly down my cheek. Mom swipes her finger, mopping up the fallen tears.

"How can you live with yourself if you stay in a job for the rest of your life that you're not happy in?"

"Mom, I *am* happy. I promise, it's just..."

"I know honeybee." Her soothing hand on my knee rubs in circles. "I was so happy when you decided you wanted to buy me out of the bakery and keep it in our family, but deep down I know you have other dreams you wanted to chase. Dreams that are not here in this little town."

"I can't go anywhere; I have to be here for you. I want to be here for you."

"You know I won't be here forever, honeybee."

Then the dam of tears breaks free.

Sean

Coming through the front door the first sound I hear are sniffles and tears. Lucy is sitting with her back to me at the dining room table sobbing. Shoulders shaking. I stand in the hallway like a shit bag with no idea if I should go in or run for the mountains.

I don't think I've ever seen Lucy look defeated before. She's the happy, positive pants, the *everything-happens-for-a-reason-and-will-work-out-in-the-end* kinda gal.

Her sobs were painful. Something pulls me to go in and comfort her.

I stay hovering outside the kitchen. What on earth do I do with a crying chick? Do I leave her alone? Pretend I didn't hear her? Go buy her chocolate?

"I can see you hovering, Sean," she says between sniffles. "Your reflection is in the glass."

Busted.

"Just come in. It's your house."

"I'm sorry. I was just going to make coffee. Got that afternoon slump after the gym."

She blows her nose noisily into an already very soggy tissue. I pass her the box for a fresh one.

"Thanks, I'm sorry. I should have stayed in my room."

"Not at all." I scoop coffee and boil the kettle. "Do you want one?"

"Sure."

I let the silence sit for a bit. My life coach liked a long silence. I usually broke it. Lucy is a tougher nut to crack.

"Are you going to tell me what's got you so upset?"

She peers up at me with her big brown eyes, tears threatening her eyelids again.

"I might be able to help, you know. It's been said that I'm real good at listening."

I place the steaming coffees between us, sitting down beside her.

"You still cream, no sugar?"

She nods with a hint of a smile. The silence continues.

"Well ..." I prompt rolling my hand in front of me.

"It's just family stuff."

"I have family."

"Okay, it's business stuff."

"I have a business."

"Has your business just imploded along with your home and ended in a soggy mess, leaving you with no work, no money, and nowhere to go?" She snaps, thumping her fist on the table, sloshing coffee.

"No! You have it all, swanning about with your online business all over the world, not a care or responsibility in sight!"

Wow!

I still, my hands around my coffee mug. "You're upset, Lucy, so I'll let that outburst go. I have done nothing wrong. I just want to help if I can."

Lucy throws her head down on the table, hair scattering, shoulders heaving with the returning sobs.

"I'm sorry." Her voice muffles into the table, each word punctuated with a sob. "I-just-don't-know-what-to-do."

"Do about what, Red?" I hover my hand over her head, nervous. Would she want me to comfort her?

"It's me; Sean. You can tell me anything."

I place my hand on her head and stroke a soothing motion over her thick hair. "Remember when you told me it was you who broke the porch swing, not Kate and I backed you up?"

A snort sounds from under the hair.

"I've got your back. Let me listen." A few more strokes with my thumb and she lifts her head.

"I don't know if I want to re-open Honeybee Bakery and it will destroy Mom."

"Okay, I wasn't expecting that, but talk to me." I lean in, ready to hear it.

She picks the coffee up wrapping her hands around the not seasonal pumpkin mug, composing herself, before telling me all about how she's always wanted to go to med school and become a surgeon and how this might be the opportunity to do it but closing the family bakery would let everyone down, letting go of everything her family has built over the last sixty-five years.

"Don't get me wrong, I love the bakery. I love what I've built since I took over. I love I am the one who gets to help the whole town celebrate every occasion, being a part of making that perfect. Weddings, baby showers, gender reveals, birthdays, it's so much fun. Even chatting to all the regulars who come in every week. But is it my dream?"

She pauses for a breath.

"I remember you talking about med school before I left. When I was away, I always pictured you in green scrubs, married to another doctor living in the city."

Her eyebrows raise and she scoffs at me.

"Well, clearly, that never happened. Dad died and Mom needed me at the bakery. I'm stuck here, where I've always been."

She tucks her hair behind her ear. "I thought this might be my opportunity to make that change; be brave. But now it just feels selfish. Am I being selfish?"

I lean back in my chair, coffee now cold. "You're not selfish. Look at me," I lift her chin with my finger, her skin so soft, "You don't have a selfish bone in your body. Do you hear me?" Her eyes glistening with unshed tears.

She nods.

"Everything you do, every decision you make, you are thinking of someone else before you. You always have. Maybe it's time to put yourself first, but first think about what your dream is. What do you really want in life? Is med school an excuse to get out of Breakridge? Are you running away?"

Pot, kettle, black Sean!

"You wanted med school when you were in your twenties and to go live a life in the city. You're thirty now. What do you really want from life *now*?"

God, I want to scoop her up and tell her it's all going to be okay. Who the hell am I to be giving life advice? When this wedding is over, I've no clue what I'm going to do.

What the hell do *I* want from life? That was my big question. Maybe we could figure it out together?

Chapter 15

Lucy

The rest of the week is a blur of bridesmaid dress fitting, and heated debates with the rest of the bridal party about the style of shoes we're going to wear and if we're having hair up or hair down for the wedding ceremony.

Out for lunch with the bridesmaids and Kate in a cute, quaint diner after yet another shoe-shopping torture session, Becca is determined to undermine me every step of the way.

"Look, I can't have my wild, thick hair down all day at a wedding in July. I'll be a sopping mess before midday."

"I'm sure Kate wants the wedding party photos to be perfect and that won't happen if the maid of honor could be mopped up from the tile floors." I punctuate my point to Becca with the straw from my Mai Tai.

"Don't exaggerate, Lucy." She sighs back.

Becca, Kate's cousin, who is clearly jealous that Kate didn't ask her to be her maid of honor, rolls her eyes. Becca is the same age as Kate and me. We played together as kids growing up. She thought because she was family that she had one up on me and hasn't been afraid to challenge me at every single maid of honor duty. She was becoming a real pain in my ass.

"I'm not exaggerating Becca. Have you seen how thick my hair is?"

She rolls her eyes. "Yeah, I don't know what you're complaining about. It's gorgeous and you keep scrapping it back in a ponytail, you need to use it to your advantage."

As she said this, she flicks her hair like she used to when she was a teenager trying to get the attention of Hudson Roads, the quarterback when she was head cheerleader.

"Easy for you; your hair dosesn't weigh you down."

"Ladies?" Kate's voice behind us. "Put your claws away," she shimmies herself into the booth next to me.

"You can all wear your hair how you feel comfortable."

All eyes are on her like she's grown an extra head. Kate has been more than just a little controlling throughout the planning of this wedding, down to the detail of the style of underwear, so we didn't have VPL.

"What?! I don't want you all to be unhappy with how you look on my big day?" She shrugs like it was no big deal. "I'm not Bridezilla you know!"

"Uh hello, do you not remember the sunflower yellow vomit dress you almost insisted we all wear?" Lisa exclaims.

We all burst into a fit of giggles at the table.

Lisa's head snaps up like a tiger spotting prey. "Hot totty at twelve o'clock."

The cute server is heading our way. Lisa pouts her lips, never willing to miss out on a bit of male attention. She is so obvious, it's a wonder she gets any guy's number. Well, I suppose she's only interested in one thing, and most guys are over the moon with that. More like a pack of dogs howling at a full moon.

Her eyelids flutter so fast I'm worried she might take flight right out of the booth.

"Hey," she stares right at the name tag on his chest for a second longer than necessary, "Paul, is it?"

He is right into this, grinning like a Cheshire cat.

"I sure am. What can I get you ladies?" he ends with a wink in Lisa's direction.

Ugh, am I just jealous I never have Lisa's kind of courage with guys? I could go on dates. I could hold a conversation, but the whole flirting thing is way past my skill set. Kate was my wing woman. Now she's well and truly off the market, what on earth would I do?

I'll be here, left on the shelf or propped on the end of a bar alone with an iced tea.

Maybe Brendan-Blue-Eyes would break my dry spell on Friday? Although is it a dry spell if you snogged the face off your best friend's brother the other night?

Come Friday, I'm so thankful to Kate when we walk through the door of Cedar Spa. The tension reverberates through my body and I'm damn well ready to leave it behind.

I have so many spinning plates on sticks, as well as Sean, being everywhere I was. I can't leave my room without crashing into his broad, hard chest in the hallway, making a cup of coffee without his warm musky scent entering the kitchen. Even hiding in my room trying to read, I can hear him singing in the damn shower. And jeez, when I hear that, I can't help but imagine him singing in that shower, taut muscles, golden skin, rubbing his blond curls into a lather.

Last night when I was brushing my teeth, he came into the very snug bathroom and stood right beside me, the warm skin of his arm gently rubbing against my shoulder. He picked up his toothbrush and started brushing, staring at me in the mirror, a challenge in his eye. Heat flushing me, I panicked, not so elegantly spat out the toothpaste, and sprinted back to my room.

I had to get out of that house. Sean was a tempting torment.

Yes, this was just what I need today.

Hit by the scent of lemongrass, my muscles immediately un-clench. The muted lights soothe my senses. Calm crashing over me in waves.

God bless my best friend.

I leave behind the days I'd just had of sifting through the rubble, pulling out any recoverable items from the bakery and apartment. My clothes, my shoes, my books were all ruined. I was thankful I had stored most of my memories in a container I rented when all my stuff was over crowding the apartment last year. Photos of Grandma and Pops, my dad and mom. Those are irreplaceable.

I'd fought with the insurance guy all day yesterday. My nerves were fraught. He'd questioned and questioned me about the bath tap running, but it turned out the overflowing bath was only the start of the problem. When the pressure of the water flooded on the floor of the apartment, there was underlying structural damage. The contractor said it might have come from an earthquake on Christmas day nearly 10 years ago, but he couldn't prove it. The damage had been an accident waiting to happen - he said this wasn't the first incident like this around these parts.

My mom's prayers have come through. The insurance is going to cover it, but in the meantime, I need to survive until the work was done. And I don't know how much longer I can tiptoe around the Larson's house avoiding Sean.

Right, today was for relaxing. No stress talk. No maid of honor nightmares or bakery disasters in sight. Just me and my bestie relaxing.

"Kate, I can't thank you enough for thinking of this."

We sit side by side as two very wonderful therapists rub and push pressure points on our feet. Boosting our circulation and clearing out toxins.

Her fingers are magical, swooshing and swirling the soles of my feet. With each little press on the sole of my foot, another layer of tension evaporates.

"You are so welcome," Kate beams. "We haven't had a girlie day like this in over a year. It's long overdue."

"Well, it's perfect timing for me." Closing my eyes, I lean back in the soft leather recliner, allowing it to envelop me in comfort. I suck in a deep breath through my nose and blow it away out of my mouth.

Bliss!

"You've been under such a lot of pressure. I know the wedding has added a lot more."

My eyes are still closed, hoping this conversation doesn't head in a stressful direction.

"I wouldn't have it any other way, you know that. The world could be on fire, and I'd still make sure you had the perfect wedding day."

"I know, I know. You are the best friend a girl could ever want." Her tone wavers.

I reluctantly open one eye to peek at her. She's looking concerned at me.

"Kate," I put a hint of warning in my tone, "don't make me leave this spa because you're getting all overprotective."

"I'm not, it's just me, your mom and Barbs were talking.."

"Oh jeez, here we go. What were you three conspiring about behind my back?" I say this in jest, but the uneasy feeling of annoyance is creeping over my relaxed state of mind.

"After your dress surprise, which was out of this world, by the way."

"I know."

I now thoroughly regret not asking for for separate massage rooms.

"Well, we were saying how maybe the flood at the bakery was a sign."

"What?"

"Well, you're tied to Breakridge because of the bakery, and you would never give it up or sell it willingly because of the sentimental value. What if you used the insurance money and went to college like you'd always dreamed?"

My eyes must have bugged out of my head.

"Kate, I don't know what I want to do. I thought you brought me here to relax, not plan the rest of my life out."

I love her dearly, but she is such a fixer. A rescuer. She wants to be everyone's hero. I'm over here just wanting to forget all the drama in my life right now, for a few hours at least, and Kate had to bring it right into the spa with us.

"Kate, really?" I can't hide my exasperation. "You might as well have packed all my problems in a bag and rolled them into the spa with us!"

The two massage therapists look at one another, finish their work quickly before fleeing out the door.

"I know, I'm sorry."

"You don't look sorry. You've scared away our therapists." I give her a raised eyebrow.

"Look, I'm leaving for my honeymoon next Sunday and I'm scared you're going to rush into something and regret it."

She is just going to keep pestering me until I give her something.

"I'm not rushing into anything," I sigh. "I've been considering many options. Sean was helping me."

"Sean?!" Her voice pitches higher, "like my little brother Sean?"

Shit.

Why did I have to say that?!

"What can he help with?" Kate seems genuinely curious.

"He has successful businesses." I'm sure there's no other reason he's being helpful. Definitely not because I kissed him in the kitchen the other night!

"I suppose he does." She concedes, hopefully dismissing this thought any further.

"I'm surprised my mom was in on your scheming and plotting to get me to leave Breakridge."

Well, not really that surprising. Had she not suggested the same thing to me only the other day?

"She wants you to be happy, Lucy." Kate places her hand on my thigh.

"I am happy! Why does everyone think I'm unhappy?"

"Are you really, though?" Her words sting somewhere deep I've been avoiding for a while.

“You spend every day making everyone else happy. All your choices are for everyone else. When was the last time you did something for you?”

“Well, I’m trying to relax today and I have a date tonight.” I say smugly.

Kate pins me with derision in her eyes. “Exactly, and who had to organize and force you to do both those things?”

She points her newly manicured finger at herself.

“It still counts,” I huff.

“I’m considering all my options. I love the bakery. How could I possibly just give it up?” It really is hard to imagine not getting up in the morning and baking bread and cakes. Not being the one responsible for peoples joy when they see the cakes that become such a part of their celebration.

“But do you love the bakery and being a baker or do you love what the bakery represents, the memories it holds?”

Is Kate right?

Am I holding onto a memory and keeping myself back?

Some spa day this is turning out to be, and now I had to get dressed up for a date with leering Brendan.

Oh goody!

Chapter 16

Sean

Melanie is a little over, yet still under, dressed for Breakridge Rivers' only restaurant. An ankle-length skirt with a slit up her leg almost as high as the waistline paired with a lace body suit, the cleavage scooping down low. Not too much left for my imagination.

Usually I don't mind a bit of skin, it's how I like it, but somehow at home it feels a little tasteless.

Via Napoli, the quaint Italian Restaurant, run by Gianna and Giuseppe Zanneti. The couple moved to Colorado from New York over twenty years ago and the town has welcomed them with open arms. Their restaurant was booming.

Walking in was a bit like coming home, having eaten here so much with the family when we were younger. Everyone spent their birthday and anniversaries here with the Zanneti's. I'm so glad that not too much has changed since the last time I was here.

The old-fashioned wooden door has a fresh coat of paint but still opens with a gentle creak. The exposed brick wall scattered with Italian posters and family photos tells the story of generations spent perfecting the recipes on the menu. There are a few more pictures added to the collection since my last visit. Mr. and Mrs. Zanneti with a few more lines than the rest, with a view of the Amalfi Coast behind them. A grin from ear to ear on both their faces, Mrs. Zanneti's eyes on the camera, Mr. Zanneti's eyes on Mrs. Zanneti.

The newest picture in the timeline was three generations of Zanneti's; now the grandchildren had arrived. With six children, I'm sure there would be many more to come.

I love Italian food and have been in many across the world, but nothing has come close to the welcoming smell of simmering sauces and freshly baked bread that has my mouth watering in Via Napoli.

Melanie mildly stomps in beside me, her lips so tightly pursed I'm not sure she'll be able to separate them again tonight. She thought I was taking her somewhere flashy in the Tesla that's been parked in my dad's drive.

When I rocked up to her house in the truck and said I had Via Napoli booked for seven pm, she glanced down at herself and growled.

She actually growled and stomped her stiletto like a toddler.

Having not said very much in the car, I'm predicting this is going to be the shortest date in history.

"Sean!" My name is yelled from the direction of the bustling open kitchen. Mrs. Gia ambles towards me, her arms outstretched. Grabbing my face in her hands, she plants a kiss on each cheek.

"Oh my goodness, it's so lovely to see you. I'd heard you were back in town. Your mama is so happy!" She spares a glance at Melanie behind me, and I swear she gives me a bit of the stink eye.

"Mrs. Gia!" I lift her hand and kiss it gently, like Mr. Zanneti showed me when I was only twelve years old.

"It's so lovely to see you, looking as young and radiant as ever."

"You have picked up some chat since we last saw you." Patting my cheek in that way your older relatives do, a loving gesture.

"We have a table booked for two tonight."

Melanie suddenly lights up like 4th July, her smile as wide as the Mississippi. Grabbing my arm, she glues herself to my bicep and looks right up into my face. Mrs. Gia's eyes widen with the obvious change in her mood.

I scan the room as Mrs. Gia leads us through the sea of red and white tablecloths and see the reason for Melanie's defrosting.

Lucy.

She's sitting at a table with mountain man from Kate and Josh's engagement party. Looking cozy together, their heads close in conversation. The light from the candle flickering highlights of fiery reds through her hair.

I heat under my collar, muscles clench tight.

What the hell is she doing with Josh's cousin? He was a slobbering dog at the garden party. His tongue lolling so far out, he might have tripped on it. He's looking at her like she's dessert.

A hard tug on my arm pulls my gaze, Melanie dragging my attention back to her.

"Is this table suitable?" Mrs. Gia points us to a table across the room from Lucy, but with a clear view.

"Perfect, thank you." Mrs. Gia looks at me, then over to Lucy and back. She gives me a look that only a woman with experience can, a knowing one. Raised eyebrows and a tight smile.

I pull out a chair for Melanie, leaving the one facing Lucy for me. I had no idea she was heading on a date tonight. How did I miss that?

Come to think of it, I haven't seen her in the house all day.

Why am I torturing myself? Why did I care if she's here with some guy? I am here with someone else.

Melanie is lovely, despite the hint of desperation lingering around her. I remember her carefree laugh from high school. She was beautiful.

But I couldn't help noticing her gaze constantly falling to my Cartier watch and cuff links. This isn't unusual for women I date, but it feels really strange when someone I've known all my life acts like this.

"So what have you been up to these past few years, Mel?" I ask, with my gaze still on the redhead across the room.

Mountain man places his hand over hers, leaning in closer, sharing an intimate moment.

Why is it so hot in here? I undo the top button of my shirt.

".... so after I graduated, my mom needed me to stay. Are you too warm?"

"Sorry?"

She lifts her finger across the table and runs her extra long nail down my chest where the button sits open.

"Are you a little warm?" A glimmer in her eye lets me know she's got other ideas. "We could skip dinner, you know?"

Removing her hand from my chest, I gently place it on the table; holding on long enough so as not to offend Mel. "I'm kind of famished. I've not eaten since breakfast."

I grab my menu, studying it intensely. I need to keep my eyes away from Lucy and Mountain Man.

Mrs. Gia takes our order, returning with a bottle of champagne. Of course, Melanie ordered the most expensive drink on the menu. Mrs. Gia doesn't have Dom Perignon, but Mel wants the best on the menu. I didn't roll my eyes, but Mrs. Gia did. I couldn't hide my smile at her obvious distaste for my date.

He keeps touching her, and her eyes are on him. Why are they on him? Look over here Lucy! I'm willing her to see me. It's a useless endeavor trying not to watch.

Her skin is radiant, and she's glowing against the navy of her satin figure hugging blouse. So tastefully dropping at her cleavage, but not too much. Mountain man must have the perfect view leaning above her. He lifts his spoon full of cream and strawberries to her lips and I nearly choke on my drink.

Lucy, distracted by my loud cough, lifts her eyes, meeting mine.

The sparks from that one look explode like a grenade in my chest. I'm surprised the whole restaurant doesn't see the spectacle or hear the crackling of excitement that pierces my ears. Her burning gaze lights me up, a dark seductiveness in her eyes. She knows exactly the effect she's having on me and it's all over her face.

Satisfaction.

I've never seen this side of Lucy Davenport and I'm not disappointed.

She is a temptress.

She is sin.

She is mine.

Her smile over Mountain Man's shoulder is filthy. Swallowing her strawberry, our eyes remain locked. She sticks her tongue out so slowly and draws it along her bottom lip. Mountain Man must be creaming in his pants, but I know that was just for me.

It takes every ounce of my restraint to remain seated and not stride over there, drag her out of this restaurant and back home to my bed. My cock is solid under this table. I have a feeling it's going to be a long night next door to Red tonight.

Chapter 17

Lucy

I am going to think of a very long and very painful payback to Kate for forcing me on this date. Okay, she didn't force me, but I could hardly say no and let him down. That's not how my mama raised me.

Brendan is regaling yet another story about how much money he has made in investments in farming and agriculture. I've already heard how lucrative his farm is, how he was the first in the state to import buffalo (I'm almost certain that's not true) to produce buffalo mozzarella and the demand for it was out of this world.

The worst part of the evening yet, had to be when he tried to make a pitch to Mrs. Zanneti on the benefits of buffalo mozzarella and how it would improve the taste of her pizza. A pizza recipe which has been in her family and passed down the generations for decades. She'd once told me her great grandmother had collected recipes in an old book and it had passed from daughter to granddaughter, then their daughter, and it would soon be her daughters and granddaughters.

Literally for decades, and Brendan thought he was going to get Mrs. Zanneti to change it.

The cringe forming inside me is uncomfortable. I'm sure my face is hiding nothing.

I couldn't help but run my finger over my throat in a 'cut it out' motion. My red nail polish must have matched the shade of my face as I wished the restaurant floor would part and swallow me up.

It would have been the most perfect excuse to cut the date short.

"So when I had the chance to invest in this new machinery ..."

What would Kate say? *Saddle up and make the most out of your date Luc, you're in a dry spell!*

I suppose Brendan is lovely to watch. He has the face of a preppy student and the body of a man that chops tree trunks with an axe all day. His arms could envelop me in a second. It isn't giving me the butterflies I hoped it might.

I like the few days' growth, past stubble, but not a beard. Soft enough to run your hand over and not flinch at the prickle.

I know this because when he picked me up from the Larson's house; he dove right in for a kiss. I only just had my wits about me enough to turn swiftly, and his gentle fuzz caught me on the cheek.

"Next time." He winked as he took me by the arm and led me to a very smelly old truck. If I was a gambling kinda girl,

I would bet the truck was older and more beaten than Ol' Betty.

Now I'm not a material girl, I don't live for the fancy things in life, but I do, however, draw the line at a truck that has the lingering aroma of manure and remnants of a hay bale sticking from the upholstery.

I had relaxed and pampered all day, only to feel like I needed a shower before I got seated at dinner.

I don't think I'm onto a winner with Brendan. Apart from his inappropriate propositioning of Mrs. Zanneti, he was harmless. Passionate about farming and buffalo mozzarella, but harmless.

I suppose the date isn't a complete blow out. Brendan would make a little arm candy for the wedding. Nothing worse than being a singleton at a wedding of a hundred and fifty guests, of whom the majority were couples and families. Yes, Mom would be there, but it's not really the same as having a man on your arm and a dance partner.

I wonder if Brendan could dance. I'm leaning in, attempting to be interested in the next farming anecdote, something about the piglet's chasing the chickens, when I hear Mrs. Zannetti shout the last name in the world I want to hear.

"Sean!"

Keeping my eyes glued on Brendan, I can't look over. I know it's him. I can feel heat rising, my pulse throbbing in my ears. Why is he here?

"Oh, isn't that Kate's brother?" Brendan glances up. I swiftly grab his hand in a clasp before he waves and draws attention to us. "And he's with that hottie from the gas station, lucky dog!"

I glare at Brendan tightening my grip, nails almost breeching his skin.

He winces and looks adequately sheepish.

The hottie from the gas station? That must be Melanie. Either that or Brendan has weird a fetish for older women as the other two employees are Mrs. Baton and Mrs. Kirk and they have an average age of sixty-seven.

What's he on a date with her for? Everyone in town has had a ride on that bike. Maybe that's why he's on a date with her.

Duh, she's a sure thing.

Ugh.

If I have to listen to his headboard banging tonight, I'll never sleep.

Even worse, if I get up for my coffee in the morning and Mel is standing in the Larson's kitchen in one of Sean's crisp white t-shirts, I think I might vomit right there on the floor.

Just when I think this date can't get any worse, Mrs. Zanneti seats Sean and Mel right in front of us.

I get a front-row seat to the show.

Yey for me.

As they walk past, Mel has sealed herself to Sean's arm like a clam.

Possessive much?

They sit down, Sean facing me. I keep my eyes averted, One hundred percent attention on Brendan.

Yes, I'm here on a date with Brendan.

Could Mel not keep her hands off him? She places a finger on his chest, running it down to the exposed gentle blond hair on his chest. Sean clasps her hand closer, smiling his winning cheeky smile.

Does he know what that smile can do to a woman? Mel must be combusting over there in the direct line of fire.

A rage is building inside me, how can he swan back into town, burn through me with his eyes every time we're in the same room, my insides are liquid, grab me in the most passionate kiss of my life and then take Melanie Winters on a date for a booty call.

I'll show him.

Our desserts have arrived and I have food envy.

"Brendan, that strawberry tart looks fantastic."

The cream rolls around his mouth as he talks. "It's fantastic. How's the cheesecake?"

"A little dry actually, can I get a bite of your strawberry and cream?"

Brendan doesn't look keen on sharing.

Strike two for Brendan.

Until I open my mouth and wait for him to feed me with his spoon.

Why do guys love the thought of feeding a woman?

Is it a dominating thing? A possessive thing?

I gaze at him until he obliges, his smile wide like he's just scored the winning touchdown. His spoon overfilled; he places it in my mouth and I scoop it all in.

I catch Sean's eyes over Brendan's large shoulder. I sit tall, back straight, my very curvaceous breasts forward, shoulders back. My confidence has me on fire. Kate would be proud. A pool of heat gathers between my legs spurring me on. Sean's eyes darken, like he knows the effect he's having on me, his gaze pinning me. I chew the large strawberry slowly, cream escaping from between my lips.

I swallow, slowly. Imagining I'm swallowing something else entirely.

I intentionally run my tongue along my bottom lip and finish with a gentle bite.

Sean's hands grip the edge of the table.

"Excuse me Brendan, I think I've dropped a little cream."

Brendan's eyes pop from his head. A grin appearing from ear to ear. He thinks he's onto a winner tonight.

Sorry Brendan.

I push out my chair, turn and head for the ladies, swaying my hips from side to side, knowing there are two sets of eyes on my round rear and quite enjoying the feeling.

A large gold-framed mirror above the hand basins elegantly decorates the ladies' room. The muted lighting only adds to the hunger in my eyes. I have never seen myself like this.

I look sexy.

And tempting.

It feels fucking fantastic compared to my usual apron and flour covered ensemble. My eyes are dark with a glimmer of mischief, red lipstick painted on my lips. Not my regular choice, but Kate helped me get ready for my date and said the red was sexy.

I agree.

Now how the hell will I get out of this date in one piece? There is no way I want to get back in that stinky truck to drive home. I'd rather walk if I had to.

No, I'll tell Brendan the prosecco has gone to my head and I have a headache. I'll get an *Uber* home and hide in my room the rest of the night.

Ready to face the music of letting Brendan down, I pull open the door to the ladies' room and almost crash into a very broad, very brooding Sean. I can't help the satisfaction thrumming through me. Both of his hands brace the door frame, blocking me in, his eyes hooded, bore into me.

The temptation to throw my arms around those broad shoulders, run my fingers through his thick waves is almost too much.

I don't. I have my feet firmly planted.

"Sean," I impress myself with such a smooth acknowledgement. I can be sexy and enticing when I want to be. The three glasses of wine definitely contributing to the courage I've found.

“Was that little creamy temptation for me or your date?”

I’d never heard Sean’s voice so husky. Is he holding himself back? His knuckles are white on the wood, fingers grip the frame and I really feel for the poor wood.

Do I keep this going?

Yes! My brain screams loudly.

“You know exactly who I was..” I look up at him through my lashes; “tempting.”

A low rumble vibrates from his chest, his hands still firmly gripping the door frame. He leans down into me, his lips caressing my ear lobe, my body responds with a delicious shiver.

“You better not regret that when I get home.” He grips my earlobe between his teeth and tugs.

Sean spins, walking back towards the restaurant. His thick thighs swagger in those tight jeans, leaving me wet and panting in the doorway of the ladies’ toilets.

Chapter 18

Sean

She is a siren. A temptation I can't resist for another second. My restraint has frayed to a tether. This last week living under the same roof, catching glimpses of her in short cotton pajamas, her nipples solid and almost piercing through the thin material with no bra in sight.

Her sweet scent constantly lingering everywhere she's been.

Tonight in Via Napoli, that last tether snapped.

Watching her sway her hips seductively for me, a fucking temptress. The urge to throw myself out of my chair and into the ladies' restroom was too much. I had to brace myself against the door frame to prevent from bursting in there and bending her over the sink.

Not how I wanted it to go down after all those years of fantasizing.

Seeing her pupils dilate like saucers under my gaze before I licked and bit her earlobe, her chest rising and falling rapidly, so close I could feel the rhythm beat through me.

She wants me as much as I need her.

And that's all I need to know.

The ten-minute drive back from Mel's is torture. Distance and time have done nothing to soften the bulge in my pants. It was just as solid as when Lucy pinned me with her fiery eyes and drew her tongue along those full lips, gathering the cream.

I know exactly where I want those plump lips.

The house is silent when I walk in. The only car in the drive is Lucy's pink Mini, returned from the garage.

Kate is over at Josh's. Mom and Dad are out at a dinner party. And when Barbs gets a drink, we all know it's a late night.

Thank the lord, because I need Lucy.

Alone.

I am going to make her scream my name - no restraints.

I pull myself up the stairs looking for any sign she's waiting for me.

Nothing.

My jaw clamps tight anticipating a knock back. I hold my fist to her bedroom door, ready to pound the wood.

The door flies open.

Standing there in that satin blouse, an extra button undone, her round breasts bounce, the edge of her lace bra teasing out. I couldn't help but run my tongue along my lips.

I'm ravenous for her—starving in a way food could never satisfy. That skirt clings to her curves like it was made for worship, tracing every sinful line of her hips. My hands ache to close the distance, to grip, to claim.

Oh, yes, please.

"Hey Red."

"Hey yourself." Her voice is breathy. Her dark eyes dare me to make a move.

Could I do this? Could I have what I've always wanted, what I've dreamed and fantasized about and then leave again?

Hell Yes.

If she gives me the green light, I'll fuck her until sunrise.

She doesn't want me forever. She wants the new look me. The guy who hits the gym, who runs a million dollar online company.

Lucy wants what every other woman wants.

And I'm going to take what I've always wanted.

Her.

Her lips pull between her teeth. She draws her gaze languidly up my body, pausing at the strain in my pants, continues all the way up, her head tilts back to meet my eyes.

I love the length of her neck, her soft red waves pulled to one side, flowing down past her shoulder.

"Say yes, Red." My voice is strangled with the force of the restraint it's taking to keep my hands to myself until I get that green light.

"Before we start, say yes because once we get going, I won't be able to stop. I've waited for you forever."

Her lips part, full and ready, forming an oh; she places both hands on my chest.

"Forever?" The question hangs in a thick silence.

I say nothing. Time scraping by.

“Yes.” she whispers.

That word is Pavlov’s bell going off in my head.

We throw ourselves forward, lips colliding, molding together. Teasing me with her tongue, she meets me with every thrust.

Her hands slide from my chest, up my neck and into my hair, tugging me closer.

My hands fill with her round ass, pulling her against my solid cock.

I love that her eyes widen in anticipation of what's coming. The feeling that I put that smile in her eyes is electrifying.

Exploring her body is like heaven. My hands can’t get enough. Her ass, her hips, her waist, drawing up to the curve of her breasts.

A slight gasp escapes her lips as my knuckles grazed the solid peak of her nipple.

“You like that?”

“Yes,” she pants.

I hold her firmly in her lower back. Her head falling back, pushing her chest towards me. I run my hand down from her neck to her chest, massaging a moan from her lips.

Too much material is still between us.

The sound of the material tearing as I rip her blouse is music to my ears, buttons scatter bouncing around the floor.

Her eyes widen. She's lit up. Reaching behind, she unclasps her black lace bra, letting her breasts bounce free, waiting for my attention.

Never one to disappoint; I dive in, drawing her nipple between my teeth, and I'm rewarded with a guttural moan.

"You're so responsive to my touch, Red. I love it."

"You need less clothes on," she pants.

Her hands land on my chest, drawing her sexy red nails down my skin to my stomach. She has my belt and buttons undone swiftly. Groaning when she reaches down, grabbing my cock, pulling up and down my length.

Like a man possessed, I can't wait any longer. I need her skin on my skin. I discard the rest of my clothes. She's standing still in her black lace panties and heels. I want to fall to my knees at her feet.

"You are so beautiful."

Her blush is lost in the heat of her face.

"Are you wet for me?" I know the answer. I can smell her arousal and it's a drug. This moment right here is when I realize once will never be enough.

Pushing that thought far away, I grab her by the hips against my body.

"Damn Red, you're made for me." Her body molds to mine.

Our lips crash together, each of us as violently passionate as the other. I thrust my tongue deeper, sliding my hand beneath the waistband of those lace panties and my fingers between her folds.

Oh, so wet.

"Sean, I need..." Lucy pants her soft voice like honey.

"I know, Red, I'm going to give you what you need right now."

My fingers pulse in and out, finding her tender bud with my thumb, I rub circles, gently at first, then faster.

"Sean, I..."

"I know, baby, just let go." I pull her nipple between my teeth and that's it. She tightens around me, digging her nails into my back as she comes apart.

"Oh my god, Sean!" My name finally on her lips is all I need to hear. If it's the last thing I hear, I'll die a happy man.

She lifts her eyes to meet mine, still full of hunger.

Oh, my girl wants more.

Dark and sultry, she pushes me onto the bed, taking control. I could get on board with this take charge Lucy.

Standing over me, legs apart, her high heels still in place; I've never been so turned on. I can't help but grab my cock and pull up and down my length.

Her eyebrow lifts. She runs her hands up and down her own body, accentuating her curves, landing on her nipples and rubbing. Her moan is almost my trigger to blow my load.

She is everything I've ever dreamed about and more.

"Red, you better get over here or I'm gonna explode all over this bed without you."

"This," her voice remains deep and sultry, she points her manicured finger between us, "this has been escalating, you've been driving me crazy!"

"Me?!"

She lowers her wet, swollen pussy on my stomach, placing her finger over my lips.

Jesus.

"This is our release." She draws her hands up and down my chest, digging her nails in. "Get it out of our systems and move on."

She grips my solid shaft in her soft hand. I hiss when she strokes me up and down at an achingly slow pace.

"Yes, you agree?"

I'd have agreed to have her poke my eyes with tiny needles right now if she'd asked me to.

"Yeah Red, anything you need."

Her stroking increases in pace, enough to have me growling. I'm pinned under her voluptuous legs. At her mercy.

"Say. It." she demands.

Faster stroking.

"One time only, no weirdness," she continues her persuasive argument.

"Yep.. one time... no weirdness."

Lies!

I can't take it anymore. Grabbing her waist, I flip her off me and onto her back.

Her giggle sends a jolt of electricity through my spine.

I need to be inside her more than I need my next breath.

"Condom?" Lucy asks between our lips.

"My wallet, hold on."

Grabbing it out, Lucy takes it from my hands, ripping the wrapping between her teeth.

I hiss as she rolls it down my shaft. A glimmer of satisfaction in her eyes at the sound.

My eyes can't get enough of her, absorbing her in, her fiery hair splayed on the pillow like a wild mane. She is a lioness, a strong, beautiful, feminine creature.

I'll never have enough.

I gaze into her chocolate eyes and drive into her up to the hilt.

Her back arches. My name screams from her lips.

"Sean!"

"I'm here Luc."

She tightens around me, squeezing me hard.

"Fuck, Sean... that feels ....."

Her head dips back, closing her eyes.

"Eyes on me Red." I demand.

She obliges.

"Good girl." I growl. Her eyes hood at this. Oh, my girl likes praise.

I find my rhythm, watching as I stroke in and out of her beautiful pussy. Pressing a finger on her clit, I rub in circles hard.

I’m so close. Watching her under me come undone is a sight I never thought I’d see.

"Lucy, baby, I need you to come; you feel so fucking good."

I grip her nipple between my teeth and that's enough to tip her over, she shatters under me.

"Sean!" Her nails deep in my back hurl me over the edge.

Spasms send me into release. My hips buck and I groan.

"Ah, Lucy!"

Her eyes have never left mine, burning into me.

If she feels an ounce of what I feel right now, once will never be enough. If I have to get on my knees and beg, Lucy Davenport will be mine and no other man will touch her again.

Chapter 19

Lucy

The morning sun warms my face, shining through a crack in the curtains. Keeping my eyes closed, a satisfied smile bunches my cheeks. The warm satiated feeling flowing through me is like nothing I've felt. The reason for this beautiful feeling flashes behind my closed eyelids.

Sean in my room.

Sean naked with his hands on me.

Sean's teeth on my nipples, his eyes burning into me.

Oh no, no, no!

The joy dissipates; I shoot bolt upright in bed.

"What have I done?" No-one in my empty bedroom can answer. Like someone is going to give me an explanation of why I was such an idiot?

What did I do?

How could I have slept with my best friend's little brother?

What would Kate say? Would she be mad at me? Would she be mad at him?

Could I tell her? Could I even keep it a secret if I wanted to?

She could read me like a book from the moment we met. How could I lie to my best friend about something so huge?

Was it huge, though? I had said it was a onetime thing. Getting this tension, this charged atmosphere broken between us.

That was it. Tension broken.

Was it wrong?

The feeling of warm satisfaction sure doesn't feel wrong. It feels like my body has woken in a warm lagoon. The water having caressed and soothed it.

I had fallen into a sound and satiated sleep after the best orgasm of my life, make that two orgasms and Sean had been there.

But I've woken up to an empty bed.

Ouch.

Was I just a booty call? A one-night stand?

That's what I wanted, wasn't it?

One night. One time. No weirdness.

"...I've waited for you forever."

What did that even mean?

No, I was the one who had made him promise this was a onetime only. A get it out of our system thing.

I'm the one in control.

This cannot, will not, happen again.

We'd satisfied that carnal attraction with the best sex I've ever had. The sexiest I've ever felt in my life.

I felt like a goddess.

He made me feel like a goddess.

There was a little sting that he'd gone and escaped in the middle of the night like it had been some drunken mistake.

The cracking sun burs through the gap in the curtains, reminding me the day has started, and I have a full schedule ahead of me.

I allow myself to revel in the morning after sensation a little longer before dragging my ass to the mirror.

Ugh.

It is going to take more than an hour to brush out the wild mane this morning.

A messy top knot it will have to be.

By the time I reach the kitchen for breakfast, everyone is around the table, deep in coffee and conversation. Josh is here, his arm around Kate. Oli has arrived and sipping his black coffee, waiting for his dad to head and open up the store.

But there's no sign of Sean.

I ignore the pang of disappointment in my stomach and force relief through my body. I don't have time for another awkward encounter in the kitchen with his family.

"Morning sleeping beauty." Kate chirps,

"Morning." I almost sing. Is my voice too high, too chirpy?

Coffee is the top priority, and lots of it. I don't understand these people who function before nine am without caffeine. And I understand those who resisted coffee at all, even less.

Don't start with me until after a good caffeine hit.

"What's got you smiling from ear to ear this morning?" Kate asks.

Oh, crap. Busted already.

"Nothing, what do you mean?" Act cool, Lucy, stay cool. "I'm fine. Nothing weird here."

"Mom, look, isn't she bouncing around that kitchen with a spring in her step and a smile as wide as the Mississippi?"

"No, I'm not."

How do I get out of this? Why am I so bloody transparent?

"Oh, the date went well with Brendan, then?" Josh winks at me above his fork full of pancakes. "He text last night saying how great his date was, didn't realize it was *that* great." he snickers.

"No, actually, I was home at a reasonable hour. Alone!"

Kate gives me a suspicious stare.

"I swear!" I hold my hand up in a girl guide's honor. "Can't a girl just wake up in a good mood?"

"A girl can." Kate points her long manicured nail at me. "You can't, Miss Worryabouteverything, when the wedding is coming up and your business is in a soggy mess."

"Thanks for the reminder." I stir my coffee vigorously, hoping she'll drop it. No such luck.

"I'll get it out of you." Her eyes follow me. "You know I will."

I have no response except to stick my tongue out at her. Change the subject quickly,

"Mr. Larson, that bacon and pancakes smells a treat. Any left for me?"

He doesn't lift his head from his morning newspaper. "Of course, love, in the oven for you."

Thank the lord. I busy myself in the oven and search for maple syrup.

"Corner cupboard above the toaster, love." Mr. Larson instructs. "Sean was up early this morning, bouncing with energy and out the door for a run."

"Up early!" Barb's said. "He was out late, too. Wasn't in his bed when we came in last night."

I snorted, coffee spurting from my lips, resulting in inhalation of the hot liquid and a fit of coughing.

"Are you alright, dear?" Mr. Larson peeks above the paper, one eyebrow raised.

Barbs and Kate are heading to Denver for her last dress fitting. I will be free from her prying questions for the day, at least. Mr. Larson and Oli head out for the day at the hardware store and Josh is off to meet Brendan for a game of golf.

With one week until the wedding, there is so much to do. I sit in the quiet house with sticky notes and my to-do list. Nothing calms me better than a well-organized to-do list. Second coffee in one hand, color pens and highlighters at the ready.

I have the wedding cake to plan and bake, a challenge given I have no bakery for the foreseeable. It will have to be in the Larson's kitchen, not ideal but better than Mom's tiny kitchenette, with only one work surface.

We have a mini bachelorette party with the girls in The Brew House. The only bar in town where everyone gathers on a Friday night to celebrate the end of the week, a few beers, and home.

The main bachelorette had been joint with the bachelors in Las Vegas back in May. Kate didn't want any events that could go wrong or have lasting effects on the wedding photos. Like a bridesmaid spraining a leg, or a groomsman falling drunk and breaking an arm.

Oh no, the photos were going to be perfect. No black eyes or broken bones to Photoshop out in Kate's wedding photo book.

Picture perfect.

I have the bridesmaid dresses and shoes to pick up. Kate and I have the favors and place cards to finalize. Kate is in full bride organizer mode. She hasn't reached Bridezilla level yet, thankfully. It's my job to keep her from getting there. But with my to-do list getting longer by the minute, I'm worried about my bridesmaid-zilla status.

I certainly won't have time to worry about any tall, blond, and buff brothers. I'm going to be so busy until the wedding I probably won't even see Sean and then I'm sure he'll be on the first flight out of here. There's no way he'll stay in Breakridge River any longer than he has to.

Good.

The last thing I need is a distraction from my plans, a distraction from my dreams.

First things first, what are my plans and dreams?

Chapter 20

Lucy

Walking out, the summer sun is high in a crisp blue sky. Shades on, I pause on the doorstep, feeling the warm rays grace my face. My pale skin would object as the day became warmer, but right now, I can enjoy the beauty of natural heat warm me from the outside in.

I can't remove the smile from my face, my cheek muscles working harder than usual. Not that I'm not a smiler, I certainly am. But this morning is gleeful.

Why, when you're in a great mood, does everything in your day run a little smoother? My newly repaired car sounds sweet when I start it, purring like a contented cat. My favorite country song blasts from the radio, and all the lights are green as I drive into town.

Does the universe know I had the best sex of my life last night and is rewarding me with beautiful sunshine and chirping birds?

Best sex of my life. How did a boy I've known my whole life become the best sex I've ever had? Have I been missing out all these years?

I'm not sure even my soggy bakery can dampen my mood this morning, despite the length of my to-do list.

Mom and I have a meeting at the bakery with the reconstruction crew, assessing the damage and how much it's going to cost us to get the bakery back up and running.

If that's what I want.

Okay, there goes my great mood.

A dose of anxiety will dampen happiness right out like a fire hose to a flame.

What am I going to do next? What do I want?

I drive down Main Street, visions of myself throughout my life flashing in front of me. Walking down with Kate as a kid to Jeff's candy store on the corner, running with Mom behind as we headed for the park, walking hand in hand with Leyland my first boyfriend heading to the movies, my Grandma and Pops taking me to work in the bakery for the first time, teaching me everything I know, everything I am today.

"Grandma, I wish you were here." I say out loud to no one. "You'd know what to do."

I know exactly what she'd say to me,

"Follow your heart darling, it'll never steer you wrong."

Words I'd heard so many times and taken for granted.

Car parked, I close my eyes and imagine my Grandma's voice telling me to follow my heart. Where would it take me? How would I know I was doing the right thing? How do I listen to my heart?

"Ugh!"

Stupid over-analytical brain. Question. Question. Question.

Never any answers.

The lights are on in the bakery already. Mom must have been up really early. If there was ever a more stubborn woman than me, it is my mother. How many times did I have to tell her not to go in alone? Especially with the bakery in the state it is right now. She's going to end up having an accident and no one will be there to help her. I was going to go in and find her in a pile of rubble one of these days.

That thought sends a shot of fear up my spine. Mom is all I have left. I have Kate and the girls, but Mom is my only family. She's my rock. There isn't a world I can imagine when she wouldn't be with me.

I storm into the bakery, almost taking the bell off the door, to find Mom sitting in a chair sipping a steaming cup of coffee and singing along to Morgan Wallen.

"Mom, are you okay?"

"Oh morning dear," she tilts her head away from the sun beating in the front window. "I'm great, just having a coffee and a rest for my legs."

Her smile is glowing, and I can't imagine why. The last time we were at the bakery a few days ago it was tears, snotters, and hankies.

"Have the contractors been already?" Have they given her great news without me?

"No love, they won't be here for another hour," her face beams. "I've had a helper this morning."

"Eh, what?" We don't have any other employees, unless Jaydon, the twelve-year-old who gets a bit of work experience on a Saturday counts. I'm sure I text him to say work was postponed until further notice.

"Who?"

"Mornin'."

The deep, throaty voice almost has my knees buckle, heat flashes through my core and up to my face. My brain immediately whisks me back to the dirty things that throaty voice whispered in my ear last night.

I turn to see Sean standing with running shorts and a sports tank on. His biceps flexed, my insides respond with a clench. How is it possible for someone to look so hot after a sweaty run and cleaning a dirty bakery?

If I'd been running and dropped into a soggy bakery, I would look like someone had sweat their tomatoes for too long and stuck them in the trash with old tea bag leaves.

But Sean looks like he's come straight off the cover of Men's Fitness. His blond waves finger combed back from his face, each muscle flexed and glistening with a sun-kissed tan all over - and yes, it was nearly all over. That thought brightens the blush on my face.

I stand silently. Lips parted and staring.

This is awkward.

"Uh, hi," I manage. I'm sure my face is now as red as the aforementioned sweaty tomatoes. Why am I so worked up? It's Kate's little brother. I am older, and cooler, he should be tomato red, not me!

I'm such a loser. This isn't high school and Sean has definitely flown past me on the Richter scale of cool.

"Sean was running past this morning when I was struggling in with some bags," she beams at him. "He helped me in and got to work on more clearing. Isn't that lovely?"

All I hear is 'struggling with some bags.'

"MOM! Why were you struggling in here yourself in the first place?"

All sweaty, dirty thoughts gone, I flap my hands around all the rubble still on the floor.

"You could have really hurt yourself."

"Oh, don't fuss," she dismisses me with a flick of her hand. "Sean was here; I was fine."

"Yep, she was fine. I was here."

His smile would drop panties, but not right now.

I look right at her. "Well, Sean won't always be here."

I can feel his gaze on the side of my head. That was a little cold. But hey, the truth hurts, baby. He would be gone, and I'd be here to clean up the mess alone.

"I'm not going anywhere fast," I hear the insinuation. "And I'm happy to help." He holds up the sweeping brush he's been working.

"Thanks for the offer, but I got it handled."

Leaning on the brush handle, raking his eyes over the fallen concrete, and the damaged glass display, he lifts his eyes to the gaping hole in the ceiling before landing on me.

"I'm offering my services while I'm here, Lucy."

Why does that sound like a double entendre sending heat right between my legs? I really need to start packing fresh panties in my bag.

"Are you going to refuse my services?"

"Oh, we'd love you to help us," Mom chips in. "Wouldn't that be wonderful, Lucy? You can't do all this yourself."

"No, Mom, I won't be doing it all myself; the contractors will be."

I couldn't think of a good enough reason to get Sean out of my bakery. To get him at a safe distance. His presence has my nerves on edge, goosebumps on my skin in hyper-awareness. I won't get any work done in here with him around.

"Lucy," he steps closer, Mom out of earshot and still humming away to the radio. "You don't have to do everything yourself." His words are a soothing balm. "You can let me help you."

Would it be the worst thing if I have to watch Sean sweat it up in my bakery? I might enjoy it, but would I get any work done with a view like that?

Can I trust him not to break his promise of 'one time only'?

"Well, I suppose a little help won't go wrong."

"Great!" His smile is wide, and memories of the boy I once knew with the cheeky grin surface.

"Put me to work, ma'am," he winks, and my panties almost fall of their own volition.

We work away, clearing the floor, and lifting the blocks of cement to the alley out back.

"So what is it you're going to do, then?" Sean breaks the silence.

"With what?"

"The bakery?" he swings his arms around. "Are you letting it go to waste? Selling up? Or making it the best bakery Breakridge River has ever had?"

I cross my arms, giving him a pointed stare. "This *is* the best bakery Breakridge has ever had."

"But don't you have dreams of expanding? I remember your grandma talking about extending and making a sit-in tea room and an expansion for the cake business."

My memory triggered and my heart sings. I can hear all this coming from my grandma's lips.

"How do you remember that? You haven't seen Grandma in over nine years." I place my hand on my heart, touched.

"I don't forget much Red."

He holds onto my gaze until I bend down, sweeping rubble into a shovel.

"And what's with the new *Red* nickname?" I blurt, trying to avoid his eyes and failing miserably when he steps closer. He wraps a long flyaway strand of hair round his finger.

"This hair." He pauses until I look up at him.

"This hair has never been so fiery, so red." With his head dipped low to my ear, he whispers, "So fiery it sets my insides alight."

I gasp, looking over at Mom, who is completely oblivious.

He grins at my embarrassment and grants me some grace. "So what are your bakery plans then?"

"I still have no idea what I'll do. I know the contractors will tell us that the insurance only covers the repairs and any remodeling will be at an extra cost and I don't have enough savings to get work like that done."

I throw my tired butt in one of the window chairs, gazing out.

"Never in a million years did I think I would still be here, you know. I imagined myself living in the city, a dog, a husband, an important job."

"You *do* have an important job."

I scoff, "Yeah, if I don't serve the cakes and coffee, who will?"

The morning flies by. It was actually great having Sean help, but I won't shout that too loudly. I even managed to get up to the apartment and rescue a few more bits before the contractors arrived.

They are a couple of good guys, they have a lot of ideas on how to improve the bakery layout but it would cost more money. Insurance would only cover the repairs, as the bakery was prior to the flood. Any remodeling would have to be paid for out of our savings, like I had thought.

I always imagined a remodel of the bakery in the future, expanding the sit-in area and updating the kitchen to allow for more oven space and more business.

This was before the thought of 'could I go to med school?'

I need to decide what I want. Where I'm going. What direction I'm taking my life.

Sean is working away in the background while Mom and I listen to the contractors. The young guy is interesting, Jamie. His eyes were definitely roving appreciatively over my dust-covered jeans and fitted t-shirt.

We had talked up and down and given the go-ahead to start work this week if we wanted. Jamie dips his head towards me, his low southern drawl,

"Ma'am, I'm not usually this forward," his eyes remained below my eye level, "but I wondered if you had plans for dinner tonight?"

Before I can get a word out, I feel a solid hard heat at my back and warm breath on my neck.

"What next darlin'?" Sean plants his lips on my neck. A shiver runs down my spine.

The look of horror on Jamie's face is priceless.

"I'm so sorry, Ma'am," he mutters his apology sprinting back to his buddies who were having a laugh at his expense, patting him on the back.

I whip around, faced with a hard, sweaty chest.

"Was that necessary?"

"Yes, he was eyein' you up like a side of beef on Christmas."

"I had noticed." I look around for Mom. Did she witness the illicit kiss? She's wiping surfaces in the back, thankfully. "And what's your problem with his eyes on me?"

He dips his lips close to my ear and growls, "I don't want anyone looking at you like that."

My breath catches.

"You don't get to decide that," I whisper. "One time only, remember?"

Why does my brain lose function around him? He seems to be functioning just fine.

Sean, still bent low, draws his tongue around the outside of my ear, whispering,

"Yes, Lucy, one time only."

He pulls back, sending me a wink that has my thighs' griping together. My poor panties.

Chapter 21

Sean

I'd had my eye on that contractor. I could see the feral look in his eyes. His courage climbing, the determination, which in turn was ratcheting up my blood pressure. When he started flirting and asked Lucy out for dinner, it took all my energy not to charge like a bull, beat my chest like a caveman or roar like a possessive lion protecting his lioness.

But she isn't my lioness.

'One time only, no weirdness.'

I promised.

So instead of raging like a bull or roaring like a lion, I towered over her possessively, planting my lips on the soft skin between her ear and shoulder.

He got the message quick.

After the contractors leave, Mrs. D looks beat.

"Why don't we head to the park for lunch and drop your mom home on the way?"

"The park?" Lucy's eyebrows raise. "Why would we go to the park?"

I make a list on my fingers, “Because it’s a beautiful hot day. We’ve worked hard, we need fresh air and a break, we need to eat and might as well enjoy the view. Take your pick.”

“Hmm.” She looks around at all the work still to be done. Her hair all messy, flying around her face and sticking out of her bun.

“The park sounds like a lovely idea,” Mrs. D chirps from the back room. “But count me out. I need a lie down.”

Lucy turns to her mom, worried. “Mom, you’ve overdone it this morning. It’s too much to be coming down here every day.”

There's less scold in her voice and more concern. “You need to have a break tomorrow.” She glances at me somewhat reluctantly. “Besides, I have Sean to help me now.”

Mrs. D beams, “Yes, you do, don’t you. Maybe I will have a little day off tomorrow after all. It’ll do me good, I’m sure.”

What a gorgeous day. The park is peaceful at lunchtime. The river soothing in the background with children’s laughter coming from the playground.

If someone told me last month that I’d be lying in the park beside Lucy Davenport back home in Breakridge River, I’d have asked what they were smoking.

She hums peacefully; a tune I recognize but can't get the name. I'm sure it's Zach Bryan.

Without a care in the world, I could sit here all day. Lucy had a blanket in the boot of Ol' Betty and we picked up snacks and a couple of iced teas at Humphrey's store.

My legs are stretched out, leaning back on my hands. Lucy's head on the opposite side of the blanket beside my feet.

I have the best view. I don't even try to hide that I'm staring at her, drinking her in.

Her shades are on, her eyes closed. Her breath is slow and even, one arm arched gracefully above her head, the fiery mane let loose from the top knot splayed around her.

The high afternoon sun illuminates the scattering of freckles on her cheeks. I've never noticed how many she had before. She has freckles, but in this light there are so many little ones. I am tempted to run my finger over her cheek.

I won't.

That would be weird.

'No weirdness.'

Her breath pulls into her chest, her curves rising and falling, bewitching me. I let my eyes graze slowly from her head, down her radiant face, those soft curves to her tiny little toes.

"Will you stop staring at me like a creep?"

"What?" Busted, I whip my gaze over to the blossom trees in my direct line of sight.

"I'm not staring. That would be weird."

"It would be weird, wouldn't it?" She lifts herself up, leaning on her elbows, staring right at me through the oversized sunglasses. "And you promised no weirdness, but I can feel your eyes burning through me over here."

"Just admiring the view. What's a guy to do?"

No point in denying it now.

"So what's the plan, then?" I ask her.

"What do you mean?" She tucks her hair away from her face, her eyes following the trail of a little robin bouncing its way across the grass.

"I mean, what's your plan with the bakery? The contractors are getting ready to start repairs and you haven't decided what you're doing."

She threw herself back on the blanket, arms covering her face.

"Why do you care?"

"Lucy, don't be dramatic. Of course I care, you're my friend."

That felt wholly un-natural. Friend doesn't feel right on my tongue, a little like I'd licked an ashtray. She looks up, lifting her shades.

"Friends, is that what we are?" Her gaze curious.

"Of course we're friends. I've known you since I can remember. Don't change the subject." I run a finger down the sole of her foot, the skin soft and warm, the tickle making her squirm away.

"I'm not changing the subject; I just don't know how to answer the question."

"Well, I said I'm here to help, so I'm going to help."

"How on earth are you going to help?"

Her scepticism makes me all the more determined.

"Lucy, I'm a businessman. Just because you can't see a physical business doesn't make it any less of a business. I'm the COO in my company. Buying, selling and trading every day, assessing risk versus reward. I'm sure I have something to contribute?"

She sits up, legs crossed, all serious now, "I guess I've never really thought about what you do. Your mom and dad don't talk about it. I think because they don't actually understand what it is you do and I haven't seen you in so long."

"Do you want a pitch?" I laugh. "Like Shark Tank style?"

Her laugh is carefree. I could listen to it on repeat.

"That's not necessary, but what is it you actually do? How have you managed to travel the world for nine years and keep a healthy bank balance?"

She slaps her hand over her mouth, "I'm so sorry, that's none of my business how you make money. Just give me a rundown of the business model."

"It's fine, don't sweat it. My parents have never understood what I do, but I think what annoys me the most is they don't even ask."

I've never said that out loud. "They've never just asked me what you have."

I shrug. She waits.

"I'm an online entrepreneur."

"That doesn't clear anything up," she laughs.

"Let me finish." I sit up, crossing my legs in front of her. "I established, built and ran a business online. Me and a college friend started a virtual assistant business. We were the creators in helping other online digital entrepreneurs connect with assistants, like a PA, but online."

"Sounds cool, but I'm still not sure how you earn from it?"

"We hosted the website and charged a commission for the connection if it was an introduction. We also provided monthly subscription services for ongoing passive income."

"It all sounds like a bit of a fairy tale. Not having to drag yourself out of bed at five am to slave over an oven and make big bucks," her eyes wide and interested.

"I can't lie, it's been an amazing experience." I flick her little toe. "So do I qualify to give business advice, then?"

"Yes, I suppose you do."

I watch her guard go up just a little. It's not something she's really comfortable talking about. I could wait her out, baby steps.

"We can start with what's going well in the bakery? Why is it worth saving?" I start her off easy.

"It's worth saving because it's a legacy. My grandma's bakery, the gift from my pops to her, my mom grew up there, I grew up there. It's literally baked into my family."

The passion in her voice for her family legacy is admirable.

"But they're not reasons alone. You know your mom would want you to follow your dream if it wasn't the bakery. She loves you."

I clasp her hand in mine, running my finger along her wrist until her chocolate eyes meet mine.

"What is *your* dream? Where do you want to be this time next year?"

"Ugh!" She throws herself back onto the blanket, the birds scattering at the shock of her loud groan.

"I don't know Sean. Why are your questions so hard?"

"Life is hard, Lucy, be intentional. Decide what matters the most to you and if it will bring you joy and happiness, do it."

She opens one eye staring at me, "What if I pick the wrong one?"

"If you listen to your heart, you won't."

Ha, listen to me giving all the big life advice. Me who ran away from my feelings, who didn't come home because I was hiding and avoiding my feelings. Although I can give myself points for progress, I did just admit to myself I had been running away.

My coach would be so proud.

"You make it sound so easy. Were you listening to your heart?"

Confession time?

"Mostly, yes, but there were parts I've ignored, and it's coming back to bite me in the ass now."

It really was biting me in the ass now, having stuffed my feelings and thoughts of Lucy down, crammed them away out of sight and out of mind for so long, I can't get her out of my head. From the second she stepped through the door with her arms full of muffins last week, my brain has tormented me with what could have been.

And now I've seen her naked. I've felt that soft skin under my fingers, heard her moan my name. Watched her sleep peacefully, her full lips parted when I placed a gentle morning kiss on her head before I left her this morning. So soft she didn't stir.

My heart has never felt such peace.

"We're not focusing on me, we're focusing on you! Let's frame it differently. What if you went to college to study medicine? How would you feel? What would be better? What would you miss the most?"

Laying on the blanket, she closes her eyes. She doesn't answer. Her brows furrow, lips pursed.

"Lucy?"

"Shhh, I'm imagining."

I can't help but smile. Her face is so serious. The temptation to run my fingers through the lengths of her hair, brush my finger over her furrowed brow to ease the tension, is so strong; my fingers twitch.

"I'm lonely in Denver; I don't know anyone. It's not homely."

"You'll make friends," I reassure her. "What about the job?"

Her eyes stay closed, engrossed in her vision. "I'd miss baking, I'd miss the chatter, I'd miss planning and making someone's big day, or their birthday or their gender reveal cake the best experience possible. I'd miss being a part of something I created, something my grandma and pops created. I'd miss my story."

She pauses, "I don't think I'd be happier being away, studying and stressing. It's not me."

She opens one eye, staring right at me.

"You-are-a-genius!"

Before I have time to congratulate her, Lucy leaps up and into my lap, locking her arms around my neck in a chokehold, her full breasts flush on me and I don't mind the feeling at all.

"Thanks Sean! You're amazing!"

My body responds immediately to her soft body on me. My cock standing to attention. I adjust myself trying to be discreet so she doesn't realize I'm hard as a rock in seconds.

Let's not make this weird now!

I can't help but shove my face into her hair, inhaling that toxic sweet cinnamon.

Okay, I let it get a little weird.

My heart skips.

Shit, I'm in deep trouble.

Chapter 22

Lucy

The weight off my shoulders is exponential. I never knew the burden of that indecision until it's gone.

Clarity is freeing.

Who knew it could feel like a physical weight? I feel like someone has come and lifted a fifty kilo weight from me and chucked it away.

It's gone.

How could I have ever thought I would sell my bakery? My Honeybee Bakery. It's in my DNA, running through my veins. I could never walk through town, passing the door, and it wasn't mine. All for a teenage fantasy where I play doctor and meet a cute surgeon. This isn't Grey's Anatomy or ER. This is real life.

And it feels great.

Am I giving up?

No.

I'm moving on, moving up and dreaming even bigger.

That someone responsible for lifting the burdensome weight?

Sean.

How could a few curious questions set my mind straight? Taking the time to answer and deeply think each scenario through. I could have done that.

But I didn't.

Sean did.

He creeps back into my thoughts again, not for the first time today after we left the bakery. Memories of last night, the sparkle in his field of green eyes when I opened my door to him. Grasping him for dear life, his breath was my next, feeling the heat running through me, pooling in my core. At that moment, I'd never felt more desired.

"before we start, say yes because once we get going, I'm not going to be able to stop. I've waited for you forever."

The look in his eyes in that moment was pleading, fraught. I couldn't have denied him even if I'd wanted to.

And believe me, I didn't want to.

Had I missed it this whole time? Did I dismiss his teenage awkwardness? Did I hurt him? Could I, or would I, have done anything differently?

"Lucy!"

"Huh?" Becca's piercing voice smashes through my peaceful thoughts.

"Where were you there?" She gulps her wine down. "You were miles away with a really weird look on your face and your cheeks are blushing."

“She’s had that look since she got out of bed this morning,” Kate says. “The one where it looks like she slept with a coat hanger in her mouth.” She winks.

“If I didn’t know any better, I’d say you *did* get lucky with Brendan last night and you’re holding out on us!”

I got lucky alright. If only she knew!

“Ha ha, you’re hilarious!” I avert my eyes and fold place cards in half like my life depends on it. There's a conveyer belt going, I fold and stack for Lisa to pen them with her beautiful calligraphy skills.

Seven sleeps until the big day and both the bachelorette's and bachelor's were having a pre-wedding party. A civil one, of course, because; photos.

The bachelors had headed to The Brew House. Saturday nights are karaoke night, all New Country hits; boots and Stetsons weren’t optional.

For the bachelorettes, a Chinese takeaway, with boxes dotted over the kitchen, and *a lot* of champagne. The bubbles have definitely gone to my head already, with three empty bottles between the five of us, my shoulders sway to the music.

In true bachelorette party style, we're all dressed in white Stetsons with net veils and silk garter bands around our thighs, white balloons and confetti covering the floor. Kate, with the ‘Bride’ sash on is prancing up and down the lounge, practising her walk down the aisle, her arm looped through Becca's, taking Mr. Larson’s father of the bride’s place.

"Is it left step, together, right step, together, left step, together?"

"Kate darling, you're overthinking it." Barbs takes Kate's face in her hands, placing a kiss on her cheek.

"Josh is going to drop to his knees as soon as you're standing at the end of that aisle. He won't care if you miss step on the way down to him."

"Thanks Mom, I guess I'm just getting a bit of the pre-wedding nerves now."

We're making our way through the one hundred and fifty place cards and favors. I've made the most delicious tablet, a wee Scottish sweet treat to honor Josh's family roots. The tablet will be placed in an organza bag and wrapped in a purple string with a thistle, sealing it closed.

Very sweet. I love making all these personal touches. I'd managed to locate a ribbon of Josh's family tartan for wrapping round the wedding cake tiers.

This wedding is coming together beautifully.

There's another idea for business expansion.

"You *were* quite chipper this morning dear." Barbs unhelpfully chips in. I really wish they would drop this good mood thing.

"Am I not allowed to be in a good mood? I can be miserable if you want me to?" I say, placing my hand on my hips, trying to be serious.

"You'd have to take that coat hanger out of your mouth if you were going to be miserable." Kate and Becca cackle.

I give in filling my flute high, “anyone want a top up?”

Four empty glasses tip my way, and I dutifully fill three with champagne.

“You hold off Lisa,” Kate points her manicured finger. “I don’t want wonky writing on those place cards!”

Lisa frowns, “I can do this in my sleep Bridezilla, don’t you fret.” She shoves her flute in my direction. “Fill me up, maid of honor.”

Not sure if I imagine it, but that last part seemed to be directed at me with a bit of a tone. I fill it high with a sickly sweet smile.

“Just a Nosecco for me, love,” Mom says, winking. I'm glad she joined us tonight after missing out on the barbecue last week. Her afternoon siesta did her good, and she had a spring in her step when I told her my plans for the bakery.

I don’t think her smile could have been wider if I’d told her she was getting a grand baby and I swear I saw a tear.

“So bride party, who’s the next one?” Lisa swirls her pen around us all.

“The next one what?” Kate said, placing name tags on each organza bag I had piled up.

“To get hitched, silly.”

“Well, the way Lucy’s been acting today, she’s more than a little smitten.’ Kate gladly throws me under the bus.

They all shriek and hoot at this. Even Mom gets in on the teasing, pinching my already rosy cheeks.

"You are all going to hell, you know that, right?" I point at each one of them as they throw wedding paraphernalia my way, humming the bridal march. "It wasn't like that with Brendan, honestly."

"Sure, we believe you," Lisa drawls sarcastically. "The lady doth protest too much!"

A whole new fit of giggles bursts from them at my expense.

I give up.

"Now not thinking about weddings, but I know who's sure looking fit." Lisa has everyone's attention, as she'd intended.

"Sean has galloped back into town like a stallion!"

"Oh-my-gawd, that's my brother, you hussy!" Kate pretends to vomit down the back of the sofa. "He's just the same, except a little more golden."

I struggle to hold back a scoff. He is not the same. Far from it.

"He ain't the same. Any woman with a pulse can see he's been working that body out, those shoulders and tattoos."

"EW, stop! I can't listen to that!" Kate shrieks, cutting Lisa off and covering her ears.

"Well, good genes certainly run in the family." Barbs lifts her chin and toasts towards Kate, who clinks her flute with a smile.

"Just sayin'" Lisa continues, "I wouldn't mind a date before he rides back out of town."

No way.

Not happening.

Really, why do I care if he has another date before he leaves? I'd had my one time. We'd gotten it out of our system. Purged that need. Dampened that flame.

Hadn't we?

"Lucy!" Kate and Becca shout.

"Oh, sorry, what was that?"

"Where'd you go there?" Kate asks. "Anyway, we were just saying, we've finished the place cards and favors, why don't we head to the Brew House for a song and dance?"

Oh hell.

In a bar, full of booze, with Sean and, from what I could hear, Lisa dripping all over him. This could be a recipe for disaster.

Chapter 23

Sean

The Brew House is jumping.

Breakridge's Saturday night highlight and I have to say it isn't disappointing. I had memories of Mom and Dad coming out on a Saturday night to the Brew House karaoke night. Claire from the top of the street would babysit us for an extra twenty bucks in her pocket. Saturday night is still karaoke night.

I've only been here a handful of times before I left and I was too young to drink. The little place was so welcoming. When I walked in, it was like I'd never left. Jon, the owner, like a lot of folks in Breakridge, had been born and raised here. He met his wife Suzi in a biker bar in Denver and she's never left his side since.

The Brew House is a rustic little joint with distressed wood panels lining the walls, lit with vintage steel cage pendant lights. The overhead exposed steel rails adding to that rustic ambiance. Dark ebony tables line the walls and dot the floor with a worn space for dancing. Just enough room to get your boots on the floor and up close with your partner.

Karaoke night has the place filled to burst. A woman in a white Stetson, a red, sleeveless checked shirt, buttons opened down her full cleavage, stands atop a wooden crate. A mic in her hand singing, I should say killing, one of my favorite Kacey Musgraves songs.

"Does every singer sound like I want to rip my ears off?" I lean into Oli's ear. His lips raise on one side with a smile.

"No, there's actually a few that carry a decent tune on a Saturday but Cassie ain't one of 'em, and she loves a Saturday karaoke."

His eyes are glued on Cassie, well, to be more specific, they were on her ample cleavage. He throws her a wink.

Give the girl her due; she never missed a beat when she winked back.

"You've been there then?"

I have to roll my eyes. Oli has a reputation around town. He has since he was a horny teenager. He takes his dark features from Mom's side, where I have the lighter tones from Dad. The girls just love that tall, broad, dark and broody vibe he had perfected by age eighteen. I don't think Mom was holding out too much hope for grand babies from Oli.

That left me and Kate to push over the cliff edge and Kate is nearly there. Xander has done his duty with grand babies, but she still loves to bend his ear, reminding him that thirty-five wasn't too old to get married and give the twins a baby brother or sister.

I love my mom, but dear God, she has empty nest syndrome and we were all feeling the pressure.

One week until Kate and Josh's wedding and the bachelors are out to toast the groom. Kate had warned us all individually and then again before we all left, there was to be no 'funny business' as she put it, so close to the wedding. Nothing that risked broken bones or facial bruising. She must have thought we were a bunch of animals.

Xander clearly wasn't paying attention to his little sister as he negotiates his way around the dance floor with a tray of what looks to be sambuca shots and another round of beers. Josh spots the tray and a look of panic crosses his face.

"If I go home wrecked, Kate will kill me."

Xander places the tray down slapping Josh on the back. "She's not got you whipped just yet, has she? Still one week until that chain tightens around your ankle, man."

Josh hesitates until Xander shoves the little glass in his hand. The rest of us all do our bachelor duty, raise our glasses and knocked 'em back.

"To Josh!" We all cheer.

Mountain Man, Brendan is here with the other best man whose name I didn't catch. I couldn't help feel a little sorry for the schmuck. At least three times, he's mentioned his date with Lucy last night. How amazing it went, how he's going to ask her to be his date at the wedding and see where it goes.

In your dreams, woolly mammoth. Not happening on my watch.

Josh is egging him on, saying how happy Lucy was this morning. The guy, thinking Lucy's morning joy was because of him, had a shit-eating grin I just want to wipe from his face.

Oli watches me closely. He pulls me in so only he and I can hear.

"What happened last night, brother?"

"Nothin', what are you talking about?" What does he think he knows?

"I'm not blind. You're still hung up on Lucy Davenport. Nothing has changed." He pokes his finger into my chest. "In fact, I'd say it's even worse."

"You don't know what you're talking about, Oli." I attempt to laugh him off.

"You bet your ass I do. Funny, you were at the bakery all day after Lucy woke up with a shit-eating grin that matched Brendan's, except I know he didn't get lucky and stay the night, and I know you weren't in your bed last night."

His face is accusing.

"How would you know if I wasn't in my bed?"

"Mom."

Ugh, this family is unbelievable. No secrets. Ever.

"Can't we just forget about the girls for one night and enjoy the bachelor night?" I try my hardest to sway the conversation. "How's the store doing?"

I take a long pull on my beer, the scent of whiskey and leather thick in the air.

"It's shit. Don't change the subject."

"Why are you getting your knickers in a bunch over Lucy, anyway?" I pin my brother with a hard glare. I might be the youngest, but I have a good three inches on Oli.

"Have you got a thing for her?"

Those words almost catch in my throat, waiting for his reply.

He holds my gaze, not fazed by my looking down at him. He knows he's letting me stew, placing his whiskey on the rocks to his lips, taking an appreciative gulp.

"Don't be fucking ridiculous. You're the only one that's hung up on Lucy. She's like my adopted sister, and I won't see her hurt."

His eyes are almost solid black, the brown so dark it would be menacing if he weren't my big brother and I knew all his weak spots.

"If you're just flying in and out of town, looking for a one-night stand, a good time, no problem. I've got names and numbers I can pass on, but leave Lucy out of it. Do not come back here and fuck her around and leave. I don't care if you're my blood, you're the one who will be worse off."

I don't think I've ever seen Oli so aggressive. He is deadly serious.

Good time Oli. Laid back Oli.

He looks like he would knock his glass over my head if I say the wrong thing.

Xander lightens us up, throwing his arms around us both.

"What are you two girls fighting about? It looks deathly serious over here."

"Nothing at all." Oli's mood lightens immediately, a spark back in his eyes. "Just catching up with little bro and setting a few things straight."

"Sounds ominous." Xander raises his eyebrows. "I'm the chief around here; I thought I did all the setting straight?"

Xander has knocked a few back. Who can blame him? It wasn't every weekend he got a break from the twins. A full time working, single dad. I take my hat off to my brother.

He had hired one of the Henderson sisters to baby-sit the twins tonight. Xander was a stickler with the twins. He hardly ever let go of the reins, keeping tight schedules. Only Mom or Kate got to watch them. And of course, everyone was tied up tonight.

It's great to see my big brother letting go for a while. He deserves it. His arms still firmly around our shoulders, he pulls us in tight.

"I'm so glad we're all here for Kate this week," he gushes.

"Xander I think you need to lay off the sambuca," Oli slips out from under our brother's tight grasp. Xander tugs me in closer, the aniseed scent strong on his breath.

"Kate is thrilled that you made it, brother. Just be careful with Lucy."

And with that, he lets me go and staggers towards the bar.

What is it with everyone and protecting Lucy? What have I done? Didn't anyone notice when she was breaking my fragile heart? Now, it's all protect Lucy.

Lucy.

The music had quietened between singers. Five white Stetsons caused a ruckus entering the bar. One with luscious red waves bouncing from underneath.

What are the hens doing here? They're supposed to be sipping champagne and making some giftie things for the wedding. Leaving us to get Josh good and drunk and perhaps tied to a streetlight on his last weekend as an unmarried man.

Gaging by his face, Josh realizes the appearance of his bride to be has saved him from his drunken fate. He leaps up, swaying slightly from the last few rounds of shots.

"Kate!" She has a 'Bride To Be' sash on, a lace garter and a phallic shaped straw hanging from her neck. Finding his feet, Josh tips the brim of her Stetson, dipping her back for a long kiss.

The place erupts in cheers, wolf whistles and calls to, 'Get a room!'

Mom teeters over in high heels with her 'Mother of the bride' sash proudly in place.

Her eyes looking for my dad, she slips her arm in his, laying her head on his shoulder. My Dad was ever the gentleman, placing a kiss on the side of her head. They really had been a role model for love since we were born.

My eyes scan the crowded room for the red head filling my thoughts. Bodies squash together, cotton shirts, sweat and whiskey. Well balanced trays of drinks negotiating through the crowd, a Shania Twain wannabe sounded through the speakers.

My eyes found the fiery, flowing hair at the bar. High-waisted Levi's hug those luscious hips with a light green shirt pulled tight around her waist. Just a little skin peeking inbetween.

A large hand rests on the small of her back. Woolly mammoth, Brendan, leaning in close to her ear.

My feet move before my brain engages, fire burning up from my soles, throwing me towards her.

He wouldn't lay another finger on her.

Mine.

I stop just short of colliding with her, placing my hands on each shoulder, I lean into her space.

"Can I speak with you?" My lips graze her ear and are in her hair when she turns her head towards me; "outside?"

"Hey man, me and the lady were talkin'" Brendan stands tall, chin raised towards me.

"Well, now she's talking with me." I stand straight, my broad shoulders back. I'm a big guy, but the woolly mammoth still has an inch or two on me.

Where is this anger coming from? I'm not an angry guy. I'm usually pretty laid back.

Never the guy in the bar causing trouble after a few drinks. I'm the peacekeeper, the negotiator. The amount of times I've had to step in between Oli and some guy over something stupid. A girl, a bet, a prank gone wrong.

My skin prickles like a shock from a cattle prod. This possessive fury is unfamiliar.

"Sean, what the hell are you doing?" Lucy stabs a finger in my chest, standing between me and Brendan.

Her fierce bite only makes it worse. She's a smoke show in her cowboy boots and Stetson. My head is swimming. I can't form any words. I stand there, breath leaving me like a raging bull, mute.

"Come on Brendan," Lucy loops her arm in his. "Let's go finish our drinks."

I watch her sashay away.

A hard hand thumps my back. "What the fuck was that?" Oli shoves me towards the door. I don't fucking know. I hate losing control. Is this some new kind of witchery Lucy Davenport has over me?

Chapter 24

Lucy

Who the hell does Sean think he is? He doesn't own me!

Where is the laid back picnic in the park, Sean? The one who worked with me at the bakery all day and helped me work through my life plan dilemma.

The Sean that's showed up here tonight is no one I've ever met. Dark, brooding and angry.

I walked into the Brew House with the girls, minus Mom, because it's too over crowded in here for her and she was tired. We were quite a sight, all in denim and white.

Brendan stands overly close while I sip my beer; an arm slipped around my waist. Kate notices winking my way. I wince.

His large fingers creep around my waist. I notice the dirt under his nails from days of hard work on the farm. Bile climbs in my throat at the thought of what's under those nails.

Brendan continues to babble away to Mr. Larson about tractor parts. Mr. Larson looking as interested as I feel.

Can I step away, excuse myself from his questionable hands? I feel bad. Brendan is a good guy. A genuine soul who is really interested in me. But how can I compare the heat that pulses through me with only a look from Sean? As unimpressed as I was with his possessive outburst at the bar, somewhere deep inside that I didn't know existed feels a thrill of excitement at that possessiveness.

I side step towards the table out of Brendan's grasp, propping myself on a high stool at the table. He doesn't get the hint.

He slides in closer, the whiskey from his breath almost knocking me out. Probably why he's feeling so bold.

I'm not really a karaoke fan, but I grab the karaoke song sheet and pretend to study it closely. Usually I'll be nodding along, but you will never catch me up there in the spotlight. I couldn't think of anything worse than having everyone's eyes on me as I screeched like a dying cat into a crackly microphone.

"Are you getting up for a song?" Brendan asks with his intoxicating breath. "We could do a duet!" His face lights up like a kid on Christmas Eve.

"Not for me. The only singing I do is in the shower!" I laugh him off.

"Good to know," he winks.

Ugh!

"I'm getting up for a song; any requests?"

Yep, 'Save Me' by Jelly Roll comes to mind!

"No requests; sing whatever you love."

Anything to get you out of my ear and off my waist. He winks, his smile wide and cute. No reaction from my body.

None. Nada. Zilch.

Why doesn't my body react? It would be so much simpler to have a date with Brendan. He's a good guy. But nope, she doesn't want a nice guy like Brendan.

He grabs the song sheet from me and squeezes his way through the crowd towards the DJ.

"What was that all about?" Kate rushes in, taking Brendan's place.

"What was what all about?" I ask innocently.

Kate witnessed the whole awkward interaction with Brendan. There is no way she's going to let it go.

"You shriveling up like a snail into her shell to get as far away from Brendan as possible?" She has one curious eyebrow lifted under her Stetson. A whiskey in one hand and a manicured finger pointed in Brendan's direction, who looks to be deep in conversation with the DJ about his song choice.

Am I that obvious? Not enough if Brendon isn't taking the hint!

"I did not." I place my beer bottle to my lips, eyes averted from Kate's questioning gaze. Everyone in the Brew House is tipsy and light-hearted. The mood light and the laughter loud above the music.

I'm not out often, but with the right company, it's a real mood lifter. I smile at the group of young guys egging each other on to approach a cute blond at the bar, or a couple wrapped in an embrace close to the exit. There was rarely trouble in the Brew House. The town is friendly, and any arguments are settled over an arm wrestle and a whiskey. It helps that Caden McBride is the bouncer. An ex-military guy with a no-nonsense face. He would lift the biggest of guys with ease and place them outside with a message.

"Lucy, don't avoid my eyes." Kate swishes her tipsy face in front of me. "You know that won't work. I see you, lady. What happened? You looked so happy this morning after your date last night."

Yes, *after* my date.

"I guess I'm just not into the whole farmer thing." I sigh, hoping she'll get the hint and stop badgering me.

"Okay, I get that, not sure I'd be into that either." Kate giggles.

"Right, mission find Lucy a great guy is back on!" She stands up so fast, her head high, and scanning the room like a meerkat.

"You won't find anyone in here, Kate." She's off her head. "If there was anyone in Breakridge for me, don't you think I'd have found them already?"

She doesn't break her scanning. "Not if you're looking at them from the wrong angle."

"What does that even mean?" My friend is three shades of crazy. I palm my face. It's no good trying to reason with her when she gets an idea in her head. I let her roll with it.

Becca squeezes her way towards us, tipping her head up towards Kate. "What is she doing?"

"Finding me a great guy, apparently." I grab Kate down hissing at her, "give me a break from guys. I just need to get my life back on track myself."

"Well, you might not be getting lucky with Brendan, but one of '*team bridesmaid'* is onto a score."

Becca inclines her head to the back of the room with a grin.

My jaw hits the floor. I want my eyes to move, to drag away from the sight that's so offending, my insides shrivel.

I'm such an idiot.

"Ugh, that's gross! I don't need to see my brother doing that!" Kate turns away.

Lisa has her body suctioned against Sean's with her palms firmly on his chest. His back to the wall, his head dipped low to her ear.

The bile from earlier threatens to appear again. Maybe I've had too much champagne and beer.

To top this moment off and make it most memorable, Brendan's voice bursts through the mic, "This one's for Lucy!"

He tips his hat in my direction.

'And I know that you can't pretend that this a fairytale and you ain't scared how it will end ... wanna take off your clothes, wanna mess up your hair...Gonna make you fall in love with me.'

His voice is surprisingly deep, he carried a lovely tone.

He looks right at me as he sings.

Kate gushes behind me. "Aww, Brendan is so sweet."

I can't help my eyes dragging back to the eyesore at the back of the room. Sean standing up tall, away from slutty Lisa's ear, her hands still firmly on his hard chest.

Bile tickles my tonsils.

I need to get out of here.

'Make that feelin' worsen, you'll be cursin''

Brendan's lyrics cut deep, but for all the wrong reasons. My feet hit the floor, my legs carrying me through the crowd like my ass is on fire. I bump and shove through to a chorus of,

"Hey, watch it!"

and

"Sorry darlin'"

Finally, I make it to the door. Caden gives me a concerned glance as I shoot through the door into the parking lot.

I inhale deeply, gasping in a lung full of fresh air. The cool night hits my skin, prickling me with goosebumps. I'm not sure if the hum in my ears is a result of the loud music or the offending sight of Lisa rubbing herself on Sean like a dog in heat.

Her hands were on him.

His lips whispering in her ear, the dirty words that were in my ear only last night.

I'm such a fool. Of course, Sean wasn't only interested in me. He was used to a different woman every night, being on a tropical island with women throwing themselves at him.

A rich great-looking guy like him. He doesn't need to stick with a frumpy older small town baker.

Tears burn threatening to fall.

Why am I so bothered by what Sean's doing? Why am I so bothered with who has their hands on him? We had our one night. We had our release.

'One time only, no weirdness.'

Is this it getting weird?

My shirt and jeans are no use in the cool evening air. I can't go back in. I can't face Kate. She saw the whole thing. She saw me.

Oh dear god, I'm going to have to tell her I had sex with her brother.

I pace back and forth in the parking lot, avoiding pot holes. The rhythmic click of my boots like an anchor. I wrap my arms around myself, attempting to generate some heat.

"Red?"

Why does that deep drawl hit me hard? One syllable is liquid gold. I stop pacing.

"What're you doing out here? You'll freeze."

"Nothing, just getting some air."

My body betrays me with a teeth chattering shiver.

"This is ridiculous." His large legs have him in front of me in two strides. Slipping out of his jacket, he pulls it around my shoulders. Leaving him in his tight jeans and white t-shirt. I stiffen under his touch.

"What's wrong Red?" The scent of pine and lavender mixed with the beer, messes with my senses, taking me right back to last night when his smell engulfed me, raptured me and remained on my pillow when I woke up this morning.

All the heat and tension from earlier and the frustration of the week swirl in me like a tornado.

And Sean is right in this tornado's path.

"What's wrong?!" I yell.

He steps back, his eyes full of confusion. It's enough space for me to stand my ground, lift my head high.

"You're kidding me right?!" My blood hums in my veins, rushing through me powering me on. My finger pokes his hard chest.

"You come barraging over to me at the bar like a bull to a red flag, all hot, bothered and psycho possessive." I stabb my finger harder for good measure, standing on my tiptoes, making myself big.

"Lucy, I..."

"No. I'm talking."

He purses his lips shut, those green gem eyes wide.

"Then I turn around and Lisa.." Her name leaves my lips in a spit of distaste, "has herself plastered on you like frosting on cake, and not the delicious frosting I make. Oh no, the sickly sweet, will turn your stomach and rot your teeth kind!"

A smile tugs at his lips. My rage isn't over.

"Don't laugh at me, Sean Larson! You didn't look like you were objecting too much to her large tits pressed against you as you whispered in her ear." My finger lands one more time right in the center of his chest.

We're chest to chest, well chest to stomach, with my head tipped high. My breath rising and falling fast, a white cloud of vapor in the cold mixing with his breath.

"Are you done?" I give a sharp nod.

"I wasn't.."

"Don't give me your lame excuses!" I cut him off, my voice shrill.

The door of the Brew House bangs open. I throw myself back from Sean's heat. From his annoyingly comforting warmth.

Josh staggers out with a very drunken Kate propped between him and Mr. Larson.

His eyebrows raise when he sees us.

"This bride to be, has had enough for the night. An *Uber* is on the way."

"Nooo, you've ad anof.." Kate lets go of her dad, spinning on one shaky heel and flings both her arms around Josh.

"Good, I'm ready to call it a night, too." I say before I slip Sean's jacket from my shoulders and I shove it in his direction. He holds it back at me, but I turn, waiting on the *Uber*.

"Can I ride in with you guys?" Sean asks.

Oh, no. Please no. Not an awkwardly silent car ride. Although I'm sure Kate will make for superb entertainment if she doesn't pass out or vomit.

"Sorry, I only ordered a six seater, us four, plus Mom and Becca will fill it."

Yes!

I feel a little bad. But not really.

"I thought you'd be staying out with Oli and Xander, and Lisa's still in there, too."

The *Uber* pulls up beside us, Barbs and Becca trot out and right into the back seat as Josh attempts to not so gracefully slip Kate in beside them.

"Are you staying, Lucy?" Sean's smooth voice carries hope. I shake my head keeping my eyes averted.

"No worries then. I'll just head back in."

In my head, all I hear is,

No worries then. I'll just head back to Lisa.

Why do I care?

I don't want to care.

But I do.

I slam the car door closed and lay my head on the cool glass. Through the tinted window, Lisa bounces out towards Sean, all toned, tanned, beautiful and confident.

Ugh.

Chapter 25

Lucy

"What the heck *was* that last night?"

Kate's loud voice assaults my ears like a thousand tiny needles piercing the drums. My tongue is like sandpaper, my eyes still blurry. How is she functioning after the state she left The Brew House last night?

"I heard Oli and Xander talking at the bar last night about how Sean better not hurt you. How could he hurt you?"

How does she remember any conversation from last night? Does she remember serenading us with Justin Timberlake in the *Uber* on the way home?

That memory is seared into my brain for eternity.

Probably not. I wasn't nearly as drunk as her and I feel like the icy hand of Hades had touched me last night but left me behind to drown in a pool of my pillow drool.

"What time is it?" I rasp through parched lips without exposing my eyes to the bright light filtering through the blinds.

"It's tell me what the fizzle is going on with you and my brother time!"

"Ugh, why are you so loud?" She pulls the blanket from my head before I can bury myself deeper in the duvet and disappear.

"Lucy Davenport!"

I open one eye to see her standing, freshly showered, hair perfect, hands on hips. Why could the universe not bless me with hangover free Sunday mornings?

"Shh," I whisper. "Keep your voice down. He'll hear you."

"He won't hear a thing. He didn't come home last night."

Sean didn't come home?

Did he go home with someone else?

Lisa.

Why is my heart racing? Bile creeps up my throat again. Not entirely sure if this is the news of Sean potentially staying out with Lisa loose legs or the bucket of booze I sipped down last night.

"Kate, I really don't feel good, and I need some caffeine." She sits on the bed beside me, her head tilted in that sympathetic head tilt people do. Irritating.

"Luc, I'm worried about you." She strokes my leg over the blanket. Tears threaten, but I'm determined I'm not crying again. All I've done for nearly two weeks is cry. I'm even fed up with my own self pity.

"I'm fine, just hungover." Closing my eyes again, her hand strokes my face.

"You're not fine. I'm going to get us a coffee and you're going to tell me every little thing that's eating at you."

There will be no arguing with her. I don't have the strength.

"And that's final. So suck it up buttercup and get ready to spill the tea. A problem shared and all that."

She skips annoyingly light-footed out of the bedroom door, humming an upbeat tune. Apart from everything else that's falling apart in my life, how am I going to tell Kate I had the best sex of my life with her little brother? I can't stop thinking about him, his lips, his voice, his tongue. And now my heart hurts at the thought of him going home with someone else.

Beating the mattress with my fist, I lie flat on my belly, pillow over my head until Suzi Sunshine returns with the caffeine.

"Right Luc, what's going on with you? And don't give me any of that bull crap about being fine and there's just a lot with the bakery."

I'm propped up on the pillows, the heat from the caffeine bringing me back to life, slightly. With the full-length mirror at the foot of the bed, I can see that I look like death warmed up compared to Kate, with her fresh face and bright eyes. What was a voluptuous full curl last night now resembles something a crow was building in the yard atop my head.

"You should be a detective, you know."

"Well, I always thought I'd make a great Miss Marple." She straightens her back, tilting her head thoughtfully. "Now quit deflecting and spill!" She orders.

Closing my eyes, not being able to look her in the eye when I say it out loud. I'm not entirely sure if the beads of sweat trailing down my spine are perspiring alcohol or Kate's intense glare.

Eyes still closed, I'm debating whether to tell a long story or just blurt it out.

"Lucy!"

"I had sex with your brother!"

Okay, blurt it out it is.

Kate's silence is ear drum shattering. I open one eye to check on her. She is staring with her mouth gaping. I'm assuming lost for words, which is a first for Kate.

"Kate...?" No words are worse than lots of words. "Say something, please."

"I.. I... when?...Why?"

This is not the reaction I was expecting.

"Are you really that shocked?"

"Lucy, you just told me you had sex with my little brother. My little brother, who we grew up giving wedges to and making fun of."

Her face has gone a shade lighter than pale. "I'm just going to need a minute."

"Okay, but just know, it was a onetime thing. We both promised, just like a get it out of our systems kind of thing. One time only, no weirdness."

The rigor I put into shaking my head for emphasis really rattles my tender brain.

"Nope, never again. It's not weird, is it? Don't let it be weird."

Words are flowing from me like vomit. I can't hold them in.

"I'm sorry Kate. Have I crossed a line, some kind of best friend code? I just.... Well, Sean was.... And then we..... It wasn't like he was your little brother... he's like all grown and big and muscles.."

"Ew, gross! Stop now!" Kate stands up, pacing the room.

My mouth suddenly dryer than the Sahara, I gulp down the rest of my coffee.

"I'm sorry."

"Stop apologizing." Her pacing slows. "You know Sean has been in love with you for years?"

Now it's my turn to be confused.

"What are you talking about? He's been gone for nine years. I haven't seen him since he left for college."

She points that manicured finger at me again. I swear I might snap it off.

"He was infatuated with you since he was a teenager. Could hardly be in the same room as you without turning bright red every time you spoke to him."

This is too much for my dehydrated brain to digest. Kate doesn't stop,

"He went away to college, and we always teased him, saying he never came back because he couldn't face you."

"You are joking, right?"

Her face is deadly serious. No grin. No joke.

"He's only just home and Mom is so happy he might stay.."

"What? He might stay?"

Sean hadn't mentioned anything about staying. How could I look him in the eye after the best sex ever when he went and slept with that hussy, Lisa?

"He said he was leaving after your wedding?"

"He told Mom he might stick around for a while."

Kate stares at me. She isn't angry. I'd seen Kate angry. When Oli stole her Jetson's lunch pack when we were nine and snapped the handle, she was mad.

When Cindy Dunn kissed her boyfriend at prom, she was livid.

Hell, just the other week when the wedding venue called her to say they had ordered the wrong table cloths, she saw red and gave the poor wedding planner a red ear down the phone.

Right now. She isn't mad.

She looks disappointed.

Is she disappointed in me? What did I do?

Okay, I *did* sleep with her little brother. But he was there too.

She put her hand back on my leg. Little tiny hammers thunder on my skull.

"Just don't break his heart, Lucy."

Wait what?

This is not the way I imagined this conversation going.

"Excuse me?" I surely didn't hear right. "Me break his heart? He's the one who went home with Lisa loose legs last night!"

"I should have known by the way he was staring at you in the bar last night. It was the night you were on a date with Brendan, wasn't it?"

"Yes."

"It's so obvious. If I wasn't so consumed with all this wedding planning, I would have noticed."

"Noticed what?"

"He's still in love with you."

She might as well have stood and mic dropped right there.

Did a bus just ride over me, stop, then reverse back? My head is spinning. Kate stands, grabbing the coffee mugs and heads for the door.

She stops before leaving, "He didn't go anywhere with Lisa last night. He spent the night on Xander's sofa after making sure my big brother was home safely. Just thought you'd want to know."

The door clicks shut.

Well shit. I feel like a class A idiot.

What the hell is Kate talking about? Sean hasn't been in love with me since he was a teenager. He didn't stay away because of me. That is ridiculous.

He maybe had a little crush on me.

I can't break his heart. She is crazy. He'd been away living up his life all over the world, girls here, there, and everywhere.

There is no way I was breaking Sean Larson's heart.

Mine, on the other hand, seems a little fragile.

Chapter 26

Sean

"Is he alive?"

"I don't know? Check if he's breathing."

Little footsteps creep closer. The giggles are a huge give-away. I smile with my head under the blanket, my neck stuck at a strange 45-degree angle on the arm of Xander's sofa. Regret for not making it back to my bed sits heavy in my gut.

Footsteps creep closer still...

3, 2, 1 ....

"Roaaaar!!" I burst from the confines of the blankets, my neck objecting painfully. Lola and Luke scream and laugh while I chase them to the kitchen door, scoop the two of them up, pretending to eat their heads.

"Who dares wake Uncle Sean?" I growl playfully.

"It was Lola!"

"No, it wasn't!!" Lola shrieks, "It was Luke!"

They are wriggling and giggling. The sound is so warm, I can't help the wide smile that spreads across my face.

"Ugh, who is being so loud?" Xander groans before he slumps himself over the breakfast bar.

"Rough night brother?" I laugh at his fragile state. "You were three sheets to the wind."

"Shhh, too many words."

I click on the coffeemaker.

"Why did we drink so much last night?" He put his head in his hands, leaning on the breakfast bar.

I bend close to the twins' ears, "Daddy isn't feeling well this morning, kids. Why don't you go play while I whip us up some eggs on toast?"

The kitchen fills with cheers and whoops. Xander grimaces like his head might explode.

"Yey Uncle Sean! Can we get bacon?"

"You sure can; now scoot!" I shoo them away to the living room before navigating my way around my brother and his kitchen.

I work around Xander, cracking eggs and humming some tune from the karaoke last night. Xander downs the remains of his first espresso.

"Better?"

"Marginally. What happened last night? How did you end up on my couch?"

If the town could see their chief right now, they might not feel so confident in his law enforcement abilities. His usually larger-than-life appearance shriveled up, shoulders hunched. The neat, not a hair out of place, Chief Larson is nowhere to be seen and there's a high probability of sparrows nesting there this morning.

"You don't remember?" I laugh.

"Oh god, what did I do?" He pales further, a worried look spreading on his face.

"You had fun brother, you had fun!" I slap him on the back, "you don't get to un-ruffle that hair much anymore, so don't fret."

I pour our second cup of coffee.

"So I didn't do anything to discredit myself or my job?"

"Discredit yourself?" I raise an eyebrow. "Unless you count absolutely murdering Johnny Cash on the karaoke, then no, you didn't do anything to 'discredit' yourself."

My stomach grumbles loudly, the scent of the bacon filling the kitchen.

"So how did you end up on my couch, then?"

"My ride left me behind."

"Sean." His tone is dripping in accusation. "I thought Oli, and I warned you about hurting Lucy."

"OH, that part you remember?" I stir the eggs vigorously.

"Yes, I remember the way you were looking at her."

"I wasn't looking at her."

Liar liar pants on fire!!

"Yep, big Brendan was all over her like white on rice and your eyes were sending fireballs in his direction."

He's enjoying this now the coffee has kicked in. Teasing me like old times. It still isn't fun for me.

"And then I remember you in a corner with Lisa." He points a finger in my direction, wagging it. "We warned you, brother. You can't just waltz back in here breaking hearts and then jet set away again, leaving us to mop up a river of tears behind you."

The eggs were scrambled, the bacon sizzling, and they were about three seconds away from being thrown in my brother's lap.

"I wasn't in a corner with Lisa." I grit through my teeth. "She cornered me, held me against the wall with her long talons in my chest, whispering a lot of dirty shit in my ear."

"So I'll ask again, why did you end up on my couch?"

"Because I told Lisa, *very* politely, that I didn't want to do said dirty things with her and she took the huff. Lucy went home with Mom, Dad and a very drunken Kate and I didn't much feel like sleeping in the room next to Lucy with a raging hard on!"

Xander's eyes pop, "Dude, keep your voice down - the kids!"

Lola and Luke are laughing uncontrollably at a movie they had playing on Netflix. I roll my eyes before whispering, "so I got your drunken ass home, paid the babysitter extra because you were an hour after you said you'd be home, tucked you in and lay my head down."

My back to him, I lay out four plates and dish up breakfast.

"What's going on, brother?"

His big brother voice is distracting my anger.

Although I'd been away from home for a long time, I did everything to keep close with my brothers. Oli and Xander had visited me the most, before Xander had the twins. Oli still took holidays with me regularly, we video called at least weekly to keep up to date. My big brothers were always keeping tabs on me wherever I was in the world.

Family is everything.

"I can't get her out of my head." I shake my head like that might make the difference. "It's like I'm sixteen all over again. She's everywhere. Wherever I go, whatever I do, she's there."

"That could be a song, mate!"

"It's not funny Xee, I can't get her out my head." I pause before I drop the next bomb, "and it's worse since we had sex the other night and I promised it was a one time only, get it out of our system situation!"

Xander's face turns pink as he chokes on a mouthful of bacon and eggs.

"She slept with you?"

"Seriously?!" I throw the tea towel his way. "I'm in real trouble, man. I thought I was over her. I thought I could come home, see her and get on with my life."

"And that didn't happen?"

"NO!" I whisper shout. "She slammed into me at the barbecue with a tray of muffins, her bouncy cinnamon hair all up in my head and I haven't gotten her out since. It's getting worse. Is there something wrong with me? This isn't normal."

Xander is clearly enjoying this. His grin wide and the hangover long gone.

"Hold that thought till I feed my kids." He lifts the two smaller portions through the living room to the dining table, sitting the kids down before joining me back at the breakfast bar.

"You need to talk to her, man."

"What do you mean? I talk to her every day. It's not helping, it's making it worse."

"This egg is great, so fluffy. How'd you get it so fluffy?"

"Can we stay on topic??"

He laughs, "I mean talk to her, tell her how you feel."

"Like a randy teenager? I don't think that will help somehow!"

This is getting nowhere. Xander isn't going to give me anything useful. I finish my eggs and bacon, down the rest of my coffee.

"Well, it's been a pleasure, but I better head back home for some more sexually frustrated torture."

"You are so dramatic, little brother. I mean, tell her how you feel. You've been in love with this girl since seventh grade. You have pined after her, and it's clearly not a crush any more. What if it's the real thing, man?"

"Like marry her and be with her forever, love?"

He rolls his eyes. "Yes dipstick. Of all the girls in all the world, and you've been there, she's the one who always has your heart."

I walk back from Xander's, the scorching sun at my back. Last night's clothes on, I must look rough. Xander's words spin around my head on a loop. Do I love Lucy? Is this what love is? This torturous feeling, the not knowing if she wants me too, the heat when I think about her, smell her, the electricity sparks when she's near, when I hear her singsong voice, see her round hips sway, press my lips on hers.

If this is love, I'm in trouble.

Lucy doesn't love me, she made me promise one time only.

I need to see her.

I pick up the pace, propelling me towards the house. I just need to figure out what I'm going to say to her when I get there.

Chapter 27

Lucy

The bag hits the floor with a thud. Mom's kitchen fills with a tsunami of flour.

"Shit!"

White powder touched every tile and every cupboard, looking like an explosion in some drug cartel's underground basement.

"Are you alright darling?" Mom shouts from the living room.

"Yes Mom, just a floury disaster. I'll get it cleaned up."

It's the fourth accident today. I'd already tossed a layer of cake in the trash because the sponge was too soggy.

I can't serve soggy cake. The bakery might be closed, but the business has to go on. I wouldn't let my customers down. Especially now I'm going all in on having the best dang bakery in Colorado. Honeybee Bakery is going to be on everyone's lips, literally.

If I could only get myself together. One burst bag of flour and messy floor to add to the soggy sponge, a burned thumb and the carton of eggs I dropped in the middle of Humphry's earlier today.

"Oh darling, what's going on?" Mom appears at the door, leaning on the frame. "Let me get the vacuum."

"No Mom, it's fine. I'll get it."

"What's going on with you today?" She pulls out a flour covered chair from the table and sits down.

"All I've heard from the other room is sighing, humming, and a few choice curse words."

Am I okay? That seems like a loaded question today. Kate's morning revelations about Sean's teenage infatuation with me, thinking he was still in love with me, not coming home to avoid me. That was a cyclone of emotion to receive in a sixty-second period before she swept out of my room.

I couldn't even question her. By the time I assembled myself fit for the world to see, she and Barbs had gone shopping.

There is no way Sean is in love with me.

Look at me.

I'm his big sister's shorter, rounder best friend. I'm not the one that guys hit on. That's Kate, with her perfectly proportioned body and blond hair and blue eyes combo.

My curves and red hair didn't grab too many second glances. Certainly not infatuation worthy.

It was a schoolboy crush. It had to be.

The little voice in the back of my head asked, *'well what is it now?'*

"I guess I'm just having a bad day." I slump in the chair beside her. "Maybe I drank too much last night."

"A bad day is all in the head."

Mom's hand touches my knee, her hand wobbly but reassuring.

"Whatever has gone on, you can turn it around. Nothing is the end of the world."

I had grown up into such a positive person because of my mom. She's a ray of sunshine on a dark day. A reminder that in the face of challenges, we have the strength to go on.

I smile at her and she reassures me with her smile back.

"I do have some good news."

"There's my girl. Good news to cheer us up. What's that then?"

After all my deliberating and talking with Sean about the business, I've never been more certain of my business plan.

"I know you were worried about my commitment to the bakery and what I was planning,"

She squeezes my knee, "I was never worried about any of those things, darling, only that you made a choice that would make you happy."

"I know Mom. And the flood has forced me to make a decision. It's forced me to consider all the things I have thought I wanted and what my future will look like."

"I understand, Lucy, the bakery is too much to keep going; it's okay." Her words are supportive, but her heart is breaking.

"No Mom, you don't understand. The bakery is my future. Sean was really helpful yesterday when we went for lunch. Talking through the business, through my mindset and what I really am passionate about."

"Oh Lucy, I'm so happy you feel that way. The bakery is in your blood. You were born a baker and you're such a savvy businesswoman."

"I have so many ideas Mom, I hope you'll get excited about them with me."

"Honeybee Bakery is yours, my love. I know you will rebuild in your vision, to build for your future, hopefully for your children."

I could see little feet running about my new vision for the bakery, teaching them how to weigh and count and mix and kneed up on a stool just like grandma did with me.

The afternoon was an improvement from the disastrous morning. I told Mom all my ideas for the new bakery and the expansion and how I planned on financing it.

I had an appointment booked at the bank later this week to secure some capital for the expansion. The builders start work tomorrow for the remodel and I'm meeting them in the morning with the updated plans.

It really feels like a massive step in the right direction.

I was so excited telling all this to Mom. The flour cleaned up and the birthday cake for Mrs. Steedman's granddaughter's tenth birthday was finished without any more accidents.

The sponge was perfect. If I do say so myself.

I dropped it off at her house on my way back to the Larson's. I'd been glad of a little distance from the house today.

Kate messaged earlier.

> *Hey girl, I know you wouldn't intentionally hurt my brother. I love you both. I don't want to see either of you get hurt. Hopefully that's it out of both your systems and we can go on as normal. See you soon. Kate xxx*

Was he out of my system?

I really don't think so.

Trying to avoid all in person contact, I run into the Larson's house heading straight for the stairs.

"Had a busy day, Luc?"

Busted.

Mr. Larson looks up as my escape is foiled.

"Oh yes, I was at Mom's filling a few orders for this week before I'm caught up with the wedding and bridesmaid stuff."

He nods in understanding. "Yep, a lot on your mind right now."

Why does that feel like it had an undertone?

"Sure do." I pull out a deep yawn. "Better get myself to bed, big day tomorrow at the bakery."

"Aren't you hungry? Sean made your favorite. Lasagna." His smile is wide, with a hint of knowing. "He kept some for you."

Was Mr. Larson a mind reader, a psychic in a past life, maybe?

I just need a hot bath, a face mask and an early night.

"That was really thoughtful of him. I can take it with me for lunch tomorrow."

I make my lame excuses and hop upstairs to draw the bubbliest bath ever.

Candles, check.

Lavender essential oil, check.

Soothing meditation play list, check.

The hot water soothes my aching shoulders as I plunge my entire self under. That moment when your head is fully under the water except your nose and lips is bliss. The world is quiet. All I can hear is the swish of water drowning out my thoughts. My hair floating on the surface, tickling my neck and chest.

Deep breath in my nose, filling my belly.

Hold, two, three, four.

Slowly out my mouth drawing out all the breath.

This is the most at peace I've felt in weeks.

I could just stay in the bath for the rest of my life. Would anyone notice? I could shrivel up in here like a prune and die in bliss.

I'm sure it wouldn't be that blissful, but at least I wouldn't have to face Kate, or Sean, or Brendan.

A loud knock on the bedroom door bursts my bliss bubble in the bathroom.

Kate. I forgot to text her back.

I'll get her later.

My eyes close, ready to drop under the water.

The knock came again. A little more urgent.

"Ugh! Can't a girl get a bath in peace?"

The cool air of the room hits my skin, covering me in goosebumps. I wrap the fluffy, not so generous towel around me before pulling the door open wide.

Not Kate.

Sean.

Oh, dear lord. He is smoldering in his jeans and, for a change, a black t-shirt taught across his chest.

My mouth waters and I can't be sure if it's Sean or the aroma of the lasagna he's holding.

"Oh shit, sorry." His eyes shoot in another direction. "I'll come back."

"Are you serious?" I whisper, gripping the tiny towel a little tighter and wishing it had a little more length. Not much modesty covered at all.

"You've seen me naked! Get in here!" I grab the front of his t-shirt and drag him in before anyone can see us, quietly closing the door.

When I turn, he's right there, in my space. Those emerald eyes glistening back at me, entrancing. He's wild and rugged, hair finger combed out of control. My hand flinches at my side, desperate to reach up and run my fingers through it.

I grip my towel tighter.

The plate of lasagna and my towel, the only things separating us.

Chapter 28

Lucy

I'm standing in a tiny towel and Sean is inches from me.

Would it be too forward to just drop my towel? Is that too forward? I mean, he has seen me naked already, and this towel isn't covering much, anyway.

He's been living rent free in my head for the last week.

Once definitely wasn't enough.

I know he feels it, too.

The buzzing between us pulses on my skin. Beads of water intensify the pulse throbbing through my veins.

His eyes lower, tracing the trickles of water from my hair running between the crevice of my full cleavage. He's looking at me like he's just returned from the desert and I'm his tall cold glass of hydration.

"I came up here to talk to you." The words are slow and gruff. "But I'm finding it hard to put the words I came to say together right now."

I know the feeling champ.

Storming in here looking like that with my favorite meal. I don't know which is making me hungrier.

Without taking his eyes from me, he places the plate on my sideboard.

They pin me, searching, asking, wanting, needing.

Or is that me?

Desire pulls in my stomach so strongly my head spins. The butterflies are no longer butterflies but huge locus on a mission to free themselves.

I can almost hear the crack of the electricity before we snap and collide in a tangle of tongues, lips and arms.

One hand furiously gripping the back of his head, my fingers pull his hair, the other still grasping the corners of the useless towel in a last-ditch attempt to keep it in place.

"Lucy." My name leaves his lips in a groan, an aching.

"Yes." my voice is throaty and breathy, gasping for air.

"Red, I need you." Lips and tongues clash in a rhythmic dance.

"Confession.."

"Uhmh," between my lips.

"Once was never going to be enough." He pulls his head up. "I knew from the moment I set eyes on you again, I would never get enough."

Is this what he said to get in all the girls' pants? It was certainly working, even though this time I was panty-less already.

I feel the longing between my thighs long before I drop the towel between us. His arm wraps around my back, pulling me tight against him. The friction of his jeans reminds me I'm the only one in my birthday suit.

I don't want to want this, but my treacherous heart thrums as Sean pulls back to take me in. I've never had eyes on me like this.

Rake over me with undisguised passion and want.

The pause is long enough to make me self conscious, but how could I feel anything but desired with the look of adoration on his face? He rips his t-shirt over his head before we collide again and I work on his jeans' button with ease, shimmying them down his hips.

His mouth on mine is demanding, his tongue invading, and I meet him with equal fever. My hands explore his body, his firm chest, the roughness of his stubble.

His fingers lace in my hair, gently pulling, angling my head to just where he needs it to deepen the kiss. A moan escapes from my lips.

Desire burns right down to my curling toes.

"Need to get you on the bed." He growls, "better access."

I don't complain when his hands find my ass. Holding me higher with a firm grip, he lifts me and I wrap my legs around his waist before he walks to the bed.

I've never had a guy lift me before. It's so sexy. Who knew being manhandled was such a turn on.

Sean throws me down and I can't help but giggle.

"Aren't you joining me?"

“Oh yes,” he drops his snug Calvin Klein underwear, releasing his solid erection before crawling between my legs.

“I want to explore every part of your body, Lucy.” He runs a finger from my ankle, making a trail of fire right up my inner thigh.

“Hmmm,” I purr, I actually purr.

“But tonight I can’t hold back. I need to have you.”

No false promises of one time only.

He doesn’t let me answer before he pounces on my solid, aching nipple. I gasp as his tongue works wonders, flicking and teasing in time with his fingers.

“Sean.” I whisper a strangled cry, aware we’re in a house full of his family.

“More, don't stop” I beg.

“I’ll give you more Red.”

He slips a finger inside me, stroking faster.

“You’re so wet.” We both groan.

I gasp when a very loud knock comes from the door.

“Lucy, are you in there?”

Oh, dear god it’s Kate. She has the worst timing.

I leap from under Sean so fast I trip on his jeans and head-butt the mirror.

“Ow!”

“Are you okay?” Kate shouts through the door.

Sean has a wide smile and is moving at a snail’s pace.

“I’m fine,” I shout, “just out of the bath, hang on!”

I make a zipper motion over my lips to Sean as I franticly search the floor for the towel. He doesn't make a move until I silent movie gesture he needs to move his ass into the bathroom.

Pronto.

He rolls his eyes but heads in that direction, grabbing each discarded item of clothing as he goes. I watch his retreating perfect, firm rear end as he goes.

Pay attention Lucy!

"Hey, what's up?" I open the door just a crack so Kate can see I'm not dressed, hoping that will dissuade her from coming in.

"Why is your face all red?"

Not a chance in hell she's not coming in.

She steps forward into the doorway until I step back out of her way. Kate has no concept of personal space or privacy. I'm genuinely shocked, but thankful she even knocked on the door before coming in. She would think twice about not knocking, if she'd been greeted by a full moon from her brother as he had his way with me when she walked in.

"Are you okay? Did you not get any of my texts? Your face is really red."

She sits down right where her brother has just vacated. How can I get her out of here rapidly?

"I'm fine." My voice is so high, I don't even believe my lie.

Her eyes scrunch, scrutinizing me.

"Lucy, what's going on?"

"Nothing, I just had a really long day in my mom's tiny kitchen and was in dire need of a scalding hot bubble bath." Is she buying it? "Just a little me time."

Her eyes are scanning the room suspiciously. I have a quick glance to make sure there are no rogue boxers or knickers lying around.

"Ha, Sean brought you his 'I love Lucy Lasagna then?'" She points to the abandoned dish on the dressing table.

"Kate! No, he just brought me some leftover dinner."

"If you say so." She leans back on the headboard and swings her legs up, getting comfortable. She isn't going anywhere fast.

"Where is Sean? He hasn't been around since dinner."

"I have no idea. I was in the bath." Can she hear the stress in my tone? "He just gave me the plate and left."

"He just gave you the plate and left?" Her tone is disbelieving.

"Of course. What else would he do?"

I laugh it off, searching for pajamas in the drawer. Goosebumps cover my legs with the useless tiny towel. "It's just lasagna."

I indicate I'm about to drop the towel and get dressed. She shuts her eyes.

"You know I've seen you naked hundreds of times growing up." Kate was never anxious about her body. She had petite little curves, all in proportion. Why should she be conscious of her body?

"Not the same as getting changed for swim club together when we were ten." I joke, "I'm decent, you can open your eyes."

Distracting, I potter around tidying up. Kate is fiddling with the end of her hair. A clear indicator she is nervous. I wonder if she knows my nervous tells? I'm sure she does.

True to form, not being comfortable in a silence longer than ninety seconds, she spits out what she wants to say.

"I'm so sorry I was a bitch this morning!"

She looks me right in the eye. "I know you wouldn't intentionally hurt my brother. I just don't want it getting weird if he goes. He'll get hurt. You'll get hurt, and I'll have to watch you hurt."

I finally sit beside her and hope that Sean isn't listening with his ear pressed against the door too hard.

"You weren't a bitch this morning. I love you for trying to protect me, and Sean." Could I quiz her about all the things she told me this morning with Sean in the other room?

"Can I ask how much of what you said this morning was true?"

"What part?"

I try to keep my voice low.

"The part about Sean being infatuated with me when we he was a teenager, the part about him maybe staying."

I was now sitting back against the headboard side by side with her, getting comfy just like we did watching movies at sleepovers, telling secrets, and giggling until we fell asleep.

Kate took my hand and squeezed it.

"You should talk to Sean."

Chapter 29

Sean

Ow!

Squatting beside the bath for over an hour, my legs cramp. I stretch each one in front of me, attempting to regain some feeling. The scent of lavender is making me sleepy.

The candles Lucy had around her bath flickered for about another thirty minutes before burning out. I've been sitting in the dark ever since. Scared to put the light on in case it made a noise, or the light shone from under the door.

I started off with my ear pressed against the door and could make out mumbled bits of conversation. Something about loving lasagna, and being a bitch. Then a lot of giggles.

How long could I survive in here? No food and only bathroom tap water. Was I going to be here all night? Could I eat the melted candle wax and survive? It was natural wax apparently.

I eventually gave in and redressed. The moment was gone when I heard the giggling start. Kate was going nowhere fast.

Bloody Kate.

I was just getting to the good part where Lucy was about to scream my name as I made her come when Kate battered on the door like the house was on fire. I had to admit that I was a little stung that Lucy felt she had to hide me in the bathroom.

Couldn't we have told Kate, told her to come back when it was a more convenient time?

I wanted to tell Lucy how I feel. Let her know I wasn't looking at any other woman last night except her. Tell her I lied when I said once was enough and it wouldn't get weird.

Finally, tell her she's been in my head for years, it didn't matter how far around the globe I was, my thoughts would often wander to the red head girl from home and wonder what she was doing, who she was with, if she was happy.

All of those well prepared words were stuck in my throat, lost in the ether, when she opened the door to her room in a tiny little towel with half a nipple peeping out at me.

Every ounce of self control evaporated. I wanted to be cool, calm and collected when I told her how much she means to me, that I wanted to stay here in Breakridge and help her build and put her stamp on the bakery.

To watch her succeed and celebrate with her.

The longing in her eyes reflected my own. Snapping my last straw of restraint, she met me move for move, pace for pace. I nearly convulsed when she wrapped her legs around me and I felt her wet core around my waist.

Then Kate interrupted.

The moment is now long gone and I'm still sitting in the dark. Alone.

Leaning on the bath with my eyes closed. The door creaks open and light shines in.

"Sorry!" Lucy pops her head around the door. "I couldn't get her to leave. She settled in, feet up on the bed and everything."

"I wondered for a while if it would be too weird if I came out after an hour."

"Yes, it might have been a teensy bit awkward. I'm so sorry you've been stuck here for nearly two hours." Her smile is apologetic.

"Has it been that long? I gave up looking."

I reach my hand up to her and pull her down beside me. It's a little disappointing that she's no longer naked but it will probably be better for a sensible conversation.

I clasp her fingers in mine, her small hand fits perfectly. I run my thumb gently along her soft skin. It's quiet, it's peaceful.

We sit in the dark, on the floor, leaning on the bath, side by side, hand in hand, for a silent few minutes.

"Sean?"

"Yes?"

"Can I ask a question?"

"Sure."

"Why did you stay away for so long?"

Sucker-punch.

How do I answer that without looking like a pathetic, needy, love sick man child?

"I was traveling; that's what us young guys do after college." I try and fail to inject a little humor. Her hand grips mine just a little tighter.

"You never came home for holidays, birthdays or special occasions."

"I'm home for this special occasion."

"It's been nine years. Most people have visited their parents after college in nine years."

"I guess I never thought it was that weird because I was always flying them to wherever I was, or Face-timing."

She exhales loudly, her chest deflating. Her hand goes a little limp in mine. I clasp it back tighter.

Here goes nothing.

I came here to be honest.

"You really want to know?"

"I really want to know." She confirms in a whisper.

Man, I'm glad we're sitting in the dark right now. How many guys get to sit with their high school crush, not just crush - that word is never big enough. High school love, infatuation and tell her what she means to him.

My tongue scrapes the roof of my mouth like sandpaper. She must be able to feel my heart beat through the palm of my sweaty hand, it's reverberating through my body.

"I didn't know how to come home and see you with someone else. Married. Kids. The whole white picket fence family life."

When I say it out loud, I feel stupid. I feel like I'm seventeen again. Weak and helpless.

"Sean... I.." Lucy's words are soft and broken.

Great, she feels sorry for me. This really is an all-time low after such a high. Sitting on a bathroom floor baring my soul, preparing for the ultimate rejection.

"I know, I'm sorry. It's weak and pathetic."

Her fingers rub on mine gently.

"I didn't know, Sean." Her body shook with the shake of her head, "and it's not weak or pathetic to be strong enough to talk about your feelings." She rests her head on my shoulder and I let out the breath I didn't know I was holding.

"Just to be clear, it wasn't all about you." I laugh, wanting to lighten the heavy mood that's descended.

"I was having the time of my life traveling and learning about business, experiencing the world, meeting friends."

"Oh, it wasn't all about me? Now my ego is bruised." She laughs and warm courage flows through me.

"I was obsessed with you before I left, and yes, I know how lame it is to tell you that. I was a seventeen-year-old spotty, awkward teenager, and you were a sophisticated twenty-two-year-old graduating and heading into the world. You barely even looked my way."

"Sophisticated! Yeah, right, I don't have enough sophistication to fill my little finger. You were Kate's little brother. I could never see you in any other way."

She might as well have taken a baseball bat to my guts. That was a sore one. I'm right back to awkward and rejected.

"You didn't let me finish." She dug an elbow into my side in the dark. "...back then. I could never see you in any other way *back then*."

I can't help the shit-eating grin that forms on my face, and I'm again, glad we're in the dark.

"What's changed?"

She's quiet for a beat.

"Me. I'm fed up with being the good girl, the one who always does what's expected. I'm overdue a little fun."

Although her giggle is infectious, that stung a little.

Just .... *A little fun?*

Her warm breath on my ear tickles, my body reacts with goosebumps and blood rushing south. I jump up, pulling her with me.

"Whoa Sean!"

"Shh." I pull her through into the light and tight against me. Both our eyes squish closed at the bright bedroom light. I plant my lips right on hers. Those soft, full lips. So kissable.

This is a gentle kiss. Nothing like the rush and race of earlier. This is the kiss I've imagined giving her so many times.

My imagination is nothing close to the reality of her. My lips explore hers and she opens up to me when I slide my tongue in, just a little. Her hungry hands are on my chest, rubbing up my neck to my hair, pulling me down.

Planting a kiss on her jaw, she tilts her head, opening up to me. I continue up to her earlobe and give it a bite.

Her gasp is like a reward; spurring me on, a growl rumbles out of me. I can't get enough.

She wobbles and I want to take the credit for it, but when I look at her, she looks drained.

"Red," I whisper in her ear, "let's rain check tonight."

Her sleepy eyelids lift and meet mine. "Are you sure?"

"I wouldn't have it any other way." Scooping her up easily, I place her gently on her bed. I deserve an award for this. The hard wood is going to be difficult to tame in the shower tonight.

I pull the blanket up to tuck her in and she reaches out, grabbing my hand.

"You're not staying for a bit?" She stifles a yawn.

"Red, I'm good, but I'm not that good. If I climb into this bed right now, there's no way I can keep my hands away from you." Her sleepy smile is cute.

"Rain check then."

I kiss her forehead, stroking her wild mane. Before I get to the door, there's a gentle snore coming from the bed.

"Rain check Red."

Chapter 30

Lucy

Today would be perfect.

The sun beat so high in the sky, it's as if the angels themselves are shining down on my happiness.

With the insurance covering the repairs, the contractors had agreed to start the work right away. I thought the work could hold off until after Kate's wedding, but I can't wait to get back behind the counter and put into action all the ideas I have for Honeybee Bakery 2.0.

A week is a long time to lose business.

The remodel is the biggest project I will have ever taken on. It feels like I'm finally growing up. Finally, taking charge of my life. I wasn't just handed this business by luck.

I hadn't realized until the flood that I didn't feel like I actually owned the bakery, like it was mine to do with anything I wanted. It still felt like my mom's business. Heck, it still felt like my grandma and pop's business. I had never made it mine, put my stamp on it. I had created recipes and added my ideas, but it wasn't me.

Now it's time for a new beginning. I would never change the name. It would forever be Honeybee Bakery. But now it was time for Honeybee to enter a new era.

Light on my feet, I float into Humphrey's store for a take-away coffee before heading to the bakery.

"Mornin' Ms. Davenport," Mr. Humphrey chirps. "I was sorry to see what happened to your grandma's bakery."

Even the town still thought of it as Grandma's bakery, but nothing is getting me down today.

"Good morning Mr. Humphry," I beam at him. "Thanks. I'm getting it all up and running again, don't worry. Honeybee Bakery will be back in business before you know it. Back and better than ever."

"Ah, that's what I like to see, a young 'un with a bit o' fight and tenacity aboot them."

Mr. Humphrey had followed his wife here to Colorado forty years ago, but his Scottish accent was still thick. I always smiled, even when I couldn't understand a word he said. Not entirely sure what a young 'un is and his 'ou' vowel sound always comes out as 'oo".

I struggled to keep up.

"What can I get you the day, lass?"

"Can I get an extra hot latte with skinny milk, please?"

"Comin' right up." He whisks away, his slight but agile body working quickly with the beans and the steamer in the milk.

"Lucy!" Mrs. Humphrey came barreling up the aisle, grasping me in a bear hug. Oh, dear lord, her compact frame is deceiving.

"How are you? The bakery is looking terrible."

She pulls back, her sparkling blue eyes searching mine. "Oh, you've got a lovely glow about you, dear. Is that a man I see in your aura?"

What in heavens?! Can't I just come in and get a coffee?!

Mrs. Humphrey is the town's local psychic. If you're looking for answers, she's the woman to sort you out. She has rules though. No lotto numbers, no information about other peoples personal thoughts or business and no match making after the Davidson's wedding disaster four years ago. But no-one talks about that anymore.

I feel the blush from my toes right to my cheeks. How on earth could she tell with a look that I had been seeing a guy?

Have I been seeing a guy? Was I 'seeing' Sean? What did he mean last night? It was just a rain check. Was it just a rain check for the best sex ever or a rain check for another soul disclosing conversation?

Why were all these questions popping up from no-where? Today is a happy day!

"Ah, you're making it more complicated than it needs to be, dear."

Did I even say a word? Mrs. Humphrey lifts my chin with her finger.

"Don't overcomplicate it dear, do what feels right in your heart." She places her hand right on top of my heart. My breathing slows and peace settles over me.

"I thought she looked a bit chipper for someone whose bakery literally went down the drain a couple weeks ago." Mr. Humphrey chimed in over the loud hiss of the milk steamer. "A new fella in the picture, eh? That'll usually put a smile on it!" He turned and winked at Mrs. Humphrey.

Her lilac wild curls, tamed messily in a bun, stray curls spring from every direction, large amethysts hang from each earlobe. Every line on her soft skin tells a story.

Diane Humphrey isn't old, maybe in her early sixties, but she has stories. She's had life. She was a woman a man literally crossed the Atlantic for.

When I turn, Mr. Humphrey places my latte in my hand and I head for the door.

"Good luck today. It's a big one!"

I leave the store with more than I went in for, slightly confused but with an extra spring in my step.

The patrons of Humphrey's usually get a little more than they bargained for.

The bell, now back above the door, tings and my head shoots up like a meerkat for the hundredth time this morning.

"Hi Mrs. Larson," I hate that disappointment laces my voice. Why was every damn person and their dog dropping in today? Everyone except the face I want to see.

We'd had a steady stream of locals dropping in with well wishes, snacks, and flasks of coffee to keep us going through the start of the renovation. Truth is, we can't really do much today, but neither Mom nor I want to be anywhere else. We'd sat at the fold-down table for the last hour making notes on new recipes and new business ideas I couldn't wait to tell her about while the contractors, Jamie and his dad had been hard at work through the kitchen in the back. If the noise level was anything to go by, there was a lot of progress, but I'm scared to pop my head round the door.

"Thought I drop you ladies in some fresh coffee for the afternoon."

Barbs couldn't look more out of place in the upside down bakery in her Capri pants and baby pink cashmere sweater.

"That's so thoughtful of you Mrs. L, I'm so hyped on coffee I think I'll be jittering through my meeting with the bank this afternoon."

To say I was nervous was an understatement. The whole new vision and remodel for the bakery is balancing on getting this loan.

"Are you waiting for someone, dear?" Mom nibbles her cheese sandwich that Mrs. Humphrey had dropped off earlier. She looks a little smug in the deckchair and table set up by the window, a knowing smile on her face.

Am I that obvious? What on earth is going on?

One day I'm happy with my little town life, okay, maybe happy is too strong a word, satisfied? I'm moderately content? Any way, I was just getting on with life. Then Sean Larson comes home with his all grown up muscle physique, tight white t-shirts, lingering looks, radiating sexy and my head can't string a thought together.

As well as knocking me out with his rock hard abs and emerald eyes, he has made me feel more than I have in a long time. Maybe ever.

Feeling confident in myself, my skin, my body. Being there as a great friend with the best business advice and serving me up honesty on a plate.

Is Mrs. Humphrey right? Am I over thinking it?

Probably yes. I should just speak to Sean. It's just a fling. A bit of fun.

Obsessed with me.

Last night he'd said he'd been obsessed with me. Passed tense, of course. When he was a seventeen-year-old with hormones raging round his body.

But now?

No one has ever been obsessed with me. Red-haired, freckled and a little round in the hips. Obsessed is a strong word. The thought of Sean obsessing over me brought a tantalizing flutter between my legs.

Oh jeez! He isn't even here, and my body is reacting. Maybe I'm the one obsessing. I need to get out of here. Need to get him out of my head.

He'll be leaving to fly off somewhere tropical this time next week. There's no way he'll stay in this small town after everything he has seen the world can offer. The town he'd run so fast from, like he was being chased out by dwarfs wielding oversized mallets.

I won't have long to obsess. I'm just a bit of fun while he's home.

We would have some fun. He'd get on a plane in a week and I'll be back to working in the bakery seven days a week.

Why shouldn't I enjoy that fun? I never let go and let my hair down, throwing caution to the wind. Maybe it's my turn to take something for myself for a change instead of being Little Miss Responsible all the time. The bakery is getting sorted. Bridesmaid duties are getting checked off the list. I deserve a little fun in my life.

For a week at least.

And Sean Larson has fun written all over him. From his bouncing soft curly hair to the cheeky dimples when he grinned at me, I could imagine the fun I could have for the next week.

I just need to make sure I don't catch any feelings. That would be just my luck. Fall hard and then Sean jets off.

Nope. Not happening. No feelings. Just fun.

I suddenly can't wait to cash in that rain check.

Chapter 31

Sean

Did I really confess my high school obsession with Lucy to her last night? That I didn't know how to come home and see her married with kids, living her life happily without me.

In the bright light of a new day, I cringe thinking about it.

I keep hoping it might have been some kind of nightmare, a figment of my imagination I had played out, a fantasy where Lucy lets go and reveals all her hidden feelings she has had for years.

Of course, she didn't, but I wasn't disappointed.

"…. I could never see you in any other way back then."

'Back then.'

But now was different, things have changed.

I've changed. She's changed.

"Ow!"

The basketball hits me square on the back of the head. "What the hell was that for?"

Oli grins like a hyena, "where the hell were you man, 'cos you weren't on the court with us!"

"Nowhere, just a little distracted."

I pick up the ball dribbling it towards the hoop that still sits high on the side of Mom's garage. We had all played here since we were old enough to pick up a ball. Dad had taught us everything we knew. Xander had been the pro, taking his skills to college.

I set up aim and let the ball go, hitting the hoop before it bounced back towards me.

"You don't say, brother!" Xander smirks, grabbing the ball from my hands.

"Could a certain red head be the cause of this distraction?" Oli taunts.

My face flushes hotter than a beach side cabana, embarrassment and irritation combined.

"Oohh, it definitely is. He can't even hide it." They are both ripping into me now. Time has transported me back to a time I had spots and braces.

Not fun.

"Shut up! You don't know what you're talking about." I intercept the ball from Xander attempting to save face. Aim for the hoop again.

Miss.

Shit.

"Oh yeah, you've got it bad, brother." Xander slaps his hand on my shoulder, pulling me into a hug. "It's just like you're seventeen again...... except this time you've actually seen her naked!"

“Shut up Xander!” I break out of his grasp, feeling my blood boil at the thought of Lucy in my brother’s head, naked.

The last place I want Lucy is in my brother’s dirty thoughts!

They both hold their hands up in surrender, laughing. I hate the ribbing I'm getting but I have missed this with them both.

“What has happened to the happy-go-lucky tech millionaire in Bali?” Oli swipes the sweat from his forehead grabbing his water.

“Nothing, I’m still here,” lies, total lies. “I’m just adjusting to life back home.”

“You mean turning back time by nine years?” Xander laughs.

“Ha ha, very funny. No, nothing is the same. I’m not the same, and Lucy is definitely not the same.”

Not the same at all. Curves are rounder, hair redder, mouth dirtier.

“Yep, it’s just the same,” Xander knocks back his head, gulping water. “You’re just as obsessed with her now as you were back then. You have that look.”

“What look?”

They look at each other, obviously something on their minds. Oli got there first.

“That far away puppy dog look. Like you’d do anything to get the girl.”

"You're a pair of dicks." I grab my water bottle and head for the house, needing a cold shower.

"Buck, buck, buck." They both start flapping their arms, clucking and imitating chickens around the drive. "Can't even admit he's got it bad."

As much as I've missed them, I've had enough of this shit today.

"Oli, you wouldn't know, *got it bad*, unless it slapped you around the head with yesterday's dirty underwear. You're such a man whore you haven't called one woman back since ...." I struggled to think of a time I'd ever know Oli to be serious about a girl, "ever!"

He swooped his hand through his hair, preening with a wink, "yep, can't tie me down!"

Pausing at the door, "I really like her man." I give in and sit down on the porch step. "I don't know what to do."

The pair of them look at each other, worried they've broken me. Neither one of them has been lucky in love or relationships. Oli's never tried and Xander's ex ran so far to the other side of the country after the twins were born. I think it's scarred him for life. I'm not sure he's been on a date since they were born.

I had the wrong audience in my hour of need.

Xander sits down beside me, serious now.

"What's changed? You've been crazy about Lucy for years, but you never came near."

Oli starts back with the chicken impression until Xander gives him the big brother glare. "Why have you gotten your knickers in a knot this past week since you've been home? Did you take my advice and tell her how you feel?"

"Yes." I drop my head between my knees. Why does talking about feelings make guys so awkward and senseless?

"Well.... What did she say?"

Oli has lost interest at this point and starts shooting balls into the hoop again. Dunk after dunk. Nothing wrong with his confidence.

"She said she didn't know how I felt back then. She couldn't feel anything back then, but now was different. Then she fell asleep."

"Huh. She fell asleep, not really telling you anything." He scratches his head. "Not how I would imagine that kind of conversation ending. Are you changing you life for this girl? Or are you breaking her heart and leaving next week?"

I don't know how to answer that question. It has spun in my head since I left Lucy's room last night. Is one week enough?

Is it enough for us to be over?

Could we be something more?

"I, ah. I don't know."

"No wonder I avoid women!" Xander stretches up, laughing. "Sounds like an unfinished conversation to me... You should head over there."

"That's not helpful, man!"

He keeps walking, grabbing the ball from Oli. I head in for a cold shower.

Chapter 32

Lucy

What. A. Day.

That bank manager grilled the hell out of me. He sat in his corner office with his fancy coffee machine and silky soft leather sofas. And I knew they were real leather, no faux leather smelled as sensual as that.

Judging me, looking down his thin pointy nose over the rim of his no-frame glasses. The pinstripe on his navy-tailored suit made him look more like a sharpened pencil sitting behind the wide mahogany desk. Grilled on every penny spent and earned by the bakery in the last year.

I'd had it all ready for him. Why was I so nervous?

I dressed in my most professional black pantsuit, which miraculously avoided the flood damage, because there was no way I was going to fit into one of Kate's skin-tight suits. Beads of sweat trickled down my back every time he lifted his head and peered at me above the edge of his glasses. I had felt like I was back in school waiting for the principal to punish me.

I pulled my hair between my fingers, fidgeting, likely looking unprofessional.

"Well Miss Davenport," he placed the papers on his desk, straightening the bottom perfectly horizontal to the edge before clasping his hands. Those three words did not sound positive. I had to persuade him.

"This is a big change, I know, but I will have the finance to repay when I am up and running again. I haven't actually stopped earning. I am still baking and fulfilling some orders."

Okay, this was stretching the truth somewhat, having only been able to complete one birthday cake and Kate's wedding cake coming up, but I had to get my point across.

He raised his hand to silence me.

"I have reviewed all your income and expenditure and your estimated earnings with the new business model, however," he paused. However, was never good. However, was the worst let down ever.

"... I am not yet convinced this is the best financial option for you. I need you to provide me with the previous two years' accounts to have a better understanding of your range of income potential."

"So it's not a no?" I clasped my hands on my lap to stop the nervous hair fiddling.

"It's a pending decision." He nodded his head firmly. "These additional accounts need to be submitted before proceeding. If you could let your accountant know."

"I don't have an accountant." I said sheepishly, "I've done the books since the bakery was my grandma's. She taught me how."

He looked at me again like a schoolmaster disappointed in a student. "Miss Davenport, this is not the 1960s when your grandpa opened the bakery. It is not the 80s or the 90s everything must be in financial order before the bank will consider lending any money. I suggest you get an accountant and have them forward me the accounts."

He turned and began typing furiously on the keyboard. The final word, I got up and left.

Sitting back in Breakridge River across from the bakery, I can't get out of the car. How can I go in and break Mom's heart? What if I didn't get the money? How would I pay for the contractors? The dream will be gone, up in a puff of smoke before it's even started. What would I do?

It's getting late, but the lights are still glowing in the bakery. That's weird. I thought Mom would have been home hours ago.

My stomach churns as I throw myself out of Ol' Betty towards the bakery, nearly taking the door from its hinges.

"Mom!"

The front is empty. Dear god, don't tell me she's through in all the construction. It would be just like her to carry on without me here.

Why does she never listen? Beads of sweat trickle down my already moist back.

"Mom, where are you?! Call out!" I rush through the back and into a pair of rock-solid arms.

"Woah, where's the fire, Red?" Firm hands clasp me firmly by both arms, my eyes still darting around, searching for a crumpled heap on the floor that resembles my mom.

"Mom, where is she?" my heart is thundering through my chest. Sean grasps my chin, tilting up, focusing my eyes on his.

"She's at home safely tucked on the sofa with a warm tea." His thumb strokes my chin so gently, his deep voice soothing my racing heart.

No, not the deep voice. Definitely not the deep voice. It was the words. Yes, the words of reassurance.

"I drove her home a couple of hours ago when she was tiring."

My whole body relaxes giving way to him. He pulls me closer, firmly against his chest. Why can't I resist resting my head on him and inhaling deeply? That now soothing pine and lavender smell hits my senses like a welcome breeze in the scorching sun.

"What happened? Are you okay?" His voice rumbles through his chest. I'm enveloped in Sean's arms and I've never felt more at peace.

"I saw the lights on and thought Mom was still here and in trouble. I always imagine the worst. She had one nasty accident when she tumbled and now I can't stop imagining her becoming so weak and falling or dropping something or tripping and hitting her head, burning herself on the oven."

His large, soft hand moves up to the back of my head beginning a stroking and kneading that almost has me drop to my knees.

"Oh. My. God. What are you doing?" Every nerve ending feels like it's being soothed and teased at the same time. My senses are so confused, they can't decide if I'm relaxed or turned on.

"It's a massage technique I learned when I was in India."

His magical fingers move to the nape of my neck. Still pressed against his chest.

"You were in In.... Ughhh," he does something with a finger on the back of my head that feels absolutely sinful.

"Red, I'm trying to soothe you, but if you keep making noises like that the soothing is going to turn into something a lot more active." He croaks.

The pressure is bubbling between us. Bubbling like an overflowing pot. Dangerously close to the edge.

Literally.

His solid length pulses on my lower stomach where all the butterflies have resurrected themselves, fighting for release.

Every nerve ending inside me ignites. My body has never reacted this way to a guy. I've never felt the desire to strip off every stitch of clothing and get skin-to-skin in my bakery like my next breath depends on it.

And that's exactly how I feel right now.

His nimble fingers continue gently rubbing, caressing, and pressing in all the right places. My eyes close, my head tilting to the side, allowing Sean access to kiss along the length of my neck. His lips soft and slow trail up to my ear. His whisper is a caress across my skin.

"Cashing in that raincheck Red?"

His lips have put me under some kind of spell. There's no other explanation for this. The burning need to get naked right here, right now, like my clothes are on fire.

I tilt my head up and let him see the need in my eyes.

He holds my gaze a few seconds before our lips collide in a vigorous attack of hands and tongues. Lips locking, teeth biting, lip pulling.

My body quivers at the urgency as Sean grapples with the buttons on the front of my shirt, my hands just as clumsily fighting with his tight jeans' button.

I pull back.

Sean hesitates, his hands hovering.

My chest is heaving to catch my breath.

I lift my lips into a smile and grab his hand, pulling him through the back and out of the sight of Main Street and into the half constructed bakery kitchen.

Mrs. Humphry's words ring in my head, *'Don't overcomplicate it, dear, listen to your heart.'*

Not entirely sure I'm following my heart, rather the burning desire between my legs right now; but I am listening, and it feels damn good.

Not waiting a minute more, we're again attacking each other. Sean swipes clutter from a work surface behind me, our lips still locked. His firm hands grip my waist, lifting me, spreading my legs.

I fumble my buttons, bloody buttons. I give in, ripping it over my head.

Sean stands back, drinking me in.

If I wasn't so horny, I might have become nervous under his gaze. No idea what has come over me. My confidence elevates through the roof every time he looks at me like nothing else matters.

With his eyes on me, I feel sexy and wanted. I grip my nipple between my fingers and rub, the thin lace increasing the friction, sending a shot right to my clit.

His pupils blow wide with desire, "you look deliciously sinful right now." His fingers work on his pants, my fingers continuing their sensual rubbing on my nipple.

"I have never seen anything so beautiful, Lucy." His dimples are deep, with a seductive smile. He unfastens his jeans, kicking them to the side. That tight t-shirt ripped over his head. I'm left staring at that delicious pronounced V. It dips below his boxers with a smattering of light hair. A tempting trail indeed.

"Lucy," I love the sound of my name like gravel on his lips, so deep I feel it rumble in my core.

"What do you want?"

He stands between my legs. I lean back on my elbows. My chest rising and falling, his hand massaging up and down between my breasts, a sensual stroke up and down.

I've never had a guy ask what I want. They took the lead and fumbled their way through until they climaxed.

"I want you to taste me." It's out of my mouth before I can even think about it. I said it with such confidence and seduction it could have been someone else's voice.

His grin widens. "I was so hoping you would say that."

Sean is calm and seductive, his hands nimble and precise, reaching behind me, unclasping my bra. My breasts fall free; his lips pull one nipple in and fingers squeeze and torture the other. My back arches in pleasure. He pulls me closer, tugging my trousers and lace panties to the floor.

"You're stunning, Red." His hands stroke my body like he can't get enough before he dips low, trailing kisses right down to my hip bone. He stops, eyes meeting mine before his teeth nibble the tender flesh and he glides a firm finger through my core.

"Hmm, so wet for me, Red. I know you're going to taste delicious."

The soft chaste kisses continue down.

"Just as sweet as one of your cupcakes, and I can't wait to be covered in your frosting."

Oh, sweet Jesus. I've never had a man talk dirty to me. Didn't think it would be my thing.

I was wrong. New kink unlocked.

With every dirty word uttered from Sean's lips, my pussy contracts in anticipation.

I want to squirm and wriggle; I try to gain friction on the teasing finger as he softly massages my sensitive nerve bundle.

Sean holds my hips firmly, his wide hands spread down my upper thighs before his mouth descends on my pussy.

"Uhhh," I gasp, my head falling back. A satisfying hum reverberates through my lips as I feel every inch of his tongue draw up my slit before he pulls my clit between his teeth.

"Oh my fucking god, Sean!"

He lifts his head, a wet grin on his face, but his fingers don't let up stroking.

"God huh, I kinda like that." He winks before descending on me again, sucking and stroking simultaneously.

A deep moan leaves my lips,

"I knew you would taste so sweet, like Red Velvet, so sweet, it's sinful." He draws his tongue along his bottom lip, his hooded eyes on me, "and it's all mine."

Those words.

Mine.

Goosebumps erupt over my body, my fingers gripping the air for dear life, needing something to hold me down.

He continues with his tongue in a pressure so sweet and delicious I'm ready to explode. He reaches a hand up over my writhing body, coating my nipple in my juices, squeezing tightly.

I moan loudly, dropping my head back. Sean's name screamed as I writhe in ecstasy. I grip his head, my fingers through his hair, riding my climax.

He stands, not giving me a moment to recover.

He pulls out a condom pack from god knows where pumping himself before rolling it down his generous length.

His fingers grip my waist, pulling me forward on the cold, now wet surface. I wrap my legs around his waist.

"Now it's my turn." He breathes heavily, our heat and sweaty skin colliding.

"I can't wait, Lucy. I can't get enough of you."

"Sean..." My words lost as his filthy words have me pooling at my core again. He pulls me close, teasing my clit with this solid length before dipping lower to fill me up. No holding back. He slams in until his body meets mine and I jerk at the fast, full intrusion, loving it.

"Ahh, you're so tight Lucy, this is going to be hard and fast." He says in an apologetic tone like I'm going to object.

He has me in a vice, increasing the pace, the slapping of our skin loud and sexy. His fingers are deep in my ass cheeks, pulling me closer with every thrust.

"Sean, don't stop," I can see him struggling to hold on.

"Couldn't if I wanted to, Red." He grits his teeth.

He continues in the same pace and rhythm and adds a firm pressure from his thumb to my clit. Enough to have me writhing all over again.

Wow!

The beginnings of my core tightening, my back arching, I moan as the strongest orgasm I've ever had erupts through me.

I throw my arms around Sean's neck, my fingernails grip the back of his shoulders. His neck arches, straining as he groans a loud release into me.

"Wow."

Did I just say that out loud?

"Thanks." his shit-eating grin is ear to ear. I playfully slap him on his firm rear end while he remains buried deep inside me.

"What?" he laughs. "That's a real ego boost, to leave a girl speechless."

An ego boost for him?

This is the sexiest I've ever felt and I'm sitting with not a stitch on in the middle of my very dusty construction site bakery kitchen. I thought sexy would be red lingerie and champagne, but clearly not.

It's the way he looks at me. Like I'm the only one he sees. Oh boy, am I in trouble?

Chapter 33

Lucy

The Larson's kitchen is full of action this morning. Kate and Barbs are at the dining table pouring over the Wedding Scrap book, I mean *bible*, wedding bible. If I said that out loud, Kate might behead me!

Ticking off the last of the to do lists, they are deep in a serious conversation about the benefits of having a fascinator in one's hair when the temperature will be hot enough to fry eggs on the sidewalk. With only four sleeps to go until my best friend is married and away on her honeymoon, it's getting pretty real.

Mr. Larson's head remains buried in the morning paper with a steaming coffee in his hand, and then there was Sean.

In the kitchen taking up all the space with his wide shoulders, crispy white t-shirt clad body smelling like pine trees in spring. Since when did spring pine trees smell sexy?

Since now.

They do now.

He's singing along to Morgan Wallen, as I try my hardest to avert my gaze. Every time I look him in the eyes, all I can hear are his filthy words from last night. The dirty words that caressed up to me from between my legs.

Jesus Lucy, get a grip on yourself.

He winks, and my insides convulse.

Sticking my head in the fridge to get the milk and cool the hell off, I feel his warm body at my back.

"Excuse me, Lucy, just need the butter." His hand grazes mine on the fridge door and it takes all my willpower not to lean back into his hard, warm chest.

He leans down, inhaling deeply like he can't get enough of my scent before stretching over my head, grabbing the butter and leaving my back cold when he moves.

It's déjà vu being in the kitchen the morning after another close encounter.

A very close encounter.

This can't come out the week of Kate's wedding. I don't want to take any shine away from my best friend with my drama.

And why would it? It's a quick fling. A romp in the sheets, or in our case, a romp in the dust and debris of the bakery.

Sean shared a lot of feelings the other night, but he's never going to change his life and move back here. He's created this amazing, high flying, millionaire life and it doesn't belong here in Breakridge River. I'd be kidding myself if I thought he'd stay here with me.

It will be fun while it lasts and boy, am I going to make the most of it? The wedding is Saturday and his flight is Sunday night. I don't even know where he's heading, just that he was only staying until the day after the wedding.

Somewhere down in the pit of my stomach, there's a twinge of pain thinking about that. Being left behind, again. Left by Kate going off and getting hitched, left by Sean, who will return to his exciting life.

I push hard to extinguish that pain. Squash it into a tiny little thought box and place it on a very busy shelf in my head alongside all the other worries I have.

For another day.

A tight nip on my bum pulls me back into the room and I jump back.

"Ow!"

"Oh what happened, are you okay?" Kate looks up from the bible.

I shoot Sean a warning look.

"Yes, all good, just stubbed my toe on Sean's big boots."

"Yeah, you are all up in her space; give a girl some room to get her brekkie." Kate's eyes bore into her brother.

Has she noticed? Is she suspicious already? Is she mad at him or me? Kate warned me not to break his heart, but what if it's my heart now at risk?

"It's a tiny little space. *Lucy* should be more careful where she puts her feet." Sean winks.

"Ugh, get over yourself brother!" Kate's eyes roll. "Lucy, where are we with all the favors and place cards?"

"Done and done." I splash milk into my coffee, thankful for the distraction.

"Kate, you know I have all this in hand. You have nothing to worry about."

"You're the best I know. I just worry you've had so much going on these last few weeks. I don't want you to burn out."

"Lucy is on top of it all. She is amazing, you know that. It will be perfect, darling." Barb sips from her second espresso of the morning and it's not yet ten am. It's no wonder she is so feisty through the day and sleeps for the dead from nine pm, unless fueled by some prosecco.

"You have the most wonderful man to marry who loves you with every fibre of his being and a best friend by your side who will go to the end of the earth for your happiness." Barb holds Kate's hand over the wedding bible.

"Isn't that right Tom?"

Mr. Larson peers over his paper, "Yes dear, wonderful Josh is a wonderful guy, will be a great day and Lucy is doing amazing."

Mr. L never appears to be listening. I'm never fooled. He's always listening. I'm so moved, Barb never really runs that deep; a tear threatens to spill.

"Thanks Mrs. L, that means a lot."

"I have the bestest friend, don't I?" Kate beams.

"The best indeed." Sean whispers from behind me for only my ears.

The next couple of days are a balancing act of bakery oversight, bridesmaid duties, and dodging Brendan.

He's too keen and I don't know why. I must have given him a green light at some point, but I don't remember ever showing that much interest. Perhaps he only sees what he wants to see. The constant flow of messages from him are off the charts.

Random pictures of his farm animals, his breakfast, asking what I'm up to, being excited to see me again on Friday. It's a little exhausting mixed in with everything else in my life right now and to top it off, making me feel heavy guilt that I just don't have those feelings for him.

The bakery and apartment remodels are coming on so fast. It's only been three full days of work and the ceiling is back in place and I have a floor in the apartment. James, the contractor, said I could even be back in the apartment as early as the end of next week with how fast they're progressing, if I don't mind the noise of the construction downstairs through the day. That would really be ideal.

I can't imagine continuing to stay at the Larson's after Kate is on her honeymoon and Sean will be away. Of course, Mr. and Mrs. L would have me there without question, but I know I won't want to be there.

With all things wedding and bakery, I haven't seen Sean. He's been with the men of the wedding doing last-minute groomsman things, which reminds me I need to check in with the best man and see if all the suits are ready.

I add this to my mental checklist as I fall through Mom's apartment door with a handful of bags full of wedding cake ingredients. All this flour, sugar, butter and icing will be the most spectacular wedding cake I've ever made. Four tiers, four flavors and the fluffiest of icing. To say I'm excited about making this cake is an understatement. A wedding cake is more than cake, it's the tone of the wedding.

It's in wedding pictures, captured and frozen in time in the memories of the bride and groom for life.

It's a pressure and an honor to be asked to make something so integral to a couple's special day, but even more so that I get to do it for my best friend.

"Darling, I thought that was you." Mom steps with frailty into the hall. "Let me help you with those bags."

"Not a chance Mom." I spin away from her towards the kitchen.

"I'm not a child, Lucy Davenport," her voice is stern, "don't treat me like one."

Placing the bags down, I rub my relieved arms.

"I know you're not a child, Mom." I pull her into a hug. Is she smaller than the last time I hugged her?

"You have been doing so much this week back and forward to the bakery. I just don't want you overdoing it, that's all."

She gives in and let me hug her.

"Are you going to let me help you bake this cake?" She breaks away and starts gathering all the bowls and spoons we're going to need. I love that baking still brings her joy. She likely feels pain or tiredness, but she is one determined lady.

The little chirp of a doorbell rings through the apartment. I'm head first, ass in the air in the depths of the corner cupboard, looking for the fourth baking bowl.

"Wow Red, what a view!"

"Ow!" I crack my head trying to get in an upright and semi decent position quickly.

"Sean! What are you doing here?" I rub my head where a bump is most definitely going to appear.

"Don't you listen to her. You don't need a reason to appear at my door, Sean Larson."

My mom is such a lush. I roll my eyes.

"Thanks Mrs. D, I love you too." He plants a kiss on my mom's head, pulling her into a one armed embrace and I swear she almost swoons.

"I'll go and let you two get on." She raises her eyebrows at me before not so discreetly winking.

"I thought you wanted to help bake the wedding cake of the year?" I ask her suspiciously.

"You know what they say, too many cooks and all that." She grabs a jacket off the hook. "Besides, Cathy next door said she's taking me for a stroll through the park."

"*Really*?" I question her with the most patronizing tone I can muster.

"Really dear, have fun, you two!"

And with that, she's out the door.

Chapter 34

Sean

It's been three days since I last had Lucy on her own. Since I heard her scream my name in her dusty bakery kitchen. We're back in the kitchen again, but this time she's in a flurry of flour and sugar.

Gorgeous.

"Are you just going to stare at me or are you whisking that egg in?"

This kitchen has so many trinkets and utensils I remember from Mrs. Davenport's old kitchen. The one above the bakery I've stood in a thousand times getting soda and chips when I used to follow Kate and Lucy around like a lost puppy. When I was seven, the guys never wanted me around. They were getting too cool and heading to high school, getting girl-friends, so the girls were left with me trailing behind them.

I used to listen to their chats, heard about boys, knew what made them laugh the most, what never to say to a girl. Those were absolutely the early years building up to my infatuation with Lucy Davenport.

She pierces me with her dark eyes, pointing her spatula at my bowl.

"Okay, okay, I'm whisking, I'm whisking!"

I whisk and whisk, trying hard not to let the batter slop over the sides. I remember something about needing a vigorous whisk for a fluffy sponge.

"Sean, don't you remember anything my grandma taught you?"

She grabs the bowl and the whisk, making quick work of it.

"It's been a few years since I was in a baker's kitchen, Red." I laugh and lean on the work surface, watching her in her element. "Cut me a bit of slack."

The utensils are like an extension of her, fleeting from one task to the next without missing a beat. She really is a master at work. She would make sure my sister had the cake of her dreams. Just like she's made sure every entity of this wedding will pull off without a hitch.

From the petals for the flower girls, wrangling the other two bridesmaids, the thoughtful little favors hand made and the dress. I still can't get the vision of her in that white dress from my mind.

There was a time I wondered if I would ever see Lucy in a white dress? Would it be our wedding day?

There's time yet, my hopeful heart reminds me.

"Why don't you want Kate to know about us?"

Shit. Where did that come from? I did not mean for that to fall from my lips.

She drops her wooden spoon in the bowl.

"Sean." She draws out my name in a warning. "I don't want to ruin Kate's big day."

She doesn't look me in the eye, picking up the whisk and continuing vigorously.

"How would you and I getting together ruin her big day?"

My tone is harsher than I intended. "Surely she would be happy for us, if we're happy?"

I step towards her, grabbing her curves into me until she looks up.

"Sean, let's get real."

"Get real?"

She looks a little awkward and places her hands on my chest. A barrier.

"This," her finger points between us as she looks at me through those long lashes, "you and me."

"Yeah, you and me?"

"Well, it's just, it's not forever, so why pretend?"

Ouch.

I've had a few punches in my time, but that one is a blow. A blow to the ego and the heart. I grip her tighter.

"What do you mean, it's not forever? Have you got a crystal ball hidden in here somewhere? A pack of tarot cards or a time machine?"

I can't help the sarcasm drip as I hunt for these unlikely objects, opening each cupboard and under the units.

"Sean, seriously." She folds her arms over her chest.

"I am serious Red, what are you talking about?"

"Well, you'll be leaving on Sunday. I'll be here in my bakery." She rolls her eyes like I'm not putting two and two together. "Ergo, this, you and me, it's not forever."

Wow!

Was she not listening the other night on the bathroom floor? Did she not hear me pour my soul out to her? Did she think I was lying? She is still talking.

"And that's fine, you know. I totally get it. Your life is somewhere else. Your business and travel and goals, they aren't here."

She takes a breath and I still can't say a word.

"So let's not pretend this is something it's not. Telling Kate would be too hard, she'd get all excited, then you would leave. She'd accuse me of breaking your heart and making you run away again."

"Wait, what?"

"It would be too hard."

"No, the last bit you said about breaking my heart?" She's getting flustered now, her red hair all fraying out from the topknot. If I wasn't so frustrated, it would be cute.

"Oh, it's nothing. Kate figured out we had a moment last week and said to me about you leaving, that they all teased you saying it was because you were in love with me and if I broke your heart, you would run again." She tucks a few wild strands of hair behind her ear; not meeting my eyes.

"Silly really. You wouldn't be staying, anyway."

"I wouldn't, huh?" I step right in front of her, toe to toe, lifting her chin with my finger so her eyes meet mine. So she can see the fire in there just for her.

"And how would you know my travel plans if you've not asked me? Do you have my itinerary?"

"No." She doesn't move from my finger. "But of course you'll be leaving. That's always been your plan."

"Plans change."

"I mean, not really. Travel plans are quite firm. Once those flights get booked, you know, it's pretty set in stone."

"Plans - change. My plans have changed."

"Sean," both her hands clasp around my wrists, "you can't change your plans for me."

I grip her wrists in mine now, firmly.

She gasps.

"Were you not listening the other night? You are the only one I would change my plans for."

If she won't hear my words, maybe she'll feel my heart. I catch her mouth on mine in a kiss so deep I can feel it down to my toes. She submits, her body leaning into me as I deepen the kiss, my arms pull her so tight against my chest I feel her breathing race.

In this kiss, I want her to feel my soul. My tongue meeting hers, merging us together. Clasping the back of her head to pull closer still, her soft hair gripped in my fingers. Greedy for more.

Her phone chirps a singsong on the counter behind her.

"Leave it," I mumble onto her lips.

She pulls back and away, her lips plump and swollen.

"I can't. I'm waiting for a call from the bank."

She grabbs the phone, tapping the screen before it stops.

"Hello, this is Lucy Davenport."

She steps right back turning away. I'm nervous for her. I want her to have everything she wants in this world. Being able to rebuild her business in her way will be an enormous achievement.

I can only hear one side of the conversation and still can't see her face. Lots of nodding and "*I see, yes.*"

Her fingers tap the counter loudly. I just want to grab her from behind and tell her it will all be fine. She doesn't have to worry.

She places the phone back on the counter before her body shudders, shoulders shaking a sob escapes. My arms are around her so fast, I turn her around and she buries her head in my chest.

"Shh, love, what did he say?"

Stupid question, really, but I had to start somewhere. It's clearly not good news.

"Whatever it is we can fix it. We can sort it together."

"I - didn't- get - enough - money." Her words are punctuated by her sobs.

"It's okay, Lucy, we'll figure it out. You still have the insurance money."

Her body stiffens under me before she shoots back out of my arms. Her face blotchy and angry.

"WE! What we? This is my business, my life and there's no-one to help me." I reach out for her hand, but she pulls it away so fast. "Sean, you wouldn't understand. You don't have to struggle, you don't have to beg the bank for money."

That's a slap to the face. "Lucy, you're not alone. I want to help you. You know I can give you the money you need."

Apparently, that's a red rag to a bull. Lucy drags her hand over her teary face, smearing flour across her cheeks before she stabs her finger right in the middle of my chest. "You don't get it Sean, you can't just swoop in here with your deep pockets and your big ideas then shoot out of town."

"Shoot out of town? Who's shooting out of town?"

Am I not being clear?

Shaking her head, her hair falls from the messy bun in disarray around her face. I want to take my hand and smooth it down, to stroke her cheek and comfort her.

"The bakery is all I have. It's my life. This little town is my life, here, with my mom, and I don't need your pity or your charity."

What the fuck has just happened? Have I transported into an alternative reality where Lucy is the mean girl?

"Look, I know you're disappointed about the bank..."

"Disappointed," she half laughs, "disappointed doesn't even come close to how I feel right now. Without that money, Sean, all the ideas and plans for expanding the bakery are gone. I'll have to let my mom down and it will be years before we are back in profit. This is the worst thing that could have happened!"

"Then let me help you." I gently cup her face in my hand, wiping a stray tear with my thumb. "If you really want to, you can pay me back, but know that I wouldn't want it."

I don't know that I've ever seen her look so sad, the fire in her dark eyes extinguished. She clasps her hand around my hand on her face, gently removing it and letting go. Her eyes avert from mine. She steps back. I feel that space like a canyon.

"You should probably just go."

"Lucy, don't shut me out."

I step forward. She steps back again.

"You don't have to do this yourself. I'm here."

"Not for long. Just go Sean."

I don't know what else to say.

She doesn't want me here.

She doesn't want me.

I turn and leave, the walls of the little apartment shuddering with the door slam as I do. I've done it again.

Fallen for Lucy Davenport and gave her my heart.

And she's crushed it with her tiny size four feet. The difference this time, she knows exactly how I feel about her, and I thought she was feeling feelings too.

I was wrong.

Chapter 35

Lucy

There's been absolutely no time to wallow in my self pity since Sean walked out and slammed the door last night. The wedding cake had to be iced, the bride needed reined in from her panic attack about her shoes being slightly off color than she ordered and Barb's hat having too wide a brim.

How can a wedding hat have too wide a brim? I don't get it, but I'm the dutiful bridesmaid, nodding my head in sympathy as Kate describes how her mom would sabotage the wedding photos with her *majestic sunburst of a hat.*

The hat was very on brand for Barbs, flamboyant and attention grabbing.

"You're overreacting, darling." Barbs lifts her prosecco. "Isn't she over reacting Lucy? The lovely woman in the bridal shop said it brought out my eyes." She bats her eyelids rapidly. If I didn't know better, I'd think she was having a seizure.

"It's a lovely hat, Mrs. L. You'll be the most beautiful mother of the bride."

"Kiss ass!" Kate mumbles in my direction.

"What's a kiss ass?" Lola, Kate's niece, has the cheekiest grin, sipping on her Cranberry Crush mocktail.

The night before the big day, Kate wants us all together. Slopping face masks, sipping prosecco bubbles, foot spas and giggles were the order of the evening. I don't much feel like the giggling but I would never mope and ruin Kate's wedding. I even manage a smile for Lisa Loose Legs (this will forever be her slut name) to keep the peace.

Lola is so excited she's getting to stay with the bachelorette's. She wanted to paint everyone's nails for the wedding. Thankfully, Becca managed to deescalate that situation with cocktail/mocktail making. Lola and my mom are on the mocktails and the rest of us have had a few glasses.

But only a few, on Bridezilla's orders, so we don't have baggy eyes in the morning. I will be glad when sane Kate is back.

The bachelors are all at Xander's house. He has the biggest place for them all to stay, that's not the Larsons. Little Luke, Lola's twin, was with the guys. He was pumped he might get a beer and to shoot hoops with all his uncles together. I can see the basketball happening but his chief of police dad give him a taste of beer at nine years old - unlikely. I wasn't bursting that bubble when I went to pick up Lola.

"Who wants another drink before we head for our beauty sleep?" I keep hostess mode on to keep me together. I will be in hostess mode for the next 24-48 hours until the end of this wedding, when I pack Kate and Josh into the cab headed for the airport and their flight to the Maldives.

I will not think about bakeries.

I will not think about bank loans.

And I certainly won't be thinking about hard chested, curly blond-haired, pine and lavender smelling men.

All hands rise at the request for one last drink and I take myself off to the kitchen.

Alone in the kitchen, my face relaxes, the perma-smile falling for a minute.

"Hey Luc, you want a hand?"

Can't a girl get a break for one minute?

Smile back in place, I turn to Kate.

"No, no, I can manage a few drinks. Get yourself back to your party."

I try to shove Kate back towards the sitting room. She stands, hands on her hips, not budging. She might be small, but she is pretty solid with hitting the gym three to four times a week. I really need to get my ass there with her.

"You might be fooling everyone else, girl, but you ain't foolin' me."

She shimmies behind me, gathering fresh glasses. "Those bags are a giveaway and the false smile must be giving you a headache."

The sigh I release in relief. "It's not been the best week, but my best friend in the world is getting married tomorrow and I will not make this week about me."

Putting that spring back in my step, I gather the ingredients for the final round of margaritas.

"Lucy, stop." Kate's hand clasps mine from the tequila bottle. "Don't do that. It doesn't matter that it's my wedding tomorrow. What kind of friend would I be if I see you suffering and just ignore you?"

Her tight hug is unavoidable.

"A really shitty one, that's what."

"All this will blow over Kate. I'm just sorry the bakery has imploded on the run up to your wedding."

"Oh, like you could have predicted when a leak would spout and planned it around the wedding like the selfish friend you are." The sarcasm drips from her, long eyelashes batting dramatically.

"Ha- ha."

"Seriously, it's not just the bakery. I don't know what's happened with you and my brother, but I can see you both hurting and it's hurting me."

"You noticed that, huh?"

"When my cocky brother comes home with a smile as wide as the Mississippi for you and you've been as giddy as a kid on Christmas morning for over a week I know something is up, but now you both look like a wet weekend on 4th July, what happened?"

"Ugh," I groan, falling back onto the breakfast bar stool, face in my hands. "Are we really doing this tonight?"

She shrugs. "Well, my diary is pretty packed tomorrow and I head off for three weeks in the sun on Sunday, so now is as good a time as any, no?"

She waits, "Well....?"

Sitting up, I point to the sitting room. "They'll be through looking for their margaritas in a minute."

She laughs, "Na, Lola was pulling out a game of Twister when I left. She'll keep them occupied for a while."

The thought of Barbs on the Twister mat brought a giggle.

"Oh dear, yeah, we should probably stay through here then." I laugh. "I better save my mom, though?"

"Ha, she was egging Lola on. She's doing the board spinning."

I'm glad Mom is having fun, and she made it tonight after a rocky afternoon. Kate pulled her stool closer to me, waiting.

"You are so stubborn."

"I prefer persistent," fluttering her lashes, "but stubborn works, too."

"Okay, okay, you got me." I hold my hands up in surrender and start telling her how amazing Sean has been this week, helpful at the bakery, with Mom and generous with his business advice. I hold back on some details, some things a sister just doesn't need to know. She nods along, waiting for the bang.

"So what changed?"

What *has* changed?

I don't know. I freaked out when he offered me money. I freaked out at the thought of him leaving. Then I freaked out at the thought of him changing his plans for me.

I usually have to make it on my own. I don't want to need to rely on anyone, especially someone who may or may not get stage fright and up and leave the country.

"He offered me money when the bank refused to give me the amount I need for the renovation at the bakery."

"Ok-ay." She stretches out the word, not quite understanding, "so what's the big deal?"

"I don't want his money Kate, I don't want to owe anybody anything."

Why couldn't anyone understand that? Mom had said the same as Kate, reminding me firmly it was his money and he was a grown ass man and if he wanted to kindly use it for the bakery, then why not?

"I want to make it myself. I want to be proud of doing it alone."

"Alone? Lucy, everyone needs help sometimes." Her voice is gentle, but her tone is harsh. "No-one builds a business *alone.*"

She says alone like it's a dirty word. "We all need help. Taking a loan from the bank is help."

I'm a little speechless.

"Is this even about the money?"

I have to get up and make margaritas before tears pool in my eyes again. I can't cry any more. Kate follows me, salting the rim of the glasses.

"I said not to break his heart."

"What if he's breaking mine?" It comes out as a whisper. The understanding is bursting from my best friend's eyes.

"Luc, what are you running from?"

"I'm not the one running! I'm staying right here. Sean is running." I hear the petulant child in my voice.

"You might not be physically running, but you're absolutely retreating."

Her words cut me sharper than the knife through the lime I'm slicing.

"You know Sean canceled his flight out? He canceled it last weekend. He doesn't have plans to go anywhere right now for the first time in over nine years, and I can only think of one reason."

This revelation has me stunned. He tried to tell me the other night. I didn't believe him. I didn't want to let myself believe him.

Kate grabs the bottle of tequila and glass before I drop them.

"What have I done, Kate?"

Lisa Loose Legs bursts into the door at the perfectly wrong time.

"We're dying of thirst in there, ladies. What's taking so long? Did you walk to Mexico for the tequila?" Her loud voice grates on my brain like nails down a chalkboard.

What have I done? Have I pushed away the only guy I've ever felt butterflies for? The big fluttery, tummy flipping, breath holding butterflies. The guy who looks at me like I'm the sun and the moon. Is he planning on sticking around forever, though? Just because he's canceled one flight doesn't mean he's changed his whole life plans.

Just for me?

Chapter 36

Sean

How am I going to get through this wedding without ripping Brendan the grinning giant's head off?

All night, all he's raved about is Lucy. How much they had in common, how often he caught the twinkle in her dark eyes staring at him, how much she was gagging for it on their second date.

They didn't even have a second date. It was the night we met the bachelorettes in The Brew House. He even described in great detail to the rest of the guys how she tried to tempt him on their first date with her *come to bed* eyes and mouth full of strawberries and cream, licking her lips for more.

"We all know what she wanted her mouth full of; am I right guys?" he chortles after a few too many whiskeys.

My mouthful of whiskey nearly sprays the table, my fingers crushing the low ball glass in my hand. I'm imagining my fingers around Brendan's neck when I squeeze a little tighter.

"Wow, let's keep it PG, little ears are here!" Xander eyeballs Luke, who hasn't picked up on a thing, watching a movie with his gramps.

"You alright there, brother?" Xander grips my shoulder, saving me from pouncing. "Your jaw is clenching so tight it might snap." He whispers under his breath behind me.

"Fine," I grit between my teeth, getting up. I need to get out of here. Kate would not be unimpressed if I gave the best man a black eye the night before her wedding. Brandan was fucking lucky I'm a thoughtful brother!

"What's eating you, man?" Oli is his usual unobservant self.

"That asshole." I jerk my thumb back toward the sitting room.

"Who?" he looks confused. "Brendan?"

"If he disrespects Lucy one more time, I'm going to shove his teeth so far down his throat!"

"He's not disrespecting her man," he laughs, taking a pull from his beer. "It's just banter at a bachelors night."

If he wasn't my brother, he might have lost a few teeth too. He clocks the seething look on my face and throws his hands up in surrender. "Okay, okay, we can change the subject. What's eating you though, seriously?"

"Lucy is blowing me hot and cold."

His eyebrow shoots up in question.

"Get your head out of the gutter, man. I mean, one minute she's all over me and I think she really wants me. Then she's yelling at me to leave or telling me I'm going to leave, anyway."

"Buy her some flowers or something. That always cheers up a girl."

Jesus, I'm talking to the wrong brother. "Flowers, really? That's all you got?"

"Well, I'm no expert, but Lucy probably thinks you're heading off on the first plane and leaving her behind, so why would she let herself fall for you?"

"Why would she think that?" Maybe he wasn't useless after all. "I canceled my flight for Sunday."

"Does she know that?" he answers around a mouthful of chips from a glittery pink bowl.

"I mean, I tried to tell her. I told her plans change."

"Well, that's vague," he rolls his eyes.

How could she still think I would leave? I've been nothing but honest about how I feel. My pathetic heart spilled out on a bathroom floor. I've never put myself in a vulnerable position like that. That's not me. I'm not that guy.

"You've gone quiet, man." Oli cracks open another beer for himself and hands one my way.

"Does that mean this is over? I don't do relationship advice."

"Prick." I grab the beer and clink the neck with his in cheers.

"Look, I've watched Josh and Kate over the last few years and from what I've seen, Josh is alway the one doing the chasing and explaining. He's whipped."

He throws back his hand with an imaginary lasso, letting out a whipping noise.

"Tell her what's in your head. Tell her you canceled your flight and tell her why."

"Hey guys," Josh throws his arms around Oli's and my shoulders, pulling our heads together. "Your sister has me on strict instructions, a good night's sleep for everyone. No bags in the wedding photos. So I'm heading to bed."

Oli let his laugh out loudly.

"Case and point, brother; case and point." He pulls away, laughing into the sitting room. "No wonder I keep my relationships short and sweet."

"What?" Josh looks confused. "What did I say?"

"Nothing, man." I pull him into a head lock. "Let's get your beauty sleep in and make you an official Larson brother tomorrow."

He laughs.

Josh is a good guy. My big sister had picked well. Even if his cousin was a total douche.

The question is, how am I going to see Lucy and convince her I'm not going anywhere? That she could put her trust in me, and all before Big Grinning Giant Brendan swoops in and steals my girl?

My foot taps impatiently. I'm standing at the bottom of the aisle with Oli, Xander and Brendan as best men and, of course, Josh. I've tried like a bear to get a hold of Lucy since early this morning.

She's either ignoring my calls and messages or totally distracted by Kate? I am choosing to believe the distraction option, as the first is too sore on my ego.

I thought about walking back to Mom and Dad's to see her in person early this morning, but Josh had jobs for us all.

Going for a run wasted my time. I should have gone right to see her, but I needed to burn off the energy built up not sleeping, turning over and over in a very tiny pink princess bed.

I had drawn the short straw to sleep in Lola's bed. All pink and frilly and not even close to full length. My wide shoulders had touched each edge when I lay on my back with my knees tucked somewhere up in my balls to fit in.

I haven't seen Lucy since she yelled at me to leave the other night. Without knowing what was going on in that pretty little head of hers, I'm going crazy. Is she still mad at me? Indifferent?

"Will you quit tapping?" Xander whispers behind me. "You'd think *you* were waiting for a bride coming down the aisle, not Josh!"

"Ha ha, you're hilarious!"

Josh has his shit together. He's breathing deeply and smiling widely at the wedding guests. Brendan claps him on the back as the tune of the wedding march played on the harp.

Only Kate would have a fucking harp at her wedding. So pretentious.

The bridesmaids enter one by one.

Lisa first.

Then Becca.

Then Lucy.

She is radiant. The soft green dress grasps her waist, enhancing her hour-glass figure. Her hair up and away from her face, elongating her neck. I want to place my mouth there and trace gently up that neck to her beautiful full lips. She comes down the aisle like an angel floating, her hips sashaying, enchanting me.

Mrs. Davenport catches my eye. She smiles at me widely, knowingly.

My gaze trails back to Lucy as she arrives to the front. Her gaze meets mine. A beautiful flush of pink covers her cheeks. It takes every ounce of willpower to stay put and not grasp her by the waist and whisk her away.

She takes her place in front of the two other bridesmaids. I'm vaguely aware of Lola and Luke coming down the aisle to a chorus of "aww's" and "ahh's," but I can't take my eyes off the breath-taking red head across the aisle from me.

In that moment, there is nothing I won't do to make her mine.

Chapter 37

Lucy

All eyes are on the bride and groom as they vow to love and cherish each other until death do they part. All eyes except one pair that have me sizzling up from the inside. My stomach flipping, my core tightening.

The desire in his eyes radiates across the aisle, it's a wonder the Bible doesn't ignite, or the smolder from his eyes set off the fire alarm. All I can think about is that he cancelled his flight. He changed his plans for me.

"You may kiss the bride." The pastor announces loudly, breaking the tension between Sean and me. The entire room bursts into whoops and cheers.

Josh takes Kate's face in both hands and presses a long loving kiss on her on her lips. All my eyes can see is me in a stunning white gown, Sean's hands grasping my face for a passionate kiss after we've pledged to love each other and forsake all others for the rest of our lives.

It played like a reel on a loop scrolling through my head.

Is that what I want?

My lips stick together, mouth as dry as the Sahara sand.

Kate and Josh walk with a wonderful bounce in their step in front of me. My heart swells with happiness for them. She and Josh are a match made in heaven.

Brendan meets me at the top of the aisle with a coat hanger type smile. As the best man and the maid of honor we have obligatory tasks to perform together.

He thrusts his hand enthusiastically my way and all I can think about is which farm animal he had in his hands last. Reluctantly, I put my hand out towards him. He grabs it firmly and bounces behind Kate and Josh just as enthusiastically. The heat on the back of my neck sends a shiver through me.

"Are you cold sugar?" Brendan leans down to my ear before wrapping his arm around my shoulder. A low rumbling growl comes from behind me.

"No, no, I'm all good, just the excitement, you know. They're so cute." I shrug out of his arm. Thankfully, all eyes are on the newlyweds, with ongoing cheers and confetti and not on the awkward embrace of the best man and maid of honor. Brendan, none the wiser, still has a shit-eating grin on his face, clasping my hand again in his enormous clammy palm.

The afternoon continues in festivity, glasses of champagne clinking, the photographer arranging bodies capturing the day beautifully. The one person I want to bump into, I can't get anywhere near. We're at opposite ends of photos. I was helping Kate around with her long train, making sure she's hydrated and make up not melting.

The heat outside is ferocious, making it the hottest day at 85 degree Fahrenheit.

Little trickles of sweat run down the back of my spine and my dress isn't half as full and thick as Kate's. Becca and Lisa have disappeared after the photos, clearly not taking bridesmaid duty seriously. I, on the other hand, have an arm full of the dress train in one arm and Kate's water bottle in the other as we head for yet another bathroom break.

"Don't look now, but my brother has his beady eyes all over you!" Kate twists around gushing in my ear.

If I'm not mistaken, Kate actually sounds excited. "He has actually tracked you around this garden all afternoon. If I didn't know him, I'd have him removed for being so creepy!" She laughs.

"Even if I wanted to, I can't look. My arms are full and my hair feels like some kind of torture device is constricting my head every time I turn my neck." I say, trying not to sound like I'm complaining. I really am. Who the hell invented bobby pins? They need to be sentenced to the death penalty for crimes against women.

We make it to the bathroom and squish the three of us in; me, Kate and the dress. I don't remember the dress being so full when I tried it on. If I'd have thought it all the way through to today, I might have picked a simple tea dress!

Kate pees while I hold her dress high.

"So..." she prompts me.

"So what?"

“Are you going to tell my brother how you feel or not?”

“Kate, I’m not sure this is the time or the place.”

“Are you serious right now?” she shrieks. “A wedding, on a beautiful day, in a gorgeous hotel, in the sun. Could it be a better day?”

Yep, she's excited.

“I swear he hasn’t taken his eyes off you since the ceremony. I’m not the only one who's noticed, by the way.”

“Who else said something?” I'm curious. Who cares if Sean is looking at me? Was it Barbs? Oh god, I hope not. She would have the next wedding planned and booked and Sean would leg it for the first flight out again.

“Lisa is so jealous. As much as he hasn’t stopped watching you, she hasn’t stopped watching him. She’s determined.”

As hot and sweaty as I already am, this has my blood simmering. “She’s such a hussie! She only wants one thing.”

“Well, I guess you better make your move before she does.” It's a dare; a challenge. She's goading me on and I know it.

What is holding me back?

Sitting through a five course meal with Brendan making jokes and innuendo under his breath beside me is frustrating. How am I going to let this guy down gently?

Damn Kate and her match making escapades. I just keep politely smiling and focusing on my goat's cheese and oatcakes. Every now and again, his hand slips under the table and rests on my knee. I was discreetly moving it at first, but after the seventh or eighth time I slap it.

Thankfully, he takes the hint; looking marginally sheepish.

Sitting at the top table in the wedding party, I'm miles away from Sean again. He's at a table with Lisa Loose Legs, of course, and she has conveniently swapped seats with Becca to be right next to him. Her breasts are so big they almost need a seat to themselves. She has her body turned towards Sean, chest sitting proudly atop the table, nipples not waiting for an invitation. A lesser man may have caved to the temptation. Sean hardly looks her way.

The satisfaction at this tickles me up more than it should have.

Every time I look up, his eye catches me with a wicked wink. It feels like a promise. Those dazzling emeralds that set me alight on the altar earlier were now quietly confident as he leans back in his seat with a lop-sided smile.

It should be illegal to look that hot at someone else's wedding. The white shirt snug on his biceps, collar now unbuttoned, revealing just a tease of hair and his dark tattoos. Suit trousers hugging his ass and thighs. I had wiped drool earlier, I'm not ashamed to admit.

One last maid of honor duty of the night and finally I can relax. The first dance. Kate had ordered that she and Josh only dance for half the song and all other wedding party couples are then invited up before the rest of the guests join.

Great.

Me and tipsy, groping Brendan have one final forced proximity dance. I sure hope it's a quick one. The DJ stands at the edge of the dance floor and announces the newly weds. Josh grasps Kate around the waist twirling her to the middle of the dance floor. The smile on her face lights the room. They've been taking dancing lessons together, and it has absolutely paid off. I squeeze a lump down my throat at the joy on my best friend's face.

The DJ announces the rest of the wedding party to join the happy couple.

"Please welcome the best man, Brendan and maid of honor Lucy to the floor!"

The guests clap and cheer except for one, as Brendan grabs my hand guiding me onto the floor.

Oh dear, I can't count the ways this might go wrong. Visions of a baby giraffe come to my mind, I'm not the most graceful on the dance floor and Brendan appears too tall and tipsy to lead me in any kind of graceful manor.

"I've been waiting to get you in my arms all night," the smell of whiskey almost knocks me out. I inadvertently lean back. How long would I have to dance to appear not rude if I leave?

One minute?

Two minutes?

As I suspect, his dance skills are as adept as mine. Kate and Josh swirl and twirl. Mr. and Mrs. Larson gaze lovingly into each other's eyes.

Marriage goals right there.

From the corner of my eye, I can see Sean locked tightly in Lisa's arms, her hands clasp possessively around his neck. He artfully swishes them through the other couples on the dance floor so swiftly, just as the next song cuts in.

"Hey Brendan," Sean's voice is sickly sweet. "Do you mind if we switch and I cut in?"

Lisa's eyes bulge from her head. The level of satisfaction in my stomach should be illegal.

"Actually, ye..." I cut Brendan off, swirling out of his grasp and towards Sean as he deposits Lisa in Brendan's direction so quickly Brendan has no choice but to catch her.

I look over my shoulder, "Thanks for the dance Brendan."

I was raised with manners, after all.

When I turn back, Sean has the widest shit-eating grin I think I've ever seen. Dimples so deep, I could drown in them.

"Finally," his voice is that gravel that sends shivers through my core. His lips graze my ear, his low growl doing things to my lady parts I've only ever read about in those smutty romance books I love so much,

"I've got you to myself."

Chapter 38

Sean

"Finally, I've got you to myself." I bend low and growl in her ear.

After watching Lucy all day, tracing her from one side of the wedding to the other, mountain man, Brendan not keeping his hands off of her; my restraint is hanging on by a very thin thread. The material of that dress revealing and caressing every curve I wanted my hands and lips on. Gravel is all that's left in my voice as I keep myself in check on the dance floor.

"Now that you have me," Lucy presses her full breasts up against my lower chest with my arms tight behind her back, "what are you going to do with me?"

"Red, don't tempt me right here in the middle of my sister's wedding. I swear I'm ready to throw you over my shoulder, smack your ass, and march right up to my hotel room."

"Is that a threat or a promise?" She teases. The satisfied hum that reverberates from her chest through mine almost has me throwing her over my shoulder like a caveman like I promised. I'm so glad for the slow tempo of this song, being able to hold her close, otherwise the enormous bulge in my Armani pants would be on show for all of Kate and Josh's wedding guests.

Lucy tilts her head back, her hooded eyes meeting mine.

"I warned you, Red, you make me feel like I'm sixteen again. Public hard ons and everything."

Her sultry laugh is music to my ears.

This is a different Lucy. A care free Lucy.

A confident Lucy.

If it were even possible, it makes her even more beautiful. We sway around the floor in time with the slow pace of the song, our legs entangled, one leg placed between mine, her warm core on my thigh. Her heat burning through to me.

With each step forward, leading her around the floor, my thigh grazes at the apex of her legs, her head tips back, eyes close.

"You are so beautiful right now," her blush under the lights is radiant.

"Can I be honest?" Her hands move from my neck, drawing them down my chest, stopping at the open collar of my shirt, tracing the tattoo there.

"Always," I prompt.

"I've not been able to get you out of my head since you came home." She looks down, embarrassed. Her fingers still trace my tattoo.

The confession hits me hard, that she's finally admitting that she wants me as much as I want her. A better feeling, a more satisfying feeling than any money in my bank could ever buy.

"You make me feel seen, that I'm the only one you see." Braver now, she looks right up at me, her pupils dilated and hungry.

"I want you. Now." Her confession is a whisper.

"Jesus," I release on a sharp breath between my teeth. I don't know how I'm going to make it up to the room, but I'm damn well going to try.

"No need to tell me twice, Red."

I reluctantly release her, turning her body swiftly so her back meets my front. I grip her hips and dip my lips to her ear as we walk towards the exit.

"You've been driving me wild in that dress the whole day, strutting up and down everywhere and anywhere but where I am. Your leg peepin' out at me or when you bent to pick up Kate's dress, your perfect cleavage; such a tease. I'm surprised there hasn't been a puddle of drool trailing behind me wherever I've gone."

I guide Lucy towards the elevator with my hand on her spine. Outside the crowded ballroom, I adjust myself and stand beside her, pushing the elevator button. I really hope we don't bump into anyone. The tension building between us right now is cataclysmic. Her fingers gently graze my thigh when she adjusts her dress, the sensation electrifying. I grip my fingers tighter into her waist until I hear her whimper.

The wait on it coming down to us is excruciating. The little number clicks down like a timer, pausing every few floors. Lucy leans into me, her confidence growing; she rubs my thigh up and down intentionally now, so close to my throbbing cock but far enough it's a total tease.

The elevator dings.

I all but throw her inside.

Press the button for the top floor.

I wait for the doors to ping closed before I swivel and pin her to the mirrored wall. One hand on each side of her head, I dip down to her eye level.

"What the fuck was that?" I playfully scold her.

"What?" Faux innocence in her eyes. She knows exactly what I'm talking about. I trace my tongue along the edge of her jaw, taking her earlobe between my teeth. She lets out a low moan that slams into my cock like a magnetic surge I can't pull away from.

"Did no-one tell you that teasing is mean?" I growl, placing my hands behind her head, fingers laced in her hair. I grip, tightly.

She groans loudly and my restraint shatters.

My lips find hers, ravenous, taking everything from her I've waited for. She meets me right there, wrapping her arms around my neck, pulling me down to get deeper. My tongue is ferociously dipping in and out of her mouth, exploring.

I find the slit in her dress, trace my hand up the inside of her thigh, and press my finger firmly on her clit through her lace panties. Her full lips part releasing a moan.

"So wet for me, Red," I pant the words between our swollen lips.

Her fingers search for the buttons on my shirt, popping a couple before the sound of the lift dings bringing us back. We separate as the doors slide open to an elderly couple, who pause. Both standing open-mouthed.

"We'll wait on the next one." The gentleman places an arm in front of his wife. He winks as the doors slide closed.

Three floors to go.

Lucy is so close beside me, I feel the heat from her skin on mine. Both of us recovering, our breaths come out ragged.

Two floors.

I glance at her in the mirror, her lips full, hair wild and escaping all directions. The silence is oppressive; a calm before a thunder storm. One of those cataclysmic fork lightening, thunder crashing, going to change the world storms.

One floor.

My door card in hand.

The lift pings.

I grab Lucy's hand, pulling her towards me and out of the elevator. There are only two rooms on the top floor; mine is to the right.

The green light flashes as I tap the card and pull Lucy through the door almost on top of me.

No more words are needed.

Lips collide like there hasn't been a pause from the interruption on the elevator. I whip her round, pressing her against the wall, my hard exterior pinning her. I rub my cock against her ass.

"Feel what you do to me, Lucy."

I need her out of that dress now. I take the zipper between my fingers and release her from the satin that has tempted me all fucking day. It pools at her feet, leaving her standing in lace underwear and heels.

I grab her hand, pulling her towards the bed.

"Absolutely stunning." My eyes are glued to her. I run my fingers along her collarbone, down over the mounds of her full tits as she works on my shirt buttons. I lower my fingers and flick her already hard nipple.

"Sean." It's a plead.

The buttons are too slow. I step back, taking control. I rip the buttons from the shirt and discard it along with my trousers.

Her eyes devour me. I've had a lot of women appreciate my body, but having Lucy look at me like she is starving and I'm her next meal is just the icing on the cake.

Stalking over to her, I grip my hard length up and down. I want her to know what she does to me, how I feel with her near me.

Insane.

She grasps my size in her hand, pre-cum oozing out, the wetness pleasurable.

"What do you want, Red?" Her answer was simple and the only one I want to hear.

"You."

I couldn't get enough of her. She pulls on my bottom lip and sucks, and I respond with a moan of my own. Her finger nails pierce into my back spurring me on.

I fill my hands with her full ass cheeks, lifting her easily onto the bed, brushing my thumb over her nipple. Her eyes roll back in her head.

"Damn, Lucy, you're so responsive."

"Mmm hmm," was all she could manage before I put two fingers inside her wet slit, massaging her clit with my thumb. Her back arches from the bed.

"*Fuck* Sean," she groans, "please, I need you inside me."

"A demanding little madam, aren't you?" I bend down, taking one of her peaked nipples in my mouth, eliciting a gasp from her lips.

A thundering on the door jolts me from her nipple with a pop. A look of confusion on her face. I wasn't imagining it. There is someone pounding on the hotel room door.

"Who the fuck is that?" I hiss. "I swear if that's fucking Brendan coming up here..."

"Lucy!"

It's Kate.

"Lucy, are you in there?" Her voice is high pitched and scared.

Lucy leaps from the bed.

"What the hell has happened? Is she mad I'm up here with you?" Her hair is wild, eyes revealing a touch of hurt.

I grab a hotel robe from the en-suite, handing it to Lucy. I pull on the sweats I had discarded earlier.

"Why would she be mad you're with me?"

"Lucy! Sean! Open the damn door!" Josh is there too. This is not good.

I pull the door open. It must have been a sight with clothes strewn behind us and Lucy's almost got fucked hair, but their faces are worse.

Kate storms into the room. "Lucy, why didn't you answer your phone?" She's looks fraught with worry.

"Kate, what's the problem?" I can't keep the accusation from my voice wondering if she has a problem with this, us. She has no right.

Kate grabs Lucy's hand.

"Kate, what is it? You're scaring me."

"Lucy," Kate's voice catches on a sob, "it's your mom."

Chapter 39

Lucy

My head is spinning, I can hear Kate's voice somewhere in the distance as I rush around the hotel room looking for my underwear. Her voice echoes in my head,

"It's your mom .... fallen .....she's hurt ...... ambulance is away."

When was the last time I saw my mom? Was it this afternoon? I've been so busy with the wedding and Kate and Sean, I hadn't even thought about my mom.

Sweat drips from every pour, cotton filling my mouth. I have to get out of here. I need to get to my mom.

"How bad is she, Kate?" Tears stream uncontrollably down my face.

"I didn't see her. Barb was with her. She went in the ambulance and I've been trying to find you." Kate grabs me in the tightest hug.

"I feel sick." My legs thankfully propel me past her and towards the toilet, where I empty my guts. A large hand rubs my back. I want it to be soothing, but all I feel is guilt strumming through me. These hands were making me feel so good, so wanted and needed only ten minutes ago. And I can't care, he's rubbing my back as every bite of food expels itself from me with gusto.

I wasn't there for my mom again. What is wrong with me?

She's all I've got left in this world, and I wasn't there for her.

"Lucy, your mom will be fine. She's a strong woman." Sean's voice is soothing and gentle like soft butter, but all I can think was I shouldn't be here. I jump up and start throwing on any clothes I can find.

Josh turns swiftly, averting his eyes from my almost buck naked body. It's nothing Kate and now Sean haven't seen. Sean hands me one of his t-shirts and sweats. I grab them, strategically avoiding his eyes.

"I have to get to the hospital." My skin burns like a million little midges biting the surface. I want to claw it off. I'm a trapped animal in a cage, a mouse in a maze, not knowing which way to turn. "Now!"

"I've got an *Uber* booked for you downstairs." I look over at Kate with gratitude.

"Thanks Kate." Tears threaten on the edge of my eyelids again.

"I'll come with you Luc," Sean offers, pulling one leg of his trousers on.

"No." I cut him off fast. His look of shock and hurt are raw. I can't let myself feel right now. I have enough guilt flooding through me to drown in without taking on a whole lot more.

"I'll be fine on my own." My voice is harsher than I want it to be. An accusation rather than a confirmation. I still can't look him in the eyes. It's not his fault. I know this, but he's the reason I wasn't there for Mom.

Isn't he?

I was here with him.

"You don't have to do this alone, Lucy," his tone is firm. "I'm here for you."

Sweats now on and t-shirt in place, I grab my shoes which I can't wear, heels from the wedding. Bare foot it is.

I turn to him.

"Here for how long?" That sounds bitter even in my ears, but I can't seem to control the words or the tone they leave my lips. T-shirt pulled on his arms above his head; he pauses. He looks like I've slapped him in the face.

"Lucy," he huffs my name, exasperated, "what do I have to do?"

"Luc," Kate cuts in, "let's not do this right now, you're hurting, let's get you to your mom." She sends a sympathetic look to her brother and I'm a mega bitch.

"I have to go." Barefoot, I head out the door with Kate on my heels.

"Who's running away now?" Hurt laces Sean's tone, but I hear the accusing undertone as I sprint out the door, down the hotel corridor.

My only thought is to get to my mom. I can't think about Sean and what he is or isn't going to do right now.

"Where is your damn phone?" Kate scolds me.

"In a tote bag in the function room somewhere on silent. I haven't looked at it since about seven am this morning when your big day started."

We careen down the spiral staircase and out the front door of the grand hotel hosting her wedding.

Kate's wedding. She's still in her gorgeous dress, now chasing me up and down.

"Kate, I'm so sorry," she looks at me, confused. "This has happened on your wedding day."

"Are you kidding me!" She grabs my arm and hoicks me back before I get to the *Uber. S*he squashes me into her for the tightest bear hug I never knew I needed.

"You are crazy if you think you're doing this yourself!"

"I'll be fine," I sniffle. "I just need to see her. Besides, you have a honeymoon in the Maldives to get to." I kiss her cheek.

"I can stay."

"You absolutely will NOT!" I almost shriek.

"Okay, okay, I'll go, but you better find your phone and keep me up to date." She shoves me in the *Uber* with a kiss.

"Love you Luc."

"Love you too." I wave, feeling a slight relief at being on the way to my mom.

It's short-lived when Sean's last words echo through my head.

"Who's running away now?"

Sean

What the hell was I thinking?

What a selfish asshole.

Her mom is being rushed to hospital and I'm putting pressure shit on her. I'm reflecting my insecurities on her on what's turned out to be one of the worst days for Lucy.

Sitting down in the bar, all the wedding guests have long gone. The bar man is looking ready to throw me out. I've already twisted his arm with a large tip to cover an extra hour behind the bar, and then some.

When Lucy threw those words back at me over her shoulder, again, that shit stung.

"Here for how long?"

Was she ever going to trust that I'm staying?

Am I staying? How long for?

Shit.

I thump my fist on the bar. How can I expect Lucy to believe I'm going to be here if it's not solidified in my fucking head yet? What is holding me back?

I love being with her, seeing her every day. I haven't thought about any travel or business trip since I'd arrived. Given it was only two weeks ago, but that was a hella long time for me not to have any travel plans.

I've never not had a flight booked to somewhere for the last nine years. Even if it was one month away or two, I had a flight booked to take me to another city or town around the world.

I've loved the freedom. I've loved the independence, and I've loved not being responsible to someone. Making decisions for myself and having no one to argue with or negotiate with. Making a shit ton of money and having fun. I've had all the best experiences of my life and I'm only twenty-six. What more could a guy want from life?

What more, indeed?

Someone to share those experiences with. Someone to plan the next trip with, to celebrate the win. To share all the fears, the highs and the lows.

The auburn, wild and wavy hair surrounding her pale freckled face. That someone has never been any other face for me.

I grab my phone, thank the overworked bar man with another few crisp hundreds before heading out.

Chapter 40

Lucy

I wake with a bitter taste in my mouth, dry and sticky. A mixture of stale champagne and vomit. That'll be there till next week.

What the hell? Where am I?

My neck cracks when I lift my head from leaning on my arms.

"Morning love." Mom's gentle voice greets me, her hand smoothing my hair.

"Mom!" everything came rushing back to me. The fear, the worry.

The wedding, Sean, Mom's fall, the ambulance.

When I arrived last night, Mom was through the ED, x-rayed, cast up and had fallen asleep with the strong pain medication. She'd fractured her arm in two places after losing her footing and slipping down a set of stairs on the way out of the hotel.

"How are you, darling? You look tired."

"Me! Mom, please don't worry about me." Sitting up straighter, I can't help the groan as my spine creaks. "You are the one in a hospital bed because you fell downstairs!"

This leaves my lips a little harsher than intend.

"You're the one who looks like you need a hospital bed more than me." Her eyebrows furrow at me.

I can't help but smile at her bite back. "Touché mother."

"Have you slept at all?" Her eyes focus on me with an intensity I haven't felt since I was seventeen and sneaking out for the night with Kate. She's clearly not pleased at what she sees. What I can only imagine is my very crumpled hair, and a smeared bridesmaid make up look.

"Well, I didn't have a cocktail of pain medication to knock me out, so probably not as well as you did."

I pour a glass of lukewarm water for myself from the jug on the bedside cabinet. "Are you in pain? Do you want me to call the nurse?"

She winces, trying to get comfortable in the not so comfortable hospital bed with the starchy sheets.

"Just a few more bruises to add to the collection, the biggest one being on my pride. I want no more pain meds. They make my head all fuzzy."

She scrunches her face at me. "Whose shirt and sweats are you wearing?" Her pain is clearly not so bad that she can't raise an accusing eyebrow at me.

Damn, I completely forgot about my post wedding, mid-steamy sex interruption attire. Sean's smell kept me awake for a while at the side of Mom's hospital bed. The potent scent of guilt at running out on him again will have that effect.

Did I really run out, though? I got the news that Mom was in the hospital; I was freaking out.

He had offered to come and support me and I shut him down. Again.

I keep shutting him out.

"*Hello*... Earth to Lucy; whose clothes are you wearing?"

"Sean's" I whisper. Heat floods my cheeks.

"Really?" Her face lights up like the Rockefeller Christmas tree. A spark in her eye I haven't seen in years. "What happened? Why don't you look happy?"

All in a space of three seconds, she's gone from excitement to happy to concerned and confused.

"I'm not sure, Mom." I fall into the lumpy chair, tipping my head back, hands palming my forehead.

I can't look at her. The expectation, the excitement. She'll have me down the aisle by the end of the month.

Wasn't that what you were just imagining yesterday?

Shut up, conscience; I don't need to hear you right now!

"Not sure about what? Not sure what happened or not sure if you're happy?"

My shoulders sag. Why do I feel like a little girl crying to my mom? The tiredness, the hangover, the guilt, the stress and worry all bubble over from my eyelids at once. I press the heel of my hands to my eyes, trying to contain it all in. Mom doesn't need this. I need to be strong.

"Darling, talk to me."

"We don't have to do this right now, Mom."

Or anytime.

"Oh yes, we do." She's having none of it. "I've seen a change in you since Sean came back to town, a spark in your eye, a curiosity, a hope."

I raise my eyebrows. "I've not been that obvious."

"Ha, don't kid yourself, girlie." She flattens the blanket on her knee with her one good working hand. "You've never been the best actress and far less a good liar. And Sean's been around a lot these past two weeks since he's been home."

I might as well give in. Mom is like a dog with a bone. She will hound me until she gets the intel she wants. I think she had a previous life as some kind of spy, coaxing secrets from foreign enemies.

"I don't know how I feel."

She looks at me with knowing in her wise eyes.

"What?!" I throw my hands up innocently.

"You're lying to me, or you're lying to yourself, which is worse." She shrugs. "I saw how that boy looked at you yesterday when you walked down that aisle. All eyes were on Kate except for Sean's."

She clasps my hand in her good hand, "his eyes were on you and no-one else the whole ceremony, the whole day."

I sigh, the thought flooding me with the wild butterflies and tightening of my core, remembering the piercing fire from Sean's eyes as I tried not to fall on my ass on the way down the aisle yesterday.

"Scratch that," Mom interrupts my memory; "Sean has looked at you that way since I can remember. From when he would drop into the bakery with hopeful eyes, then realized you weren't in and turn and leave."

"I didn't know."

"He was young then; it was a crush. You wouldn't have thought of him as any more than your best friend's kid brother."

She lifts my chin with a finger to meet her eyes. "The question is, how does he make you feel now?"

I can't stop the smile from turning my lips and filling my cheeks with blush. I don't even have to say a word and my mom is mirroring what I imagine my grin looks like.

"Like I'm lit up, everything has a brighter sparkle, my stomach flutters when he looks at me."

It's not the only thing that flutters, but that's too much information. "I feel seen. He see's me."

"You're the only one he sees Honeybee, you're all he's ever seen." Despite the pain clear from her flinching, she looks giddy.

"It doesn't matter what I feel. He's leaving anyway. There's no point." I sigh.

"He's leaving?" she asked confused, "he doesn't look like he's leaving."

"Mom, it's Sean." I say this like she should understand what I mean. "He can't stay in one place for more than a few weeks, never mind make life plans."

"Plans shmans, has he said he's leaving? Does he have a flight booked?"

I hesitate a little too long.

"Lucy Davenport, you always tell me you leave a guy behind in the rear view because you want that all-consuming love, that love feeling that makes you nervous, not scared, nervous, but happy nervous. The one where you don't know what's coming in life, but you know that with the other person, it doesn't matter because you know they'll be there. A love that fills you up and flows from you like a rainbow on a beautiful stormy day." Her eyes soften; "a love like me and your dad."

"That is what I've been waiting for." A tear threatens at the mention of my dad and their unbreakable love.

"Sean is that. I can see it in him. I can see it in you. And you're just about to throw it all away because you're scared to get hurt."

"What?" That's a slap. "I am not scared!"

"If you have his clothes on, where is he?" She puts her smug face on, "I know Sean, and given half a chance, he would be here in this hospital for you and for me."

I can't help the embarrassment flooding my face. A soft knock at the door interrupts us. Thank you heavens.

A tired eyed nurse pops her head around the door,

"Hi Mrs. Davenport, how are you feeling?"

"I'm feeling fine, dear; thank you."

The nurse places a pile of clothes on the side table. "I can see how fine you are, Mrs. Davenport; your heart rate is telling me another story."

She pulls out some medication from the locked drawer in the bedside table. Hopefully, she'll get back to sleep and I can get some rest.

The nurse inclines her head to the pile of clothes she laid down. "That's for you, Miss Davenport."

"Oh." I place my hand on top and find my phone tucked into the pocket of a hoodie I don't recognize, along with my sneakers underneath. I recognize the smell of the hoodie, a familiar pine and lavender.

"A guy has sat out in the waiting area all night," her tired face has a little blush.

"What did this guy look like?" I question, her obvious reaction irritating me.

"Oh, tall with blond curly hair." She's more than a little flustered; "em, I thought he was maybe your brother or something? He said to give these to you."

I stare up at her and I can feel my mom's eyes burning the side of my face.

"No. Not my brother. Is he still here?"

"No, he left about ten minutes before I could get in here, but he was here a while. I said I could have shown him in but he said he was happy outside as long as he knew Mrs. Davenport was going to be alright and you were in here with her."

"Aw Lucy," Mom gushes, "he is just the sweetest boy."

I pick up my phone to check all my messages while the nurse put observation devices on Mom and gives her pain medication.

I hadn't looked at my phone since yesterday morning before all the wedding preparations. My inbox is overflowing.

All from Sean.

0742 Sean: Lucy, I don't know what this is. I'm going crazy after leaving you the other night. Can I see you before the wedding? x

0824 Sean: I'm here. I'm not going anywhere. I canceled my flights. I want to stay.

0825 Sean: for you. X

1006 Sean: I'm outside my Moms. Can you come out? I need to see you x

1007 Sean: Kiss you xx

I sit with my mouth wide open. He's been trying to tell me all along and I've been shutting him out. I had about a hundred missed calls from Kate and Josh's phone numbers before more messages and missed calls from Sean.

0025 Sean: Answer your phone! I'm worried about you and your mom x

0045 Sean: Lucy!

0210 Sean: I'm coming to the hospital. I need to see you're okay.

0624 Sean: I found your phone. I'm sorry for all the messages. I'm outside just now but I'll be away by the time you get your phone back. The nurse told me your mom is going to be okay. I'm glad. I think I need to get away for a little while. You don't know what you want. You keep shutting me out. I'll be back soon. I promise.

What the fuck?

He's leaving.

Again.

Chapter 41

Lucy

My mom's words echo in my head as I push Ol' Betty down the freeway.

"He's what you've been waiting for..... Why are you letting him go?"

I've never relied on anyone.

Since Dad died, and Grandma and Pops, it's been me and Mom. I've taken care of her and the bakery for so long now I don't know how to stop. I don't know how to let anyone in, let anyone help.

My foot is to the floor, Ol' Betty whines in frustration. I don't think she's moved this fast since the 1990s. Still, I keep my foot to the floor.

There is no way I can miss him.

"I need you to keep going, old girl." I rub the steering wheel encouragingly, lovingly. Thankful it's Sunday and there's not a lot of traffic on the road, I swerve around a few elderly drivers out for a stroll that slows me down. I earn a few shaking fists and tooting horns. I can't care.

The gut wrenching feeling when I read Sean's message was creeping back in, a sickening feeling that I might be too late. That I might have pushed him away one too many times.

'I think I need to get away for a little while. You don't know what you want. You keep shutting me out. I'll be back soon. Promise.'

I keep shutting him out.

The thought of not seeing him today was a scarier feeling than letting him in. Scarier than letting him go.

In these last two weeks, I've felt more excitement, more hope, more alive than I ever have in my life.

During the shittiest two weeks, he was there. He comforted and guided, was patient.

I pushed and pushed away. Mom is right.

Turning up the stereo in the car to shake those thoughts from my head; my foot on the gas pedal to the floor.

All the calls I tried from the hospital went to voicemail. He needs to know everything. I don't want him to go; I don't need time.

I need him.

His phone went to voicemail. My messages are unread.

I pull into the Larson's street, almost two wheeling into the driveway. My legs are ahead of my brain, diving out and towards the front door. He has to still be here.

I can't be the reason he leaves again.

I throw myself through the door, shouting his name.

"Sean!" my voice is laced with desperation.

"Through here Lucy." There's hustle and bustle in the kitchen.

I made it in time, relief floods through my racing heart. Until I get into the kitchen.

Mr. Larson is at the table, the newspaper spread wide and the twins are running around playing tag.

"Where's Sean?" I don't care how I sound right now or how I look running in like there's a fire on my ass. My eyes are wide and searching for anything that tells me he's still here. I need to tell him how I feel. I don't want him to leave.

"He headed to the airport in Denver about an hour ago." Mr. Larson's eyes are full of sympathy.

My heart sinks through the floor. The little energy I had from the whirlwind drive home evaporates. I slump in the dining chair opposite Mr. Larson.

"Hey Lucy, why are you sad?" Lola barrels towards me, her innocent question inviting the gathering drops of tears to my eyelids.

"I'm okay, sweetie, just had a long night with my mom." I try to put a smile on my face to reassure her. It's forced, but I know my eyes are not lying about the depth of my sadness.

"Hey kiddos, why don't you both go to the garden and play, I'll be out with a snack shortly." Their Gramps tells them.

"Cheese and crackers for me please Gramps!" Luke shouts loudly

"EW! Strawberries and raspberries for me Gramps!"

"Cheese and crackers, strawberries and raspberries coming up." Mr. Larson shoos them out the door to the garden before grabbing the cutting board and getting busy chopping little cheese blocks and fruit.

"Do you want to talk about it?" He gently asks.

I look at him; Mr. Larson isn't usually one for the deep and meaningful chats. "You don't have to say anything, dear, but I have a few things, if that's okay?"

I nod, not used to this unusual dynamic. Without Barbs or Kate here being the center of attention, Mr. Larson is such a firm presence. I'm not sure I have words to put together right now.

"I was so glad to have my youngest home these last two weeks."

Oh no, is he going to tell me off for chasing Sean away again? I'm not sure my heart could handle any more guilt than it's already drowning in.

"He's traveled and made so much of himself. I'm so proud of him. I suppose I haven't told him as much as I should have over the years."

Smiling, I nod, not entirely sure where this is going. He places a steaming coffee in front of me.

"Thank you." I wrap my hands around the mug, drawing in comfort from the warmth of the mug.

"You know, since your dad died, I've looked out for you. I've thought of you just like one of my own, Lucy. Walking

Kate down the aisle yesterday, seeing the joy in her face with Josh had my heart swelling up." He places a hand on his heart, taking a deep breath. I don't think I've seen this amount of emotion from Mr. Larson in all my time in this family.

"I want that for you, Lucy," he looks up from the chopped cheese and fruit to look me in the eye, "and I want that joy for my son."

The chopping continues. "These last two weeks I've seen changes in you both. I've watched the smiles and the lingering looks from you both when you thought no one was looking."

"Mr. Larson... I.." I'm shocked.

Here I was thinking he never paid much attention. I think we all assume he's not paying attention to our dramas.

He held up a hand to pause me; "I had to say something today because it looks to me like you both are about to throw something very special away and I can't stand by and watch it. You are not ready to break down your defence wall around your heart and my son is running. Again."

Wow, had Mr. Larson been reading one of Barb's romance novels?

"I.. I don't know what to say, Mr. Larson, it's been a hurricane kind of two weeks, but I'm gutted Sean has left."

He glances at his watch.

"He hasn't left yet."

I don't miss the insinuation in his voice. "His flight to Doha doesn't leave for another two and a half hours." He winks.

Excitement ignites low in my belly. Could I make it? Was I going to rush back to Denver to the airport?

Hell Yes!

I leap up from my chair, almost throwing the coffee over the table; forcing Mr. Larson in a hug before I rush back out the door and into Ol' Betty.

The nausea inducing sound of Sean's voicemail comes through the Bluetooth and this time I leave a message;

"Sean, it's me Lucy. Don't go. Don't get on the plane. I know it's taken me a minute, but I *do* know what I want. I want you. Please don't go."

Chapter 42

Sean

The departure lounge is brimming with families and kids running up and down, sickly happy couples that I just don't want to see. The kids' excitement at watching the planes take off from the floor to ceiling windows is palpable. If I was in a better mood, I might have absorbed their contagious energy.

Not today.

Today a beautifully curvy, delicious red head has sucked my soul out. The memory of her whimpering my name is torture. It's the only thing I can hear right now. I've had many girls whimper my name, but nothing hit like hearing it from *her* lips.

She's ruined me.

Once just a dream; I could imagine what she might feel like under my touch, imagine her scent when I had my nose buried in her hair, imagine the sounds she would make when my fingers touched her.

Now, it wasn't in my imagination. I had the reality. The full frontal experience and it was playing on repeat in my head torturing me.

How the fuck am I going to get Lucy Davenport out of my head now? I don't stand a chance.

One hundred thousand miles?

Gallons of whiskey?

A few new women?

Not one of those options sounds appealing. Yet here I am, sitting in another departure lounge.

The couples in the lounge hold my attention. Their sparkly eyes and carefree smiles at each other. A tentative kiss on the top of a head when she's cuddled in his arm.

I'm sitting here alone. One backpack filled with all my permanent possessions. All I really have fits in one backpack.

It would be funny if it weren't so pathetic.

I have to leave. Lucy needs space. I want her to acknowledge her feelings for me are more than just a two-week fling.

That I matter enough to fight for.

I know it wasn't just me. She felt it too. I could see it in her eyes, feel it in her touch.

She is made for me.

I sat in the waiting room of the hospital last night hoping to all gods that she would come out and I could hold her, tell her it's going to be fine. Better than fine because if she would let me in, we could face anything and everything together.

My fingers had re-written the last message I sent her at least twenty times before I left her phone and clothes with a nurse. I hadn't even decided I was leaving.

Having no sleep and I'd barely eaten, this seemed like the best decision. Get away from it all. Get away from her, from the pressure, from my perfect family.

What the hell was I sticking around my dead hometown for, anyway? There isn't anything for me there. I could be in Doha and partying with my friends and any girl I wanted in less than twelve hours.

Friends? More like acquaintances. People I've met on travels who usually wanted or needed something. Business advice, investing advice or investment in their start-up.

And would any of the girls I could be with be anything close to being with Lucy?

What the fuck am I doing here?

'This is the last boarding call for flight AA243 to Doha. Please make your way to departure gate eighteen. Repeat, this is the last boarding call for flight AA243 to Doha. Please make your way to departure gate eighteen.'

I pick up my rucksack and head.

Lucy

Ol' Betty is really pissed at me now. Shuddering under my feet when I pull into the airport parking. I have about twenty-five minutes until departure and I've already bought the cheapest ticket online and checked in to get me there.

I called Sean's phone non stop since leaving Breakridge, voicemail every time. What the hell is wrong? He never had his phone off.

I'd imagine a million things I could say when I saw him. I imagine it like it's one of my favorite romcom movies playing out. He sees her across the room; their eyes collide and they rush into each other's arms...

'Don't go, I need you.'

'Stay, I want you to stay.'

'We have the best mind blowing sex I've ever had in my life; stay!'

'I think I'm falling for you...'

Nothing sounds right. I'm hoping that the right words will flow from me when I see him. Either that or the adrenaline rush would cause me to vomit on his shoes the minute I see him.

If I see him. I only have eighteen minutes to hustle through security. Thankfully, the gods are on my side or answering my prayers because there's no queue in the usually congested airport security.

I have no luggage, no handbag, no carry on. The lady in security looks at me strangely when all I put in the little plastic tray is my phone and car keys.

"I'm running to stop a guy from leaving." I blurt out, not knowing why I'm explaining myself to a complete stranger.

But the energy is bursting from me. I fear my red, panting face makes me look slightly suspicious. I don't want detained and strip searched before I could get to the departures.

She looks at me like I have two heads, but wishes me luck.

I'm gonna need it.

I check the departure board. Flight to Doha is gate eighteen, a nine minute walk from security.

'This is the last boarding call for flight AA243 to Doha. Please make your way to departure gate eighteen. Repeat, this is the last boarding call for flight AA243 to Doha. Please make your way to departure gate eighteen.'

The announcement shocks me and sends me flying along up the corridor towards gate eighteen. I almost tackle two girls walking arm in arm and I shoulder check a businessman in my haste. I don't think I've moved this fast since a sports day in senior year when Kate and I came second in the three-legged race.

She would be proud of me right now.

My heart races with the exertion and excitement, propelling me even faster. I have to get to him. He couldn't leave thinking I don't care, or I don't want him. I want to tell him every time he looks at me with want in his eyes, I feel flutters, more than butterflies, the kind of excitement and wanting that has me on edge. His hands, his voice, his words make me feel everything I've never felt. Everything I need.

Like someone's first pick.

Like I'm the only woman that ever matters.

Now, if I could remember all those words when I see him, that would be perfect. I stumble into an almost empty departure lounge. A few people sit on seats with heads buried in books or phones or Kindles.

I don't see him or his tight white t-shirt covered body, his broad shoulders or blond curly head of hair.

Standing at gate eighteen, the attendant is closing the door.

"Can I help you, ma'am?" She's perky, about twenty-two, with her lips painted precisely in red to match her fitted skirt and blazer uniform.

"Is that the flight to Doha?" My heart thunders up my throat as I croak the words out, pointing to the plane taxiing away from the gate towards the runway.

"I'm so sorry, ma'am, yes it is. Did you have a ticket for this flight?"

My words are gone, along with the adrenaline. I fall back into the seated area.

I'm too late.

He's gone.

Again.

Chapter 43

Lucy

It was a long night at the Larson's. With Mom still in the hospital for another night, Kate and Josh left for their honeymoon and Sean gone; I feel alone.

Barbs and Mr. Larson try their best to cheer me up. Barbs had a bottle of wine ready when I got back, and Mr. Larson had made the best sticky ribs on the barbecue.

Mom has been messaging me non stop. Obviously, it isn't her dominant hand broken with the frequency of texts she's tapping in.

Mom: How are you, sweetie?

Mom: Did you make it on time?

Mom: Oh honey, were you too late?

Not helping Mom!

After I force down some ribs and wine, I grab the rest of the bottle and head up to my room. I can't look at Barb's sad face anymore.

"Barbs, I'm sorry, it's my fault he left." I need to get it out of there. The heavy weight of responsibility and guilt was squishing my lungs. It is my fault her youngest son, who she was ecstatic about being home, has left.

Again.

She totters around the kitchen island and grasps me in her arms. "Darling, it's not your fault." Her tears soaking into my shoulder said otherwise but I'm not arguing, "Sean has scared easily again, I just hope he sees sense soon and comes back to you. To us."

My eyes are on the clock. He will still be in the air. I've stopped looking to see if my messages remain unread.

It just hurts.

Barbs pulls back, dabbing a tissue under her eyes. Not sure the already soggy tissue made a blind bit of difference.

My queue to leave is another sympathetic look from Mr. Larson. "You know we love you too Lucy, we want you all to be happy."

"Thanks guys, it's been the longest day. I'm going to head up to my room." I grab the wine and my glass and head up the stairs.

Three glasses in and I'm wide awake scribbling in my journal. I'm not entirely sure the writing will be legible in the morning, but who cares? All this raw emotion needs to be purged if I stand a chance of getting to sleep tonight. Adele's 21 album is playing on repeat; if I wasn't sad enough, that was absolutely going to finish the pity party off.

What would Kate say if she walked in on me now? She would have a fit, grab me up, make me get dressed and head out on the town.

But Kate isn't here.

I'm alone.

Is this how it's going to be? Was Mom right? Had I pushed everyone away, anyone who wanted to help, anyone who cared apart from her? I just wanted to be independent. To stand on my own two feet, be able to say I did this on my own.

I look down at my journal. The words are hazy, but the last sentence is clear.

I don't want to be alone.

Tears drip from the corner of my eyes, dropping into the almost empty wine glass I'm holding like a pillow to my chest.

Anger combats the sadness. If I wasn't worth fighting for, then Sean Larson is not worth my tears. I pull the sleeve of my shirt over my eyes, attempting to mop up the tears, only smudging mascara over it and my face.

Looking in the mirror, there are two of me looking back. I look like a warrior.

Yes!

That's me, Lucy the warrior.

Warriors are tough.

Warriors are brave.

Warriors don't need help.

So, what is this warrior's next move?

Get out of this house. I need to get back into my apartment. First thing tomorrow. Monday morning, I'm calling the bank, accepting their offer and getting the apartment sorted. Getting Honeybee Bakery up and running is my top priority and I can make small renovations towards my dream of expanding.

The first thing to do is get to the bakery early tomorrow and ask the contractors to prioritize my apartment. I'll be home by the end of the week. In my own space with my own things.

That sounds like bliss right now.

Screw Sean and his big ideas, motivating me to be more, to do more, and then pissing off and leaving me. I pump my hand in the air to celebrate me, then collapse back on the bed, wine glass, journal, pen, smudged mascara-face and all.

Chapter 44

Lucy

I called the hospital this morning for an update on Mom. The nurse was happy to tell me Mom would be ready to come home later this afternoon. I'm sure she's driving the nurses mad. She's texted me every twenty minutes with instructions and to make sure I won't be late.

After lunch, me and Ol' Betty will take another trip back to the city. The old girl won't be pleased. No rush today though, no flight to catch, no man to chase down.

Only me.

After finishing that bottle of wine last night, I'm in no fit state to drive to the bakery this morning, never mind all the way to the city. That will definitely have to wait until the blood alcohol ratio has lowered.

I tactically escaped from the Larson's house before Mr. Larson returned from the store and Barbs is out at her daily morning yoga. The house is peaceful, and I wish I could have stewed in a bubble bath and relaxed, but I can't risk another session of pity from the two of them.

My self esteem is low enough without them both reminding me that my best friend was on her honeymoon celebrating with the love of her life and my could-have-been boyfriend/ lover/ person had jumped a flight and run away.

Yes, the best thing was for me to get my shit together and get out of here. Start building myself and my business up again. Get Mom home and get her better.

Before escaping, I haphazardly stuff my belongings into the suitcase with the tiny bit of hope that I might be back in my own space by this time tomorrow. It doesn't matter if the apartment isn't perfect. I only require a floor to walk on and a bed to sleep in. I'm not high maintenance.

After I unload the suitcase into Ol' Betty's trunk and lock up; I walk to the bakery making mental notes of all the things I need to check off my to-do list today.

The sticky summer Colorado heat is not shifting. It really isn't helping my case of the alcohol sweats I have going on down my back and in my bra. I wish I had taken the time to shower this morning. In my haste to get out the door, I had the quickest baby wipe wash and scraped my hair into an unruly top knot before splashing some cold water on my face in a vain attempt to regain consciousness.

No man will ever understand sweaty under boob and how uncomfortable these big girls can get. Half nine in the morning and I'd had already soaked through to my shirt.

Great.

Happy Monday Lucy.

On the bright side, it could only get better, one would hope. It couldn't possibly get any bloody worse, could it?

I turn the corner onto Main Street, there's a lot of hullabaloo halfway down the street.

What on earth is going on? Knowing my luck, there's been an asteroid land on Main Street or a herd of elephants, like in Jumanji. Ooh, maybe someone has found a little baby dragon egg and there's a group of archaeologists digging up the street.

I need more sleep.

I really hope there isn't another bloody burst pipe. That would just top off all my disasters; the bakery/apartment construction would have to be put on hold.

I pick up my pace as fast as my washing machine stomach will let me. I need a better look at what was going on. The closer I get, I can see the hullabaloo of people and vehicles are outside the bakery. Some kind of drilling or electric sawing noise jiggles my brain, making it all a little foggy.

Even stranger than an asteroid or a baby dragon; is that Mr. Larson's car in front of Xander's truck and the contractor's van?

Nothing in this picture is making any sense in my brain.

Was I still asleep in the Larson's and dreaming I had done my entire morning already? I hate when that happens because you just have to get up and do it all again.

I grip the skin of my arm and pinch.

'Ow!' Nope, definitely awake.

When I reach the bakery, the noise is deafening. No-one hears me come through the door. People buzzing about with wood and tools. Mr. and Mrs. Humphry from the store, Xander and Oli, Mr. and Mrs. Larson, Jamie, the contractor.

And right in the middle of them all was the last person I expect to see. My jaw hits the very dusty floor.

Standing with his back to me, the classic white tee hugging his muscular frame along with the darkest blue boot cut jeans. His blond curls stuck up in every direction like when he's run his fingers through it over and over. He was giving direction to Oli.

Oli looks up, eyes wide. His lips move; "She's here."

"What is going on?!" I struggle to get my voice heard above the buzzing and banging.

Sean spins around, his face a picture of shock. Like I'm the one that isn't supposed to be here. Like I'm the one who got on a plane to leave the country yesterday and just showed up out of nowhere!

"Surprise!" He recovers with the widest grin and that dimple.

I don't know if I'm going to cry or vomit; or both.

After the cry of '*surprise*', all tools are downed, eyes on me. Then, if the tears hadn't sprung already, I definitely might after everyone erupts into clapping and cheering.

Am I back in a dream where I stand naked in the school cafeteria and everyone is staring and jeering at me? Never one for being the center of attention, my face flushes with heat before the tears spout.

Thankful it's tears and not vomit, I don't know where to look.

Sean rushes over and grabs me tightly between his arms.

"Lucy, shh." He strokes my unruly hair, pulling me tightly in, "please don't cry."

"I.. I... you.... you .... Le..ft." I struggle, beating my weak fists on his chest. His laugh grumbles in his chest through me.

"I never left Red." He lifts my chin to face him, "how could I leave knowing what I'd be leaving behind?"

"The airport..... you ..... a flight?" I still can't quite put words together to string a full sentence. Thankfully, everyone isn't staring directly at me anymore.

"I went to the airport." He bobs his head, "I couldn't get on the plane. Not without telling you how much I love you and I never want to be without you. We could be here in Breakridge, an apartment in the city, a hut in Bali, but I don't ever want to be there without you."

All at once that all-consuming feeling I've been hoping and waiting and wishing for pours through me like warm and welcoming tea on a chilly day. The feeling of being chosen, being the one, the only one.

That all consuming love, the butterflies, the roar of heat, want and need.

He hasn't taken his eyes off me and I realize I've been quiet for a pause too long, my lips slightly parted but nothing coming out.

"I, I love you too." The words fall from my lips so naturally, it's like I've had them on pause all this time and just hit the play button.

It's the truth. My truth. I've never felt as deeply about anyone as I do about him. I've waited on that all-consuming, ground-breaking love story and here he is, sweeping me off my feet.

I can't hold myself back; and I don't care who's here in my very overcrowded and noisy bakery. I throw my hands up and around his neck.

"Sean Larson, I should never have let you run away. I should have trusted you. I should have told you how much I want you, how much I want us. How much I need you."

His answer is a panty dropping smile followed by his warm, soft lips pressing against mine, his thick arms encircling me, gripping me tight like he can't let go.

I don't ever want him to let go.

"But what's all this?" I gesture with my arm around my bakery, which looks more like a bakery than it has done in the last two weeks.

"Well, I knew you'd never agree to a loan from me and I wanted to surprise you, so please, please don't be mad. I called everyone in to get all hands on deck and make this the best surprise for you. Well, the best surprise after me, of course." He chuckles.

"Sean, I, I don't know what to say; I can't pay for all this." My heart skips at the thought of the cost of all this work that had already been done.

"Lucy, it's a gift from me to you." Grabbing my arms, he spins me. "all these people here love you and want to help you. Sometimes we all need a little help from our friends. You don't have to do all this alone."

"So you're not leaving?"

"I am where you are, Red." His face is in my hair.

"Mmm, cinnamon." That low hum from his throat sends a jolt through me.

"It's always been you. Even when I wasn't here, it was you. The best decision I've ever made was to come home and I only wish I'd come home sooner."

It doesn't escape me that we're still standing in the middle of the bakery with everyone working around us. Barbs is behind the counter with a broom in her hand and tears in her eyes watching us.

"Are you going to let me seal this deal with a kiss?" He swoops down to plant one on my lips and I stop him short with a finger to those full lips.

"I thought this was one night only?" I say with a cheeky glint in my eye.

A grin covers Sean's face. He swerves my finger, planting his face on my neck and inhaling his lips at my ears.

"Red, you're so sweet it's sinful. One night would never be enough." His words send my stomach into somersaults. "I've waited long enough for forever with you; let's start forever today."

He was my love story I didn't know I was looking for. And in the middle of bakery construction, he lifts me easily, firm hands on my ass, up to his lips for a kiss I'll never forget. Deep and loving, teasing and satisfying all in one. I'll never get enough.

"I love you Sean Larson."

His answering growl is deep and loud before he whispers in my ear, "How long until we can get out of here?"

I laugh before looking around at the community around me. Everyone has pulled together to make this really special. Everyone who cares enough to take time to help me. I wasn't alone. I've never been alone. It has taken Sean to show me I can let my guard down and accept those helping hands.

I'd never be alone again, and that thought is wonderful.

Epilogue

Sean

It's the big day!

The re-launch of HoneyBee Bakery.

Lucy hasn't slept, so I haven't slept. The excitement is palpable. After I'd rallied family and friends around Lucy and the bakery re-model, it was all anyone could talk about. The re-launch is a whole town event. Everyone has turned up to celebrate with Lucy.

I couldn't have been more proud of my girl.

She is an absolute smoke show, in her white linen shirt unbuttoned to her sexy cleavage and a summery skirt, the slit just above her knee teasing at what lies beneath. How did I get so lucky?

"Hey." I swoop in, grabbing her waist. "You look as delicious as those mini muffins." I plant my teeth on her neck, nibbling. She wriggles and giggles under me.

"Sean!" She tries to right herself up while I dip her lower, "will you behave for two minutes!"

"Absolutely not." I confess. "Where's the fun of behaving?"

"Will you two get a room?" Kate strides over, batting me on the back.

"Put my bestie down and make yourself useful." She shoves the tray of champagne flutes into my hands, nodding her head towards all the guests.

Kate and Josh returned from honeymoon last week after three weeks away in the sun. Josh hasn't killed her yet, so I think that's a win for the longevity of their marriage. Three weeks with my sister would be intense.

We decided not to tell them when they were away that me and Lucy had made it official. Lucy was worried about what her best friend would say, how she would react. I knew my sister. She would be happy for us, and I was right.

She'd thrown her arms around us both, almost knocking our heads together shouting, "It's about frickin' time! When's the wedding?"

Lucy almost choked on her barbeque wings at that comment. It had taken me enough effort to get her to realize she could have someone care about *and* take care of her without taking all her control. She is an independent woman. I loved it.

I love her.

"Will you stop making doe eyes at Lucy and go hand out those flutes of bubbly?" Kate rolls her eyes.

"FYI, I love your doe eyes." Lucy reaches on her tiptoes to peck me on the cheek.

While I did the rounds with my tray, I keep my eyes on my woman. I love the sound of that.

My woman.

I would have run a mile even considering those words about any other relationship I've ever had.

"Oh, Sean, be a darling and help me over to the chairs." Mrs. Davenport was a peach and absolutely on the road to recovery. Her arm is still in a cast, but all the black and blue bruises were healing well. She didn't require a hand, but I knew fine well she just loves being on my arm. She's proud of her daughter and proud of me and I couldn't help swell with pride myself.

I offer her my free arm. "Come on, let's get you a front-row seat to the show."

She links her good arm in mine and practically bounces over to the seat beside my mom.

"Hi Mom," I drop her a wink, "having a good time?"

"Oh yes, son, so glad you're here." A few drinks and Barbs is gushing already, wait until after the grand opening and speeches. She'll be bubbling, I'm sure.

When everyone has a glass of bubbly and one of Lucy's tasty mini muffins in their hands, I nod over to Lucy.

She stands in front of the gorgeous new front of HoneyBee Bakery, a gigantic yellow ribbon fastened across the display window and door.

Lucy clinks her flute with a little fork, trying to get everyone's attention.

"Hello everyone!" finding her voice, I watch as all eyes are on her.

"If I can have your attention for a moment. I don't want to prattle on, but I have a few thank you's before I cut the ribbon for the official opening of the brand new HoneyBee Bakery."

This garnered some cheers from the crowd.

"Thanks everyone. Thank you all for coming today and to everyone who has helped me put this old place back together brick by brick. The bakery has been here for a long time now and I know a lot of you knew it when my grandma and pops started the business many years ago and have supported it ever since."

She has a little stumble at the memory of her grandma and pops. I will her on, she's practiced this speech over and over.

"You've seen it through with my mom and dad, and now I have the responsibility of taking the reins. I would have loved for them to see what their business has become today. Extended and catering for towns beyond the boundary of Breakridge River. I think they would be proud."

"I know they would be proud, darling!" Mrs. Davenport shouts.

"Thanks mom. A huge thank you to my mom. My beautiful mother, who has worked all her days to show me baking and business through all the challenges life has thrown her way; she has never shown me wrong." Lucy sends a beautiful smile, a tear in her eye for her mom. Keep going Red, you can do it. I cheer her on in my head.

"And a final thank you goes to someone I never knew I needed; I never knew I loved. Sean."

Wait, this wasn't in the rehearsed speech. I smile at Lucy, love radiating from me.

"Sean, you brushed back into Breakridge just when my life turned upside down. You've guided, helped and loved me. You've put just as much blood, sweat and tears into this re-launch as I have. It's as much yours as it is mine. Thank you."

With that, Lucy turns with the biggest pair of scissors, ready to cut the ribbon.

"Can I say a few words before you officially open?" I speak up.

This wasn't in the original plan; Lucy looks at me with a question.

"Sure."

I step up beside her, planting my lips on hers, a chaste kiss before turning to the crowd of waiting faces.

"Coming home seemed to be the hardest thing I would ever do. It took me nine years to get on a plane headed for Colorado and there was only one reason," I look at Lucy. "I never wanted to come home and find out what I had missed out on for all these years."

I'm interrupted by the crowd's collective, "awww!"

I can see Barbs with her nose in a tissue and tears in her eyes; Dad has his arm around her, his grin wide.

My smile is beaming; I can feel my cheeks burning. "How lucky was I, that the girl of my dreams was still here, baking her delicious goodness into this town and no-one had the sense to snap her up!"

Lucy's face is turning a deeper shade of red, hating to be the center of attention.

"Lucy, you might hate being the center of attention, but you are the center of my world and I can't wait to see what we can build and make together. Be that here in Breakridge or anywhere else, life may take us."

Standing in front of everyone we love, I grab the woman of my dreams into a passionate kiss, dipping her low. I can hear everyone whoop and cheer in the crowd.

"One night's not enough, eh?" She nips my earlobe with her teeth.

"One lifetime will never be enough, Lucy Davenport. I love you."

I peck her nose before setting her upright on her feet. Lucy turns to the crowd.

"Let's get this bakery open!"

She grabs the scissors in one hand and my hand in the other and we cut the ribbon to the start of this new chapter in our lives together.

Epilogue II

Sean

1 year later

It's a year to the day since we cut the ribbon to the brand new HoneyBee Bakery. I couldn't be more proud of Lucy over this last year.

She's worked so hard to expand beyond the boundaries of Breakridge River, taking on larger weddings and events in the rural hotels around Northern Colorado. With a little bit of encouragement and marketing expertise, we have a website up and running and an Instagram page. Lucy's cakes have grown so much online, orders are through the roof.

She was gaining confidence in her skills and started writing a recipe book.

My girl is a legend.

"What are you swooning about now?" Kate prods me in the arm, her smile teasing.

"What?" I say, innocently.

"You are staring into space with hearts in your eyes, brother," Xander slaps me on the back.

We're all back where it started last year when I surprised Lucy by coming home. I asked everyone that has helped us over the last year, all our friends and family, to come down to the bakery before opening time for another big surprise.

Lucy is upstairs in the apartment getting herself ready to open up for the day while we creep around here quietly.

Brendan and Lisa huddle over a table, smiling hearts at each other. Josh had the best idea not long after their wedding that Brendan needed a woman in his life, and that someone might be Lisa. Lucy had scoffed, thinking there was no way Brendan would go for, in her words, *'such a loose leg hussie.'*

They've been a vision of love for over six months now.

Kate waddles over to Josh with her round belly; she is ready to pop any day now. Mom and Dad are absolutely overjoyed that they are getting another grandchild. Thankfully, keeping them off mine and Lucy's back for a while.

"Hey son," my dad catches my attention. "Are you all ready?"

"I sure am."

He shuffles from foot to foot awkwardly.

"Are you okay Dad?"

"I am son," he puts an arm around my shoulder. No easy feat when I have a good four inches on him.

"I'm really good. So is your mother. You know we're so proud of you, son. So proud of everything you've done, all your business success and especially coming home and being the man you are today for Lucy." His voice breaks a little before he pulls me down for a man hug and slaps on the back.

"I know Dad." I smile.

"I don't tell you enough. We are so proud of you."

Mom is looking over, tears in her eyes already.

"Right, let's get sorted; she'll be down just now."

The clock is ticking towards eight am; Lucy will be down any minute. Everyone is here, everyone in our lives who matters is standing quietly with poppers to surprise Lucy when she comes in.

The door to our apartment squeaks before my Honeybee springs through like sunshine.

"SURPRISE!!" the whole crowd shouts and cheers.

Lucy's face resembles a scream before she stumbles back into the door.

"What the heck is going on here?" She gasps, one hand on her chest. "Y'all almost gave me a heart attack."

My heart pounds when I step out of the crowd towards her. Her eyes are full of confusion when I lift her hand and pull her towards me.

"Lucy..."

"Sean, what is this? What are you doing?" she interrupts, whispering.

I hope my wide smile is reassuring.

"Lucy, I stayed away from Breakridge for the longest time. I thought that being away from here, building my life with no roots, and being free was what I wanted. The life I craved."

Why is my hand shaking? This is a lot harder than I thought it would be. I'd rehearsed so many times in the mirror and even with Kate pretending to be Lucy.

"I couldn't have been more wrong. Even after everything I learned, all the sights I've seen, all the money I earned in those nine years, I have never been happier than I have been this last year with you."

My girl blushes bright. Bright enough to match her beautiful hair.

"This last year has felt like more than coming home. It has felt like I have had a piece of me returned that I never knew was missing. And that piece was you in my life. You in my heart. We have had the best time over the last year and I want to make the best memories with you for the rest of our lives. I've wasted a lot of years without you, Lucy, and I don't intend on wasting one more."

Stepping back, my hands still shaking slightly, I drop to one knee. I reach round and pull a little box from my back pocket and when I look up to Lucy; she has both hands over her mouth; her eyes are bulging.

You could hear a pin drop in our busy little bakery.

"Lucy, one lifetime will never be enough with you. Will you make me the happiest man alive and do me the honor of being my wife?"

The silence is deafening; my words hang in the air. The hardest thing I have ever done in my life is wait for this one tiny answer. One word is just about to change my life. Beads of sweat trickle down my back, my knee shaking on the ground.

She is as still as a statue. Her hands haven't moved from her lips.

"Lucy...?"

"Yes." It whooshes out of her in a whisper before she shouts, "YES!"

Relief courses through me. I jump up and wrap my arms around her, our lips clashing in a deep kiss, all our friends and family cheering.

"Oh, my god Sean!" she gasps. "How did you plan all this? And everyone came?"

The whooping continues.

"Of course they came; they all love you. I've been planning this for over a month."

She pulls her head back a little, smirking. "You must have been pretty confident of my answer to have an audience this big."

"I was until the second I popped the question and you fell silent!" I laugh, dipping my head to her ear, "are you ready to have me call you, *my wife?*"

Satisfyingly, I feel a shudder run through her at my words. I pull back and take the ring from the box. Sliding it perfectly onto her finger.

"She said YES!" I shout out before I crush my lips to hers again. I will never get enough of this woman. I will give her the world.

"Lucy, I can't wait to see what our life will bring us. A couple of little baking Larson's hopefully," she laughs at this, "but not before you have your dream wedding and a trip around the world."

She bats her big brown eyes at me. "All I need is you, Sean Larson, all I need is you."

Hear more from Ash Rose...

So you loved Sean and Lucy's tale? Do you want to be the first to hear news about Xander and Gabby's story?

A single dad, second chance, romantic suspense story.

Ash is off writing this story as we speak!

So if you want access to everything first before anyone else then sign up here!

First offer of beta reads, ARC copies, cover reveals, character art and any bookish related stuff!

About the author

Ash Rose is a small town romance author with a love for beautifully passionate, spicy love stories always with a happy every after.

Ash lives in the middle of the woods somewhere in Scotland with her very patient other half, two kids, a husky and a pug.

When she's not writing, she's training children's nurses, wrangling kids or hiding somewhere with a book.

Connect with Ash on:

Tiktok @ashrose.author

Instagram @ash.roseauthor

Email: hello@ashroseauthor.com

Acknowledgements

Getting to write this page is an absolute achievement. It's the final piece of the puzzle. Writing a book is hard. Editing is harder and wrangling the self publishing world is harder still.

But I am so very thankful for all of the friends I have met on this bookish, self-publishing journey.

I can honestly say this book would not have made it to where it is today without the support of 'strangers' I met on Booktok. You are the best cheerleaders and have kept me motivated to get Sean and Lucy's story to you in the best version it can be.

To everyone who took the time to beta read and send your thoughts and comments; every single reply was catalogued and changed something in the story. Your feedback was invaluable.

To Lora (@taleswithlora) who I also met on Booktok and has created an absolutely beautiful cover design for my debut book. You are a creative genius.

To my other half, Greg. My number one fan. My cheerleader. My go to hype man. For listening to my rants and raves about characters, plot holes, publishing issues and general bookish nonsense. Thank you.

To my little humans (who aren't so little anymore), Charlie and Rhiannon. You are the reason I do anything. Love you both always.

Until next time in Breakridge

Ash x

Printed in Dunstable, United Kingdom

70886797R00215